Robert Browning was born in Camberwell in
1812 and educated by private tutors. His
parents were wealthy enough to allow him to
travel and to be a poet as if it were a pro-
fession. He became known by literary figures
such as Wordsworth and Landor after the
publication of *Paracelsus* in 1835, but he was
unrecognized by the public until *Men and
Women* appeared twenty years later. He was
therefore almost unknown when in 1846 he
eloped with Elizabeth Barrett. For the next
fifteen years they lived in Italy, where much
of Browning's best work was inspired and
composed. After his wife's death in 1861 he
lived mainly in London. He achieved fame
with *The Ring and the Book* which was pub-
lished in 1868-9. He died in 1889 in Venice,
and was buried in Poets' Corner in West-
minster Abbey.

BROWNING

A Selection by
W. E. WILLIAMS

PENGUIN BOOKS

Penguin Books Ltd, Harmondsworth, Middlesex, England
Penguin Books, 625 Madison Avenue, New York, New York 10022, U.S.A.
Penguin Books Australia Ltd, Ringwood, Victoria, Australia
Penguin Books Canada Ltd, 2801 John Street, Markham, Ontario,
Canada L3R 1B4
Penguin Books (N.Z.) Ltd, 182–190 Wairau Road, Auckland 10,
New Zealand

—

This selection first published in Penguin Books 1954
Reprinted 1963, 1964, 1966, 1968, 1971, 1973, 1974, 1976, 1977

—

Made and printed in Great Britain
by Hunt Barnard Printing Ltd, Aylesbury
Set in Monotype Walbaum

LIST OF CONTENTS

LIST OF CONTENTS

INTRODUCTION

In Browning's lifetime, and for many years afterwards, there existed numerous Browning Societies. Their chief aim was to elucidate the philosophic subtleties which were thought to be concealed in the master's work; and their members were in the habit of threading the maze of his obscurer poems in quest of some theological or scientific revelation. What they found was nobody's business, least of all Browning's. He was not a deep thinker and he has very little light to throw upon the religious and scientific controversies of Victorian England. But Browning was a great and original poet. Original because he brought to English poetry some remarkable innovations of style; and great because he used those innovations to illuminate many kinds of human behaviour. He could not, as they say, develop a thesis, and the more pages he spends on that endeavour, the more unconvincing and tedious he becomes. But he could, with the poet's instantaneous intuition, reveal in a flash the motives which make men and women behave as they do.

There are two legends about Browning. The first is that he is 'deep': the second that he is 'difficult'. Many of those who believed he was deep also believed that he deliberately concealed his profundities so as to evoke in his readers the alertness and percipience required to participate in a quest for truth. He concealed his message, they held, in obscurities of form and expression which the faithful, by diligent reading and discussion, could ultimately unravel. Browning can, indeed, be difficult, but not because he devised his poems, so to speak, as cross-word puzzles. He is not really very difficult at all, once the reader has become familiar with his method and idiom. Many of his best poems are monologues: dramatic pieces, in the first person, about some vital experience in the life of an imaginary narrator. It does not take long for the reader, hitherto unfamiliar with Browning, to appreciate the novelty of his poetic method. He is acting a long series of parts – a medieval bishop, an alchemist, a horseman riding for the last time with the woman he loves, an eccentric scholar, a celebrated musician, a wandering pilgrim. He is a poetic quick-change artist assuming in succession one guise after the other.

The really 'difficult' element in Browning is his occasional obscurity of language. This can arise from several causes. Sometimes the poet becomes involved in a kind of private shorthand of syntax or idiom which may take a bit of working-out. Many of these lapses are no doubt due to the pace at which Browning composed, and the indifference he so often showed in revising his work for the printer. So copious and impetuous a poet must often be slap-dash, and many of Browning's obscure and misshapen phrases are simply blemishes he never bothered to correct. He did not practise the fastidious craftsmanship of Tennyson; poetry came cascading out of him in a welter of words.

There is, too, a bogus element in some of his obscurity. Flattered by the false reputation of being a sage and a prophet he indulged at times in the kind of oracular utterance which the Browning Societies appeared to expect of him –

I cannot feed on beauty for the sake of beauty only,
Nor can drink in the balm from lovely objects for
    their loveliness,

8

I still must hoard and heap and class all truths with
    one ulterior purpose:
I must know!

But despite the mannerisms and affections, Browning's
real stature does not diminish. They are the flourishers of
a flamboyant personality, the gesticulations of a vivid
talker —

No more wine? then we'll push back chairs and talk.

And as he develops the poetic monologue it becomes
abundantly clear that he has penetrated deep into the
motives which animate human behaviour. People are his
passion: men and women, revealed through their ambi-
tions and failures and loves and hatreds. He has very little
to say about nature, but he is fascinated by human nature,
and endowed with a rare poetic insight into its qualities
and complexities. The newcomer to Browning can get the
measure of the man by reading, first, *The Bishop Orders
His Tomb* and, second, *In a Year*.

Browning was born in Camberwell in 1812, and died
in Venice at the age of 77. He was buried in Poet's Corner
in Westminster Abbey. The only dramatic event in his
life was his elopement, when he was 33, with Elizabeth
Barrett. For the next fifteen years they lived in Italy,
where so much of Browning's best work was inspired and
composed. After her death, in 1861, he lived mainly in
London. One of the last poems he wrote, almost from his
death-bed, was the *Epilogue to 'Asolando'* which concludes
this selection.

W.E.W.

SONGS FROM 'PIPPA PASSES'

I

The year's at the spring
And day's at the morn;
Morning's at seven;
The hill-side's dew-pearled;
The lark's on the wing;
The snail's on the thorn:
God's in his heaven –
All's right with the world!

II

A king lived long ago,
In the morning of the world,
When the earth was nigher heaven than now:
And the king's locks curled,
Disparting o'er a forehead full
As the milk-white space 'twixt horn and horn
Of some sacrificial bull –
Only calm as a babe new-born:
For he was got to a sleepy mood,
So safe from all decrepitude,
Age with its bane so sure gone by,
(The gods so loved him while he dreamed)
That, having lived thus long, there seemed
No need the king should ever die.

Among the rocks his city was:
Before his palace, in the sun,

He sat to see his people pass,
And judge them every one
From its threshold of smooth stone.
They haled him many a valley-thief
Caught in the sheep-pens, robber-chief
Swarthy and shameless, beggar-cheat,
Spy-prowler, or rough pirate found
On the sea-sand left aground;
And sometimes clung about his feet,
With bleeding lip and burning cheek,
A woman, bitterest wrong to speak
Of one with sullen thickset brows:
And sometimes from the prison-house
The angry priests a pale wretch brought,
Who through some chink had pushed and
     pressed
On knees and elbows, belly and breast,
Worm-like into the temple, – caught
He was by the very god,
Who ever in the darkness strode
Backward and forward, keeping watch
O'er his brazen bowls, such rogues to catch!
These, all and every one,
The king judged, sitting in the sun.

His councillors, on left and right,
Looked anxious up, – but no surprise
Disturbed the king's old smiling eyes
Where the very blue had turned to white.
'Tis said, a Python scared one day
The breathless city, till he came,
With forky tongue and eyes on flame,
Where the old king sat to judge alway;

But when he saw the sweepy hair
Girt with a crown of berries rare
Which the god will hardly give to wear
To the maiden who singeth, dancing bare
In the altar-smoke by the pine-torch lights,
At his wondrous forest rites, —
Seeing this, he did not dare
Approach that threshold in the sun,
Assault the old king smiling there.
Such grace had kings when the world begun!

III

You'll love me yet! – and I can tarry!
   Your love's protracted growing:
June reared that bunch of flowers you carry,
   From seeds of April's sowing.

I plant a heartful now; some seed
   At least is sure to strike,
And yield – what you'll not pluck indeed,
   Not love, but, may be, like.

You'll look at least on love's remains,
   A grave's one violet:
Your look? – that pays a thousand pains.
   What's death? You'll love me yet!

THE LOST LEADER

I

JUST for a handful of silver he left us,
  Just for a riband to stick in his coat –
Found the one gift of which fortune bereft us,
  Lost all the others she lets us devote;
They, with the gold to give, doled him out silver,
  So much was theirs who so little allowed:
How all our copper had gone for his service!
  Rags – were they purple, his heart had been proud!
We that had loved him so, followed him, honoured him,
  Lived in his mild and magnificent eye,
Learned his great language, caught his clear accents,
  Made him our pattern to live and to die!
Shakespeare was of us, Milton was for us,
  Burns, Shelley, were with us, – they watch from their
    graves!
He alone breaks from the van and the freemen,
  – He alone sinks to the rear and the slaves!

II

We shall march prospering, – not thro' his presence;
  Songs may inspirit us, – not from his lyre;
Deeds will be done, – while he boasts his quiescence,
  Still bidding crouch whom the rest bade aspire:
Blot out his name, then, record one lost soul more,
  One task more declined, one more footpath untrod,
One more devils'-triumph and sorrow for angels,
  One wrong more to man, one more insult to God!

Life's night begins: let him never come back to us!
　There would be doubt, hesitation and pain,
Forced praise on our part – the glimmer of twilight,
　Never glad confident morning again!
Best fight on well, for we taught him – strike gallantly,
　Menace our heart ere we master his own;
Then let him receive the new knowledge and wait us,
　Pardoned in heaven, the first by the throne!

'HOW THEY BROUGHT THE GOOD NEWS FROM GHENT TO AIX'

[16—]

I

I SPRANG to the stirrup, and Joris, and he;
I galloped, Dirck galloped, we galloped all three;
'Good speed!' cried the watch, as the gatebolts undrew;
'Speed!' echoed the wall to us galloping through;
Behind shut the postern, the lights sank to rest,
And into the midnight we galloped abreast.

II

Not a word to each other; we kept the great pace
Neck by neck, stride by stride, never changing our place;
I turned in my saddle and made its girths tight,
Then shortened each stirrup, and set the pique right,
Rebuckled the cheek-strap, chained slacker the bit,
Nor galloped less steadily Roland a whit.

III

'Twas moonset at starting; but while we drew near
Lokeren, the cocks crew and twilight dawned clear;
At Boom, a great yellow star came out to see;
At Düffeld, 'twas morning as plain as could be;
And from Mecheln church-steeple we heard the half-chime,
So, Joris broke silence with, 'Yet there is time!'

IV

At Aershot, up leaped of a sudden the sun,
And against him the cattle stood black every one,
To stare thro' the mist at us galloping past,
And I saw my stout galloper Roland at last,
With resolute shoulders, each butting away
The haze, as some bluff river headland its spray:

V

And his low head and crest, just one sharp ear bent back
For my voice, and the other pricked out on his track;
And one eye's black intelligence, – ever that glance
O'er its white edge at me, his own master, askance!
And the thick heavy spume-flakes which aye and anon
His fierce lips shook upwards in galloping on.

VI

By Hasselt, Dirck groaned; and cried Joris, 'Stay spur!
'Your Roos galloped bravely, the fault's not in her,
'We'll remember at Aix' – for one heard the quick wheeze
Of her chest, saw the stretched neck and staggering knees,
And sunk tail, and horrible heave of the flank,
As down on her haunches she shuddered and sank.

VII

So, we were left galloping, Joris and I,
Past Looz and past Tongres, no cloud in the sky;
The broad sun above laughed a pitiless laugh,
'Neath our feet broke the brittle bright stubble like chaff;
Till over by Dalhem a dome-spire sprang white,
And 'Gallop,' gasped Joris, 'for Aix is in sight!'

B–2   17

VIII

'How they'll greet us!' – and all in a moment his roan
Rolled neck and croup over, lay dead as a stone;
And there was my Roland to bear the whole weight
Of the news which alone could save Aix from her fate,
With his nostrils like pits full of blood to the brim,
And with circles of red for his eye-sockets' rim.

IX

Then I cast loose my buffcoat, each holster let fall,
Shook off both my jack-boots, let go belt and all,
Stood up in the stirrup, leaned, patted his ear,
Called my Roland his pet-name, my horse without peer;
Clapped my hands, laughed and sang, any noise, bad or
    good,
Till at length into Aix Roland galloped and stood.

X

And all I remember is – friends flocking round
As I sat with his head 'twixt my knees on the ground;
And no voice but was praising this Roland of mine,
As I poured down his throat our last measure of wine,
Which (the burgesses voted by common consent)
Was no more than his due who brought good news from
    Ghent.

SOLILOQUY OF THE SPANISH CLOISTER

I

GR-R-R – there go, my heart's abhorrence!
  Water your damned flower-pots, do!
If hate killed men, Brother Lawrence,
  God's blood, would not mine kill you!
What? your myrtle-bush wants trimming?
  Oh, that rose has prior claims –
Needs its leaden vase filled brimming?
  Hell dry you up with its flames!

II

At the meal we sit together:
  Salve tibi! I must hear
Wise talk of the kind of weather,
  Sort of season, time of year:
Not a plenteous cork-crop: scarcely
  Dare we hope oak-galls, I doubt:
What's the Latin name for 'parsley'?
  What's the Greek name for Swine's Snout?

III

Whew! We'll have our platter burnished,
  Laid with care on our own shelf!
With a fire-new spoon we're furnished,
  And a goblet for ourself,

Rinsed like something sacrificial
    Ere 'tis fit to touch our chaps —
Marked with L. for our initial!
    (He-he! There his lily snaps!)

IV

Saint, forsooth! While brown Dolores
    Squats outside the Convent bank
With Sanchicha, telling stories,
    Steeping tresses in the tank,
Blue-black, lustrous, thick like horsehairs,
    — Can't I see his dead eye glow,
Bright as 'twere a Barbary corsair's?
    (That is, if he'd let it show!)

V

When he finishes refection,
    Knife and fork he never lays
Cross-wise, to my recollection,
    As do I, in Jesu's praise.
I the Trinity illustrate,
    Drinking watered orange-pulp —
In three sips the Arian frustrate;
    While he drains his at one gulp.

VI

Oh, those melons? If he's able
    We're to have a feast! so nice!
One goes to the Abbot's table,
    All of us get each a slice.

How go on your flowers? None double
  Not one fruit-sort can you spy?
Strange! – And I, too, at such trouble,
  Keep them close-nipped on the sly!

VII

There's a great text in Galatians,
  Once you trip on it, entails
Twenty-nine distinct damnations,
  One sure, if another fails:
If I trip him just a-dying,
  Sure of heaven as sure can be,
Spin him around and send him flying
  Off to hell, a Manichee?

VIII

Or, my scrofulous French novel
  On grey paper with blunt type!
Simply glance at it, you grovel
  Hand and foot in Belial's gripe:
If I double down its pages
  At the woeful sixteenth print,
When he gathers his greengages,
  Ope a sieve and slip it in't?

IX

Or, there's Satan! – one might venture
  Pledge one's soul to him, yet leave
Such a flaw in the indenture
  As he'd miss till, past retrieve,
Blasted lay that rose-acacia
  We're so proud of! *Hy, Zy, Hine* . . .
'St, there's Vespers! *Plena gratiâ*
  Ave, Virgo! Gr-r-r – you swine!

THE LABORATORY

ANCIEN RÉGIME

I

Now that I, tying thy glass mask tightly,
May gaze thro' these faint smokes curling whitely,
As thou pliest thy trade in this devil's-smithy –
Which is the poison to poison her, prithee?

II

He is with her, and they know that I know
Where they are, what they do: they believe my tears flow
While they laugh, laugh at me, at me fled to the drear
Empty church, to pray God in, for them! – I am here.

III

Grind away, moisten and mash up thy paste,
Pound at thy powder – I am not in haste!
Better sit thus, and observe thy strange things,
Than go where men wait me and dance at the King's.

IV

That in the mortar – you call it a gum?
Ah, the brave tree whence such gold oozings come!
And yonder soft phial, the exquisite blue,
Sure to taste sweetly, – is that poison too?

V

Had I but all of them, thee and thy treasures,
What a wild crowd of invisible pleasures!
To carry pure death in an earring, a casket,
A signet, a fan-mount, a filigree basket!

VI

Soon, at the King's, a mere lozenge to give,
And Pauline should have just thirty minutes to live!
But to light a pastile, and Elise, with her head
And her breast and her arms and her hands, should drop
  dead!

VII

Quick – is it finished? The colour's too grim!
Why not soft like the phial's, enticing and dim?
Let it brighten her drink, let her turn it and stir,
And try it and taste, ere she fix and prefer!

VIII

What a drop! She's not little, no minion like me!
That's why she ensnared him: this never will free
The soul from those masculine eyes, – say, 'no!'
To that pulse's magnificent come-and-go.

IX

For only last night, as they whispered, I brought
My own eyes to bear on her so, that I thought
Could I keep them one half minute fixed, she would fall
Shrivelled; she fell not; yet this does it all!

X

Not that I bid you spare her the pain;
Let death be felt and the proof remain:
Brand, burn up, bite into its grace –
He is sure to remember her dying face!

XI

Is it done? Take my mask off! Nay, be not morose;
It kills her, and this prevents seeing it close:
The delicate droplet, my whole fortune's fee!
If it hurts her, beside, can it ever hurt me?

XII

Now, take all my jewels, gorge gold to your fill,
You may kiss me, old man, on my mouth if you will!
But brush this dust off me, lest horror it brings
Ere I know it – next moment I dance at the King's!

THE CONFESSIONAL

[SPAIN]

I

IT is a lie – their Priests, their Pope,
Their Saints, their . . . all they fear or hope
Are lies, and lies – there! through my door
And ceiling, there! and walls and floor,
There, lies, they lie – shall still be hurled
Till spite of them I reach the world!

II

You think Priests just and holy men!
Before they put me in this den
I was a human creature too,
With flesh and blood like one of you,
A girl that laughed in beauty's pride
Like lilies in your world outside.

III

I had a lover – shame avaunt!
This poor wrenched body, grim and gaunt,
Was kissed all over till it burned,
By lips the truest, love e'er turned
His heart's own tint: one night they kissed
My soul out in a burning mist.

IV

So, next day when the accustomed train
Of things grew round my sense again,
'That is a sin,' I said: and slow
With downcast eyes to church I go,
And pass to the confession-chair,
And tell the old mild father there.

V

But when I falter Beltran's name,
'Ha?' quoth the father; 'much I blame
The sin; yet wherefore idly grieve?
Despair not – strenuously retrieve!
Nay, I will turn this love of thine
To lawful love, almost divine;

VI

'For he is young, and led astray,
This Beltran, and he schemes, men say,
To change the laws of church and state;
So, thine shall be an angel's fate,
Who, ere the thunder breaks, should roll
Its cloud away and save his soul.

VII

'For, when he lies upon thy breast,
Thou mayst demand and be possessed
Of all his plans, and next day steal
To me, and all those plans reveal,
That I and every priest, to purge
His soul, may fast and use the scourge.'

VIII

That father's beard was long and white,
With love and truth his brow seemed bright;
I went back, all on fire with joy,
And, that same evening, bade the boy
Tell me, as lovers should, heart-free,
Something to prove his love of me.

IX

He told me what he would not tell
For hope of heaven or fear of hell;
And I lay listening in such pride!
And, soon as he had left my side,
Tripped to the church by morning-light
To save his soul in his despite.

X

I told the father all his schemes,
Who were his comrades, what their dreams;
'And now make haste,' I said, 'to pray
The one spot from his soul away;
To-night he comes, but not the same
Will look!' At night he never came.

XI

Nor next night: on the after-morn,
I went forth with a strength new-born.
The church was empty; something drew
My steps into the street; I knew
It led me to the market-place:
Where, lo, on high, the father's face!

XII

That horrible black scaffold dressed,
That stapled block . . . God sink the rest!
That head strapped back, that blinding vest,
Those knotted hands and naked breast,
Till near one busy hangman pressed,
And, on the neck these arms caressed . . .

XIII

No part in aught they hope or fear!
No heaven with them, no hell! – and here,
No earth, not so much space as pens
My body in their worst of dens
But shall bear God and man my cry,
Lies – lies, again – and still, they lie!

THE LOST MISTRESS

I

ALL'S over, then: does truth sound bitter
  As one at first believes?
Hark, 'tis the sparrows' good-night twitter
  About your cottage eaves!

II

And the leaf-buds on the vine are woolly,
  I noticed that, to-day;
One day more bursts them open fully
  — You know the red turns grey.

III

To-morrow we meet the same then, dearest?
  May I take your hand in mine?
Mere friends are we, — well, friends the merest
  Keep much that I resign:

IV

For each glance of the eye so bright and black,
  Though I keep with heart's endeavour, —
Your voice, when you wish the snowdrops back,
  Though it stay in my soul for ever! —

V

Yet I will but say what mere friends say,
  Or only a thought stronger;
I will hold your hand but as long as all may,
  Or so very little longer!

LOVE

So, the year's done with!
   (*Love me for ever!*)
All March begun with,
   April's endeavour;
May-wreaths that bound me
   June needs must sever;
Now snows fall round me,
   Quenching June's fever —
   (*Love me for ever!*)

MEETING AT NIGHT

THE grey sea and the long black land;
And the yellow half-moon large and low;
And the startled little waves that leap
In fiery ringlets from their sleep,
As I gain the cove with pushing prow,
And quench its speed i' the slushy sand.

Then a mile of warm sea-scented beach;
Three fields to cross till a farm appears;
A tap at the pane, the quick sharp scratch
And blue spurt of a lighted match,
And a voice less loud, thro' its joys and fears,
Than the two hearts beating each to each!

PARTING AT MORNING

ROUND the cape of a sudden came the sea,
And the sun looked over the mountain's rim:
And straight was a path of gold for him,
And the need of a world of men for me.

A WOMAN'S LAST WORD

I

Let's contend no more, Love,
   Strive nor weep:
All be as before, Love,
   – Only sleep!

II

What so wild as words are?
   I and thou
In debate, as birds are,
   Hawk on bough!

III

See the creature stalking
   While we speak!
Hush and hide the talking,
   Cheek on cheek!

IV

What so false as truth is,
   False to thee?
Where the serpent's tooth is
   Shun the tree –

V

Where the apple reddens
   Never pry –
Lest we lose our Edens,
   Eve and I.

VI

Be a god and hold me
   With a charm!
Be a man and fold me
   With thine arm!

VII

Teach me, only teach, Love!
   As I ought
I will speak thy speech, Love
   Think thy thought —

VIII

Meet, if thou require it,
   Both demands,
Laying flesh and spirit
   In thy hands.

IX

That shall be to-morrow
   Not to-night:
I must bury sorrow
   Out of sight:

X

— Must a little weep, Love,
   (Foolish me!)
And so fall asleep, Love,
   Loved by thee.

EVELYN HOPE

I

BEAUTIFUL Evelyn Hope is dead!
  Sit and watch by her side an hour.
That is her book-shelf, this her bed;
  She plucked that piece of geranium-flower,
Beginning to die too, in the glass;
  Little has yet been changed, I think:
The shutters are shut, no light may pass
  Save two long rays thro' the hinge's chink.

II

Sixteen years old when she died!
  Perhaps she had scarcely heard my name;
It was not her time to love; beside,
  Her life had many a hope and aim,
Duties enough and little cares,
  And now was quiet, now astir,
Till God's hand beckoned unawares, –
  And the sweet white brow is all of her.

III

Is it too late then, Evelyn Hope?
  What, your soul was pure and true,
The good stars met in your horoscope,
  Made you of spirit, fire and dew –
And, just because I was thrice as old
  And our paths in the world diverged so wide,
Each was nought to each, must I be told?
  We were fellow mortals, nought beside?

IV

No, indeed! for God above
   Is great to grant, as mighty to make,
And creates the love to reward the love:
   I claim you still, for my own love's sake!
Delayed it may be for more lives yet,
   Through worlds I shall traverse, not a few:
Much is to learn, much to forget
   Ere the time be come for taking you.

V

But the time will come, – at last it will,
   When, Evelyn Hope, what meant (I shall say)
In the lower earth, in the years long still,
   That body and soul so pure and gay?
Why your hair was amber, I shall divine,
   And your mouth of your own geranium's red –
And what you would do with me, in fine,
   In the new life come in the old one's stead.

VI

I have lived (I shall say) so much since then,
   Given up myself so many times,
Gained me the gains of various men,
   Ransacked the ages, spoiled the climes;
Yet one thing, one, in my soul's full scope,
   Either I missed or itself missed me:
And I want and find you, Evelyn Hope!
   What is the issue? let us see!

VII

I loved you, Evelyn, all the while.
  My heart seemed full as it could hold?
There was place and to spare for the frank young
    smile,
  And the red young mouth, and the hair's young
    gold.
So, hush, – I will give you this leaf to keep:
  See, I shut it inside the sweet cold hand!
There, that is our secret: go to sleep!
  You will wake, and remember, and understand.

A TOCCATA* OF GALUPPI'S

[Galuppi was a famous Italian composer of the eighteenth century. He was in London from 1741 to 1744.]

I

OH Galuppi, Baldassaro, this is very sad to find!
I can hardly misconceive you; it would prove me deaf and
blind;
But although I take your meaning, 'tis with such a heavy
mind!

II

Here you come with your old music, and here's all the
good it brings.
What, they lived once thus at Venice where the mer-
chants were the kings,
Where Saint Mark's is, where the Doges used to wed the
sea with rings?

III

Ay, because the sea's the street there; and 'tis arched by
... what you call
... Shylock's bridge with houses on it, where they kept the
carnival:
I was never out of England — it's as if I saw it all.

*An overture.

IV

Did young people take their pleasure when the sea was
    warm in May?
Balls and masks begun at midnight, burning ever to
    mid-day,
When they made up fresh adventures for the morrow, do
    you say?

V

Was a lady such a lady, cheeks so round and lips so red, –
On her neck the small face buoyant, like a bell-flower on
    its bed,
O'er the breast's superb abundance where a man might
    base his head?

VI

Well, and it was graceful of them – they'd break talk off
    and afford
– She, to bite her mask's black velvet – he, to finger on his
    sword,
While you sat and played Toccatas, stately at the clavi-
    chord?

VII

What? Those lesser thirds so plaintive, sixths diminished,
    sigh on sigh,
Told them something? Those suspensions, those solutions –
    'Must we die?'
Those commiserating sevenths – 'Life might last! we can
    but try!'

VIII

'Were you happy?' – 'Yes.' – 'And are you still as
    happy?' – 'Yes. And you?'
– 'Then, more kisses!' – 'Did *I* stop them, when a million
    seemed so few?'
Hark, the dominant's persistence till it must be answered
    to!

IX

So, an octave struck the answer. Oh, they praised you, I
    dare say!
'Brave Galuppi! that was music! good alike at grave and
    gay!
I can always leave off talking when I hear a master play!'

X

Then they left you for their pleasure: till in due time, one
    by one,
Some with lives that came to nothing, some with deeds as
    well undone,
Death stepped tacitly and took them where they never
    see the sun.

XI

But when I sit down to reason, think to take my stand nor
    swerve,
While I triumph o'er a secret wrung from nature's close
    reserve,
In you come with your cold music till I creep thro' every
    nerve.

XII

Yes, you, like a ghostly cricket, creaking where a house
was burned:
'Dust and ashes, dead and done with, Venice spent what
Venice earned.
The soul, doubtless, is immortal – where a soul can be
discerned.

XIII

'Yours for instance: you know physics, something of
geology,
Mathematics are your pastime; souls shall rise in their
degree;
Butterflies may dread extinction, – you'll not die, it
cannot be!

XIV

'As for Venice and her people, merely born to bloom and
drop,
Here on earth they bore their fruitage, mirth and folly
were the crop:
What of soul was left, I wonder, when the kissing had to
stop?

XV

'Dust and ashes!' So you creak it, and I want the heart
to scold.
Dear dead women, with such hair, too – what's become of
all the gold
Used to hang and brush their bosoms? I feel chilly and
grown old.

'DE GUSTIBUS—'

I

YOUR ghost will walk, you lover of trees,
    (If our loves remain)
    In an English lane,
By a cornfield-side a-flutter with poppies.
Hark, those two in the hazel coppice –
A boy and a girl, if the good fates please,
    Making love, say, –
    The happier they!
Draw yourself up from the light of the moon,
And let them pass, as they will too soon,
    With the bean-flowers' boon,
    And the blackbird's tune,
    And May, and June!

II

What I love best in all the world
Is a castle, precipice-encurled,
In a gash of the wind-grieved Apennine.
Or look for me, old fellow of mine,
(If I get my head from out the mouth
O' the grave, and loose my spirit's bands,
And come again to the land of lands) –
In a sea-side house to the farther South,
Where the baked cicala dies of drouth,
And one sharp tree – 'tis a cypress – stands,
By the many hundred years red-rusted,
Rough iron-spiked, ripe fruit-o'ercrusted,
My sentinel to guard the sands

To the water's edge. For, what expands
Before the house, but the great opaque
Blue breadth of sea without a break?
While, in the house, for ever crumbles
Some fragment of the frescoed walls,
From blisters where a scorpion sprawls.
A girl bare-footed brings, and tumbles
Down on the pavement, green-flesh melons,
And says there's news to-day – the king
Was shot at, touched in the liver-wing,
Goes with his Bourbon arm in a sling:
– She hopes they have not caught the felons.
Italy, my Italy!
Queen Mary's saying serves for me –
    (When fortune's malice
    Lost her – Calais) –
Open my heart and you will see
Graved inside of it, 'Italy'.
Such lovers old are I and she:
So it always was, so shall ever be!

HOME-THOUGHTS, FROM ABROAD

I

OH, to be in England
Now that April's there,
And whoever wakes in England
Sees, some morning, unaware,
That the lowest boughs and the brushwood sheaf
Round the elm-tree bole are in tiny leaf,
While the chaffinch sings on the orchard bough
In England – now!

II

And after April, when May follows,
And the whitethroat builds, and all the swallows!
Hark, where my blossomed pear-tree in the hedge
Leans to the field and scatters on the clover
Blossoms and dewdrops – at the bent spray's edge –
That's the wise thrush; he sings each song twice over,
Lest you should think he never could recapture
The first fine careless rapture!
And though the fields look rough with hoary dew,
All will be gay when noontide wakes anew
The buttercups, the little children's dower
– Far brighter than this gaudy melon-flower!

HOME-THOUGHTS, FROM THE SEA

Nobly, nobly Cape Saint Vincent to the North-west died
  away;

Sunset ran, one glorious blood-red, reeking into Cadiz
  Bay;

Bluish 'mid the burning water, full in face Trafalgar lay;

In the dimmest North-east distance dawned Gibraltar
  grand and gray;

'Here and here did England help me: how can I help
  England?' – say,

Whoso turns as I, this evening, turn to God to praise and
  pray,

While Jove's planet rises yonder, silent over Africa.

ANY WIFE TO ANY HUSBAND

I

My love, this is the bitterest, that thou —
Who art all truth, and who dost love me now
  As thine eyes say, as thy voice breaks to say —
Shouldst love so truly, and couldst love me still
A whole long life through, had but love its will,
  Would death that leads me from thee brook delay.

II

I have but to be by thee, and thy hand
Will never let mine go, nor heart withstand
  The beating of my heart to reach its place.
When shall I look for thee and feel thee gone?
When cry for the old comfort and find none?
  Never, I know! Thy soul is in thy face.

III

Oh, I should fade — 'tis willed so! Might I save,
Gladly I would, whatever beauty gave
  Joy to thy sense, for that was precious too.
It is not to be granted. But the soul
Whence the love comes, all ravage leaves that whole;
  Vainly the flesh fades; soul makes all things new.

IV

It would not be because my eye grew dim
Thou couldst not find the love there, thanks to Him
  Who never is dishonoured in the spark

He gave us from his fire of fires, and bade
Remember whence it sprang, nor be afraid
  While that burns on, though all the rest grow dark.

V

So, how thou wouldst be perfect, white and clean
Outside as inside, soul and soul's demesne
  Alike, this body given to show it by!
Oh, three-parts through the worst of life's abyss,
What plaudits from the next world after this,
  Couldst thou repeat a stroke and gain the sky!

VI

And is it not the bitterer to think
That, disengage our hands and thou wilt sink
  Although thy love was love in very deed?
I know that nature! Pass a festive day,
Thou dost not throw its relic-flower away
  Nor bid its music's loitering echo speed.

VII

Thou let'st the stranger's glove lie where it fell;
If old things remain old things all is well,
  For thou art grateful as becomes man best:
And hadst thou only heard me play one tune,
Or viewed me from a window, not so soon
  With thee would such things fade as with the rest.

VIII

I seem to see! We meet and part; 'tis brief;
The book I opened keeps a folded leaf,
　　The very chair I sat on, breaks the rank;
That is a portrait of me on the wall –
Three lines, my face comes at so slight a call:
　　And for all this, one little hour to thank!

IX

But now, because the hour through years was fixed,
Because our inmost beings met and mixed,
　　Because thou once hast loved me – wilt thou dare
Say to thy soul and Who may list beside,
'Therefore she is immortally my bride;
　　Chance cannot change my love, nor time impair.

X

'So, what if in the dusk of life that's left,
I, a tired traveller of my sun bereft,
　　Look from my path when, mimicking the same,
The fire-fly glimpses past me, come and gone?
– Where was it till the sunset? where anon
　　It will be at the sunrise! What's to blame?'

XI

Is it so helpful to thee? Canst thou take
The mimic up, nor, for the true thing's sake,
　　Put gently by such efforts at a beam?
Is the remainder of the way so long,
Thou need'st the little solace, thou the strong?
　　Watch out thy watch, let weak ones doze and dream!

XII

– Ah, but the fresher faces! 'Is it true,'
Thou'lt ask, 'some eyes are beautiful and new?
  Some hair, – how can one choose but grasp such wealth?
And if a man would press his lips to lips
Fresh as the wilding hedge-rose-cup there slips
  The drew-drop out of, must it be by stealth?

XIII

'It cannot change the love still kept for Her,
More than if such a picture I prefer
  Passing a day with, to a room's bare side:
The painted form takes nothing she possessed,
Yet, while the Titian's Venus lies at rest,
  A man looks. Once more, what is there to chide?'

XIV

So must I see, from where I sit and watch,
My own self sell myself, my hand attach
  Its warrant to the very thefts from me –
Thy singleness of soul that made me proud,
Thy purity of heart I loved aloud,
  Thy man's-truth I was bold to bid God see!

XV

Love so, then, if thou wilt! Give all thou canst
Away to the new faces – disentranced,
  (Say it and think it) obdurate no more:
Re-issue looks and words from the old mint,
Pass them afresh, no matter whose the print
  Image and superscription once they bore!

XVI

Re-coin thyself and give it them to spend, —
It all comes to the same thing at the end,
   Since mine thou wast, mine art and mine shalt be,
Faithful or faithless, sealing up the sum
Or lavish of my treasure, thou must come
   Back to the heart's place here I keep for thee!

XVII

Only, why should it be with stain at all?
Why must I, 'twixt the leaves of coronal,
   Put any kiss of pardon on thy brow?
Why need the other women know so much,
And talk together, 'Such the look and such
   The smile he used to love with, then as now!'

XVIII

Might I die last and show thee! Should I find
Such hardship in the few years left behind,
   If free to take and light my lamp, and go
Into thy tomb, and shut the door and sit,
Seeing thy face on those four sides of it
   The better that they are so blank, I know!

XIX

Why, time was what I wanted, to turn o'er
Within my mind each look, get more and more
   By heart each word, too much to learn at first;
And join thee all the fitter for the pause
'Neath the low doorway's lintel. That were cause
   For lingering, though thou calledst, if I durst!

XX

And yet thou art the nobler of us two:
What dare I dream of, that thou canst not do,
  Outstripping my ten small steps with one stride?
I'll say then, here's a trial and a task —
Is it to bear? — if easy, I'll not ask:
  Though love fail, I can trust on in thy pride.

XXI

Pride? — when those eyes forestall the life behind
The death I have to go through! — when I find,
  Now that I want thy help most, all of thee!
What did I fear? Thy love shall hold me fast
Until the little minute's sleep is past
  And I wake saved. — And yet it will not be!

TWO IN THE CAMPAGNA

I

I WONDER do you feel to-day
   As I have felt since, hand in hand,
We sat down on the grass, to stray
   In spirit better through the land,
This morn of Rome and May?

II

For me, I touched a thought, I know,
   Has tantalized me many times,
(Like turns of thread the spiders throw
   Mocking across our path) for rhymes
To catch at and let go.

III

Help me to hold it! First it left
   The yellowing fennel, run to seed
There, branching from the brickwork's cleft,
   Some old tomb's ruin: yonder weed
Took up the floating weft,

IV

Where one small orange cup amassed
   Five beetles, — blind and green they grope
Among the honey-meal: and last,
   Everywhere on the grassy slope
I traced it. Hold it fast!

V

The champaign with its endless fleece
    Of feathery grasses everywhere!
Silence and passion, joy and peace,
    An everlasting wash of air —
Rome's ghost since her decease.

VI

Such life here, through such lengths of hours,
    Such miracles performed in play,
Such primal naked forms of flowers,
    Such letting nature have her way
While heaven looks from its towers!

VII

How say you? Let us, O my dove,
    Let us be unashamed of soul,
As earth lies bare to heaven above!
    How is it under our control
To love or not to love?

VIII

I would that you were all to me,
    You that are just so much, no more.
Nor yours nor mine, nor slave nor free!
    Where does the fault lie? What the core
Of the wound, since wound must be?

IX

I would I could adopt your will,
    See with your eyes, and set my heart
Beating by yours, and drink my fill
    At your soul's springs, — your part my part
In life, for good and ill.

X

No. I yearn upward, touch you close,
   Then stand away. I kiss your cheek,
Catch your soul's warmth, – I pluck the rose
   And love it more than tongue can speak –
Then the good minute goes.

XI

Already how am I so far
   Out of that minute? Must I go
Still like the thistle-ball, no bar,
   Onward, whenever light winds blow,
Fixed by no friendly star?

XII

Just when I seemed about to learn!
   Where is the thread now? Off again!
The old trick! Only I discern –
   Infinite passion, and the pain
Of finite hearts that yearn.

MISCONCEPTIONS

I

THIS is a spray the Bird clung to,
    Making it blossom with pleasure,
Ere the high tree-top she sprung to,
    Fit for her nest and her treasure.
    Oh, what a hope beyond measure
Was the poor spray's, which the flying feet hung to, —
So to be singled out, built in, and sung to!

II

This is a heart the Queen leant on,
    Thrilled in a minute erratic,
Ere the true bosom she bent on,
    Meet for love's regal dalmatic.
    Oh, what a fancy ecstatic
Was the poor heart's, ere the wanderer went on —
Love to be saved for it, proffered to, spent on!

LOVE IN A LIFE

I

Room after room,
I hunt the house through
We inhabit together.
Heart, fear nothing, for, heart, thou shalt find her —
Next time, herself! — not the trouble behind her
Left in the curtain, the couch's perfume!
As she brushed it, the cornice-wreath blossomed anew:
Yon looking-glass gleamed at the wave of her feather.

II

Yet the day wears,
And door succeeds door;
I try the fresh fortune —
Range the wide house from the wing to the centre.
Still the same chance! she goes out as I enter.
Spend my whole day in the quest, — who cares?
But 'tis twilight, you see, — with such suites to explore,
Such closets to search, such alcoves to importune!

LIFE IN A LOVE

ESCAPE me?
Never –
Beloved!
While I am I, and you are you,
 So long as the world contains us both,
 Me the loving and you the loth,
While the one eludes, must the other pursue.
My life is a fault at last, I fear:
 It seems too much like a fate, indeed!
 Though I do my best I shall scarce succeed.
But what if I fail of my purpose here?
It is but to keep the nerves at strain,
 To dry one's eyes and laugh at a fall,
And, baffled, get up and begin again, –
 So the chace takes up one's life, that's all.
While, look but once from your farthest bound
 At me so deep in the dust and dark,
No sooner the old hope goes to ground
 Than a new one, straight to the self-same mark,
I shape me –
Ever
Removed!

IN THREE DAYS

I

So, I shall see her in three days
And just one night, but nights are short,
Then two long hours, and that is morn.
See how I come, unchanged, unworn!
Feel, where my life broke off from thine,
How fresh the splinters keep and fine, –
Only a touch and we combine!

II

Too long, this time of year, the days!
But nights, at least the nights are short.
As night shows where her one moon is,
A hand's-breadth of pure light and bliss,
So life's night gives my lady birth
And my eyes hold her! What is worth
The rest of heaven, the rest of earth?

III

O loaded curls, release your store
Of warmth and scent, as once before
The tingling hair did, lights and darks
Outbreaking into fairy sparks,
When under curl and curl I pried
After the warmth and scent inside,
Thro' lights and darks how manifold –
The dark inspired, the light controlled!
As early Art embrowns the gold.

IV

What great fear, should one say, 'Three days
That change the world might change as well
Your fortune; and if joy delays,
Be happy that no worse befell!'
What small fear, if another says,
'Three days and one short night beside
May throw no shadow on your ways;
But years must teem with change untried,
With chance not easily defied,
With an end somewhere undescried.'
No fear! – or if a fear be born
This minute, it dies out in scorn.
Fear? I shall see her in three days
And one night, now the nights are short,
Then just two hours, and that is morn.

IN A YEAR

I

NEVER any more,
   While I live,
Need I hope to see his face
   As before.
Once his love grown chill,
   Mine may strive:
Bitterly we re-embrace,
   Single still.

II

Was it something said,
   Something done,
Vexed him? was it touch of hand,
   Turn of head?
Strange! that very way
   Love begun:
I as little understand
   Love's decay.

III

When I sewed or drew,
   I recall
How he looked as if I sung,
   – Sweetly too.
If I spoke a word,
   First of all
Up his cheek the colour sprung,
   Then he heard.

IV

Sitting by my side,
　　At my feet,
So he breathed but air I breathed,
　　Satisfied!
I, too, at love's brim
　　Touched the sweet:
I would die if death bequeathed
　　Sweet to him.

V

'Speak, I love thee best!'
　　He exclaimed:
'Let thy love my own foretell!'
　　I confessed:
'Clasp my heart on thine
　　Now unblamed,
Since upon thy soul as well
　　Hangeth mine!'

VI

Was it wrong to own,
　　Being truth?
Why should all the giving prove
　　His alone?
I had wealth and ease,
　　Beauty, youth:
Since my lover gave me love,
　　I gave these.

VII

That was all I meant,
  – To be just,
And the passion I had raised,
  To content.
Since he chose to change
  Gold for dust,
If I gave him what he praised
  Was it strange?

VIII

Would he loved me yet,
  On and on,
While I found some way undreamed
  – Paid my debt!
Gave more life and more,
  Till, all gone,
He should smile 'She never seemed
  Mine before.'

IX

'What, she felt the while,
  Must I think?
Love's so different with us men!'
  He should smile:
'Dying for my sake –
  White and pink!
Can't we touch these bubbles then
  But they break?'

X

Dear, the pang is brief,
  Do thy part,
Have thy pleasure! How perplexed
  Grows belief!
Well, this cold clay clod
  Was man's heart:
Crumble it, and what comes next?
  Is it God?

MEMORABILIA

I

Ah, did you once see Shelley plain,
  And did he stop and speak to you
And did you speak to him again?
  How strange it seems and new!

II

But you were living before that,
  And also you are living after;
And the memory I started at –
  My starting moves your laughter.

III

I crossed a moor, with a name of its own
  And a certain use in the world no doubt,
Yet a hand's-breadth of it shines alone
  'Mid the blank miles round about:

IV

For there I picked up on the heather
  And there I put inside my breast
A moulted feather, an eagle-feather!
  Well, I forget the rest.

THE PATRIOT

AN OLD STORY

I

It was roses, roses, all the way,
  With myrtle mixed in my path like mad:
The house-roofs seemed to heave and sway,
  The church-spires flamed, such flags they had,
A year ago on this very day.

II

The air broke into a mist with bells,
  The old walls rocked with the crowd and cries.
Had I said, 'Good folk, mere noise repels –
  But give me your sun from yonder skies!'
They had answered, 'And afterward, what else?'

III

Alack, it was I who leaped at the sun
  To give it my loving friends to keep!
Nought man could do, have I left undone:
  And you see my harvest, what I reap
This very day, now a year is run.

IV

There's nobody on the house-tops now –
  Just a palsied few at the windows set;
For the best of the sight is, all allow,
  At the Shambles' Gate – or, better yet,
By the very scaffold's foot, I trow.

V

I go in the rain, and, more than needs,
  A rope cuts both my wrists behind;
And I think, by the feel, my forehead bleeds
  For they fling, whoever has a mind,
Stones at me for my year's misdeeds.

VI

Thus I entered, and thus I go!
  In triumphs, people have dropped down dead.
'Paid by the world, what dost thou owe
  Me?' – God might question; now instead,
'Tis God shall repay: I am safer so.

MY LAST DUCHESS

FERRARA

THAT'S my last Duchess painted on the wall,
Looking as if she were alive. I call
That piece a wonder, now: Frà Pandolf's hands
Worked busily a day, and there she stands.
Will't please you sit and look at her? I said
'Frà Pandolf' by design, for never read
Strangers like you that pictured countenance,
The depth and passion of its earnest glance,
But to myself they turned (since none puts by
The curtain I have drawn for you, but I)
And seemed as they would ask me, if they durst,
How such a glance came there; so, not the first
Are you to turn and ask thus. Sir, 'twas not
Her husband's presence only, called that spot
Of joy into the Duchess' cheek: perhaps
Frà Pandolf chanced to say 'Her mantle laps
Over my lady's wrist too much,' or 'Paint
Must never hope to reproduce the faint
Half-flush that dies along her throat:' such stuff
Was courtesy, she thought, and cause enough
For calling up that spot of joy. She had
A heart – how shall I say? – too soon made glad,
Too easily impressed; she liked whate'er
She looked on, and her looks went everywhere.
Sir, 'twas all one! My favour at her breast,
The dropping of the daylight in the West,
The bough of cherries some officious fool
Broke in the orchard for her, the white mule

She rode with round the terrace – all and each
Would draw from her alike the approving speech,
Or blush, at least. She thanked men, – good! but thanked
Somehow – I know not how – as if she ranked
My gift of a nine-hundred-years-old name
With anybody's gift. Who'd stoop to blame
This sort of trifling? Even had you skill
In speech – (which I have not) – to make your will
Quite clear to such an one, and say, 'Just this
Or that in you disgusts me; here you miss,
Or there exceed the mark' – and if she let
Herself be lessoned so, nor plainly set
Her wits to yours, forsooth, and made excuse,
– E'en then would be some stooping; and I choose
Never to stoop. Oh sir, she smiled, no doubt,
Whene'er I passed her; but who passed without
Much the same smile? This grew; I gave commands;
Then all smiles stopped together. There she stands
As if alive. Will't please you rise? We'll meet
The company below, then. I repeat,
The Count your master's known munificence
Is ample warrant that no just pretence
Of mine for dowry will be disallowed;
Though his fair daughter's self, as I avowed
At starting, is my object. Nay, we'll go
Together down, sir. Notice Neptune, though,
Taming a sea-horse, thought a rarity,
Which Claus of Innsbruck cast in bronze for me!

THE BOY AND THE ANGEL

MORNING, evening, noon and night,
'Praise God!' sang Theocrite.

Then to his poor trade he turned,
Whereby the daily meal was earned.

Hard he laboured, long and well;
O'er his work the boy's curls fell.

But ever, at each period,
He stopped and sang, 'Praise God!'

Then back again his curls he threw,
And cheerful turned to work anew.

Said Blaise, the listening monk, 'Well done;
I doubt not thou art heard, my son:

'As well as if thy voice to-day
Were praising God, the Pope's great way.

'This Easter Day, the Pope at Rome
Praises God from Peter's dome.'

Said Theocrite, 'Would God that I
Might praise him, that great way, and die!'

Night passed, day shone,
And Theocrite was gone.

With God a day endures alway,
A thousand years are but a day.

God said in heaven, 'Nor day nor night
Now brings the voice of my delight.'

Then Gabriel, like a rainbow's birth,
Spread his wings and sank to earth;

Entered, in flesh, the empty cell,
Lived there, and played the craftsman well;

And morning, evening, noon and night,
Praised God in place of Theocrite.

And from a boy, to youth he grew:
The man put off the stripling's hue:

The man matured and fell away
Into the season of decay:

And ever o'er the trade he bent,
And ever lived on earth content.

(He did God's will; to him, all one
If on the earth or in the sun.)

God said, 'A praise is in mine ear;
There is no doubt in it, no fear:

'So sing old worlds, and so
New worlds that from my footstool go.

'Clearer loves sound other ways:
I miss my little human praise.'

Then forth sprang Gabriel's wings, off fell
The flesh disguise, remained the cell.

'Twas Easter Day: he flew to Rome,
And paused above Saint Peter's dome.

In the tiring-room close by
The great outer gallery,

With his holy vestments dight,
Stood the new Pope, Theocrite:

And all his past career
Came back upon him clear,

Since when, a boy, he plied his trade,
Till on his life the sickness weighed;

And in his cell, when death drew near,
An angel in a dream brought cheer:

And rising from the sickness drear
He grew a priest, and now stood here.

To the East with praise he turned,
And on his sight the angel burned.

'I bore thee from thy craftsman's cell
And set thee here; I did not well.

'Vainly I left my angel-sphere,
Vain was thy dream of many a year.

'Thy voice's praise seemed weak; it dropped —
Creation's chorus stopped!

'Go back and praise again
The early way, while I remain.

'With that weak voice of our disdain,
Take up creation's pausing strain.

'Back to the cell and poor employ:
Resume the craftsman and the boy!'

Theocrite grew old at home;
A new Pope dwelt in Peter's dome.

One vanished as the other died:
They sought God side by side.

THE ITALIAN IN ENGLAND

THAT second time they hunted me
From hill to plain, from shore to sea,
And Austria, hounding far and wide
Her blood-hounds thro' the country-side,
Breathed hot and instant on my trace, —
I made six days a hiding-place
Of that dry green old aqueduct
Where I and Charles, when boys, have plucked
The fire-flies from the roof above,
Bright creeping thro' the moss they love:
— How long it seems since Charles was lost!
Six days the soldiers crossed and crossed
The country in my very sight;
And when that peril ceased at night,
The sky broke out in red dismay
With signal fires; well, there I lay
Close covered o'er in my recess,
Up to the neck in ferns and cress,
Thinking on Metternich our friend,
And Charles's miserable end,
And much beside, two days; the third,
Hunger o'ercame me when I heard
The peasants from the village go
To work among the maize; you know,
With us in Lombardy, they bring
Provisions packed on mules, a string
With little bells that cheer their task,
And casks, and boughs on every cask

To keep the sun's heat from the wine;
These I let pass in jingling line,
And, close on them, dear noisy crew,
The peasants from the village, too;
For at the very rear would troop
Their wives and sisters in a group
To help, I knew. When these had passed,
I threw my glove to strike the last,
Taking the chance: she did not start,
Much less cry out, but stooped apart,
One instant rapidly glanced round,
And saw me beckon from the ground.
A wild bush grows and hides my crypt;
She picked my glove up while she stripped
A branch off, then rejoined the rest
With that; my glove lay in her breast.
Then I drew breath; they disappeared:
It was for Italy I feared.

An hour, and she returned alone
Exactly where my glove was thrown.
Meanwhile came many thoughts: on me
Rested the hopes of Italy.
I had devised a certain tale
Which, when 'twas told her, could not fail
Persuade a peasant of its truth;
I meant to call a freak of youth
This hiding, and give hopes of pay,
And no temptation to betray.
But when I saw that woman's face,
Its calm simplicity of grace,
Our Italy's own attitude
In which she walked thus far, and stood,

Planting each naked foot so firm,
To crush the snake and spare the worm –
At first sight of her eyes, I said,
'I am that man upon whose head
They fix the price, because I hate
The Austrians over us: the State
Will give you gold – oh, gold so much! –
If you betray me to their clutch,
And be your death, for aught I know,
If once they find you saved their foe.
Now, you must bring me food and drink,
And also paper, pen and ink,
And carry safe what I shall write
To Padua, which you'll reach at night
Before the duomo shuts; go in,
And wait till Tenebrae begin;
Walk to the third confessional,
Between the pillar and the wall,
And kneeling whisper, *Whence comes peace?*
Say it a second time, then cease;
And if the voice inside returns,
*From Christ and Freedom; what concerns
The cause of Peace?* – for answer, slip
My letter where you placed your lip;
Then come back happy we have done
Our mother service – I, the son,
As you the daughter of our land!'

Three mornings more, she took her stand
In the same place, with the same eyes:
I was no surer of sun-rise
Than of her coming. We conferred
Of her own prospects, and I heard

75

She had a lover – stout and tall,
She said – then let her eyelids fall,
'He could do much' – as if some doubt
Entered her heart, – then, passing out,
'She could not speak for others, who
Had other thoughts; herself she knew:'
And so she brought me drink and food.
After four days, the scouts pursued
Another path; at last arrived
The help my Paduan friends contrived
To furnish me: she brought the news.
For the first time I could not choose
But kiss her hand, and lay my own
Upon her head – 'This faith was shown
To Italy, our mother; she
Uses my hand and blesses thee.'
She followed down to the sea-shore;
I left and never saw her more.

How very long since I have thought
Concerning – much less wished for – aught
Beside the good of Italy,
For which I live and mean to die!
I never was in love; and since
Charles proved false, what shall now convince
My inmost heart I have a friend?
However, if I pleased to spend
Real wishes on myself – say, three –
I know at least what one should be.
I would grasp Metternich until
I felt his red wet throat distil
In blood thro' these two hands. And next,
– Nor much for that am I perplexed –

Charles, perjured traitor, for his part,
Should die slow of a broken heart
Under his new employers. Last
– Ah, there, what should I wish? For fast
Do I grow old and out of strength.
If I resolved to seek at length
My father's house again, how scared
They all would look, and unprepared!
My brothers live in Austria's pay
– Disowned me long ago, men say;
And all my early mates who used
To praise me so – perhaps induced
More than one early step of mine –
Are turning wise: while some opine
'Freedom grows license,' some suspect
'Haste breeds delay,' and recollect
They always said, such premature
Beginnings never could endure!
So, with a sullen 'All's for best,'
The land seems settling to its rest.
I think then, I should wish to stand
This evening in that dear, lost land,
Over the sea the thousand miles,
And know if yet that woman smiles
With the calm smile; some little farm
She lives in there, no doubt: what harm
If I sat on the door-side bench,
And, while her spindle made a trench
Fantastically in the dust,
Inquired of all her fortunes – just
Her children's ages and their names,
And what may be the husband's aims
For each of them. I'd talk this out,

And sit there, for an hour about,
Then kiss her hand once more, and lay
Mine on her head, and go my way.

So much for idle wishing – how
It steals the time! To business now.

THE ENGLISHMAN IN ITALY

Fortù, Fortù, my beloved one,
    Sit here by my side,
On my knees put up both little feet!
    I was sure, if I tried,
I could make you laugh spite of Scirocco.
    Now, open your eyes,
Let me keep you amused till he vanish
    In black from the skies,
With telling my memories over
    As you tell your beads;
All the Plain saw me gather, I garland
    — The flowers or the weeds.

Time for rain! for your long hot dry Autumn
    Had net-worked with brown
The white skin of each grape on the bunches,
    Marked like a quail's crown,
Those creatures you make such account of,
    Whose heads, — speckled white
Over brown like a great spider's back,
    As I told you last night, —
Your mother bites off for her supper.
    Red-ripe as could be,
Pomegranates were chapping and splitting
    In halves on the tree:
And betwixt the loose walls of great flintstone,
    Or in the thick dust

On the path, or straight out of the rockside,
    Wherever could thrust
Some burnt sprig of bold hardy rock-flower
    Its yellow face up,
For the prize were great butterflies fighting,
    Some five for one cup.
So, I guessed, ere I got up this morning,
    What change was in store,
By the quick rustle-down of the quail-nets
    Which woke me before
I could open my shutter, made fast
    With a bough and a stone,
And look thro' the twisted dead vine-twigs,
    Sole lattice that's known.
Quick and sharp rang the rings down the net-poles,
    While, busy beneath,
Your priest and his brother tugged at them,
    The rain in their teeth.
And out upon all the flat house-roofs
    Where split figs lay drying,
The girls took the frails under cover:
    Nor use seemed in trying
To get out the boats and go fishing,
    For, under the cliff,
Fierce the black water frothed o'er the blindrock.
    No seeing our skiff
Arrive about noon from Amalfi,
    – Our fisher arrive,
And pitch down his basket before us,
    All trembling alive
With pink and grey jellies, your sea-fruit;
    You touch the strange lumps,

And mouths gape there, eyes open, all manner
    Of horns and of humps,
Which only the fisher looks grave at,
    While round him like imps
Cling screaming the children as naked
    And brown as his shrimps;
Himself too as bare to the middle
    — You see round his neck
The string and its brass coin suspended,
    That saves him from wreck.
But to-day not a boat reached Salerno,
    So back, to a man,
Came our friends, with whose help in the vineyards
    Grape-harvest began.
In the vat, halfway up in our house-side,
    Like blood the juice spins,
While your brother all bare-legged is dancing
    Till breathless he grins
Dead-beaten in effort on effort
    To keep the grapes under,
Since still when he seems all but master,
    In pours the fresh plunder
From girls who keep coming and going
    With basket on shoulder,
And eyes shut against the rain's driving;
    Your girls that are older, —
For under the hedges of aloe,
    And where, on its bed
Of the orchard's black mould, the love-apple
    Lies pulpy and red,
All the young ones are kneeling and filling
    Their laps with the snails

Tempted out by this first rainy weather, —
    Your best of regales,
As to-night will be proved to my sorrow,
    When, supping in state,
We shall feast our grape-gleaners (two dozen,
    Three over one plate)
With lasagne so tempting to swallow
    In slippery ropes,
And gourds fried in great purple slices,
    That colour of popes.
Meantime, see the grape bunch they've brought you:
    The rain-water slips
O'er the heavy blue bloom on each globe
    Which the wasp to your lips
Still follows with fretful persistence:
    Nay, taste, while awake,
This half of a curd-white smooth cheese-ball
    That peels, flake by flake,
Like an onion, each smoother and whiter;
    Next, sip this weak wine
From the thin green glass flask, with its stopper,
    A leaf of the vine;
And end with the prickly-pear's red flesh
    That leaves thro' its juice
The stony black seeds on your pearl-teeth.
    Scirocco is loose!
Hark, the quick, whistling pelt of the olives
    Which, thick in one's track,
Tempt the stranger to pick up and bite them,
    Tho' not yet half black!
How the old twisted olive trunks shudder,
    The medlars let fall

Their hard fruit, and the brittle great fig-trees
    Snap off, figs and all,
For here comes the whole of the tempest!
    No refuge, but creep
Back again to my side and my shoulder,
    And listen or sleep.
O how will your country show next week,
    When all the vine-boughs
Have been stripped of their foliage to pasture
    The mules and the cows?
Last eve, I rode over the mountains;
    Your brother, my guide,
Soon left me, to feast on the myrtles
    That offered, each side,
Their fruit-balls, black, glossy and luscious, —
    Or strip from the sorbs
A treasure, or, rosy and wondrous,
    Those hairy gold orbs!
But my mule picked his sure sober path out,
    Just stopping to neigh
When he recognized down in the valley
    His mates on their way
With the faggots and barrels of water;
    And soon we emerged
From the plain, where the woods could scarce follow;
    And still as we urged
Our way, the woods wondered, and left us,
    As up still we trudged
Though the wild path grew wilder each instant,
    And place was e'en grudged
'Mid the rock-chasms and piles of loose stones
    Like the loose broken teeth

Of some monster which climbed there to die
    From the ocean beneath –
Place was grudged to the silver-grey fume-weed
    That clung to the path,
And dark rosemary ever a-dying
    That, 'spite the wind's wrath,
So loves the salt rock's face to seaward,
    And lentisks as staunch
To the stone where they root and bear berries,
    And . . . what shows a branch
Coral-coloured, transparent, with circlets
    Of pale seagreen leaves;
Over all trod my mule with the caution
    Of gleaners o'er sheaves,
Still, foot after foot like a lady,
    Till, round after round,
He climbed to the top of Calvano,
    And God's own profound
Was above me, and round me the mountains,
    And under, the sea,
And within me my heart to bear witness
    What was and shall be.
Oh, heaven and the terrible crystal!
    No rampart excludes
Your eye from the life to be lived
    In the blue solitudes.
Oh, those mountains, their infinite movement!
    Still moving with you;
For, ever some new head and breast of them
    Thrusts into view
To observe the intruder; you see it
    If quickly you turn

And, before they escape you surprise them.
    They grudge you should learn
How the soft plains they look on, lean over
    And love (they pretend)
— Cower beneath them, the flat sea-pine crouches,
    The wild fruit-trees bend,
E'en the myrtle-leaves curl, shrink and shut:
    All is silent and grave:
'Tis a sensual and timorous beauty,
    How fair! but a slave.
So, I turned to the sea; and there slumbered
    As greenly as ever
Those isles of the siren, your Galli;
    No ages can sever
The Three, nor enable their sister
    To join them, – halfway
On the voyage, she looked at Ulysses
    No farther to-day,
Tho' the small one, just launched in the wave,
    Watches breast-high and steady
From under the rock, her bold sister
    Swum halfway already.
Fortù, shall we sail there together
    And see from the sides
Quite new rocks show their faces, new haunts
    Where the siren abides?
Shall we sail round and round them, close over
    The rocks, tho' unseen,
That ruffle the grey glassy water
    To glorious green?
Then scramble from splinter to splinter,
    Reach land and explore,

On the largest, the strange square black turret
    With never a door,
Just a loop to admit the quick lizards;
    Then, stand there and hear
The birds' quiet singing, that tells us
    What life is, so clear?
— The secret they sang to Ulysses
    When, ages ago,
He heard and he knew this life's secret
    I hear and I know.

Ah, see! The sun breaks o'er Calvano;
    He strikes the great gloom
And flutters it o'er the mount's summit
    In airy gold fume.
All is over. Look out, see the gipsy,
    Our tinker and smith,
Has arrived, set up bellows and forge,
    And down-squatted forthwith
To his hammering, under the wall there;
    One eye keeps aloof
The urchins that itch to be putting
    His jews'-harps to proof,
While the other, thro' locks of curled wire,
    Is watching how sleek
Shines the hog, come to share in the windfall
    — Chew, abbot's own cheek!
All is over. Wake up and come out now,
    And down let us go,
And see the fine things got in order
    At church for the show
Of the Sacrament, set forth this evening.
    To-morrow's the Feast

Of the Rosary's Virgin, by no means
  Of Virgins the least,
As you'll hear in the off-hand discourse
  Which (all nature, no art)
The Dominican brother, these three weeks,
  Was getting by heart.
Not a pillar nor post but is dizened
  With red and blue papers;
All the roof waves with ribbons, each altar
  A-blaze with long tapers;
But the great masterpiece is the scaffold
  Rigged glorious to hold
All the fiddlers and fifers and drummers
  And trumpeters bold,
Not afraid of Bellini nor Auber,
  Who, when the priest's hoarse,
Will strike us up something that's brisk
  For the feast's second course.
And then will the flaxen-wigged Image
  Be carried in pomp
Thro' the plain, while in gallant procession
  The priests mean to stomp.
All round the glad church lie old bottles
  With gunpowder stopped,
Which will be, when the Image re-enters,
  Religiously popped;
And at night from the crest of Calvano
  Great bonfires will hang,
On the plain will the trumpets join chorus,
  And more poppers bang.
At all events, come – to the garden
  As far as the wall;

See me tap with a hoe on the plaster
    Till out there shall fall
A scorpion with wide angry nippers!

    – 'Such trifles!' you say?
Fortù, in my England at home,
    Men meet gravely to-day
And debate, if abolishing Corn-laws
    Be righteous and wise
– If 'twere proper, Scirocco should vanish
    In black from the skies!

A LIGHT WOMAN

I

So far as our story approaches the end,
  Which do you pity the most of us three? –
My friend, or the mistress of my friend
  With her wanton eyes, or me?

II

My friend was already too good to lose,
  And seemed in the way of improvement yet,
When she crossed his path with her hunting-noose
  And over him drew her net.

III

When I saw him tangled in her toils,
  A shame, said I, if she adds just him
To her nine-and-ninety other spoils,
  The hundredth for a whim!

IV

And before my friend be wholly hers,
  How easy to prove to him, I said,
An eagle's the game her pride prefers,
  Though she snaps at a wren instead!

V

So, I gave her eyes my own eyes to take,
  My hand sought hers as in earnest need,
And round she turned for my noble sake,
  And gave me herself indeed.

VI

The eagle am I, with my fame in the world,
    The wren is he, with his maiden face.
— You look away and your lip is curled?
    Patience, a moment's space!

VII

For see, my friend goes shaking and white;
    He eyes me as the basilisk:
I have turned, it appears, his day to night,
    Eclipsing his sun's disk.

VIII

And I did it, he thinks, as a very thief:
    'Though I love her — that, he comprehends —
One should master one's passions, (love, in chief)
    And be loyal to one's friends!'

IX

And she, — she lies in my hand as tame
    As a pear late basking over a wall;
Just a touch to try and off it came;
    'Tis mine, — can I let it fall?

X

With no mind to eat it, that's the worst!
    Were it thrown in the road, would the case assist?
'Twas quenching a dozen blue-flies' thirst
    When I gave its stalk a twist.

XI

And I, – what I seem to my friend, you see:
　　What I soon shall seem to his love, you guess:
What I seem to myself, do you ask of me?
　　No hero, I confess.

XII

'Tis an awkward thing to play with souls,
　　And matter enough to save one's own:
Yet think of my friend, and the burning coals
　　He played with for bits of stone!

XIII

One likes to show the truth for the truth;
　　That the woman was light is very true:
But suppose she says, – Never mind that youth!
　　What wrong have I done to you?

XIV

Well, any how, here the story stays,
　　So far at least as I understand;
And, Robert Browning, you writer of plays,
　　Here's a subject made to your hand!

THE LAST RIDE TOGETHER

I

I SAID – Then, dearest, since 'tis so,
Since now at length my fate I know,
Since nothing all my love avails,
Since all, my life seemed meant for, fails,
    Since this was written and needs must be –
My whole heart rises up to bless
Your name in pride and thankfulness!
Take back the hope you gave, – I claim
Only a memory of the same,
– And this beside, if you will not blame,
    Your leave for one more last ride with me.

II

My mistress bent that brow of hers;
Those deep dark eyes where pride demurs
When pity would be softening through,
Fixed me a breathing-while or two
    With life or death in the balance: right!
The blood replenished me again;
My last thought was at least not vain:
I and my mistress, side by side
Shall be together, breathe and ride,
So, one day more am I deified.
    Who knows but the world may end to-night?

III

Hush! if you saw some western cloud
All billowy-bosomed, over-bowed
By many benedictions – sun's
And moon's and evening-star's at once –
   And so, you, looking and loving best,
Conscious grew, your passion drew
Cloud, sunset, moonrise, star-shine too,
Down on you, near and yet more near,
Till flesh must fade for heaven was here! –
Thus leant she and lingered – joy and fear!
   Thus lay she a moment on my breast.

IV

Then we began to ride. My soul
Smoothed itself out, a long-cramped scroll
Freshening and fluttering in the wind.
Past hopes already lay behind.
   What need to strive with a life awry?
Had I said that, had I done this,
So might I gain, so might I miss.
Might she have loved me? just as well
She might have hated, who can tell!
Where had I been now if the worst befell?
   And here we are riding, she and I.

V

Fail I alone, in words and deeds?
Why, all men strive and who succeeds?
We rode; it seemed my spirit flew,
Saw other regions, cities new,
   As the world rushed by on either side.

I thought, – All labour, yet no less
Bear up beneath their unsuccess.
Look at the end of work, contrast
The petty done, the undone vast,
This present of theirs with the hopeful past!
   I hoped she would love me; here we ride.

VI

What hand and brain went ever paired?
What heart alike conceived and dared?
What act proved all its thought had been?
What will but felt the fleshly screen?
   We ride and I see her bosom heave.
There's many a crown for who can reach.
Ten lines, a statesman's life in each!
The flag stuck on a heap of bones,
A soldier's doing! what atones?
They scratch his name on the Abbey-stones.
   My riding is better, by their leave.

VII

What does it all mean, poet? Well,
Your brains beat into rhythm, you tell
What we felt only; you expressed
You hold things beautiful the best,
   And pace them in rhyme so, side by side.
'Tis something, nay 'tis much: but then,
Have you yourself what's best for men?
Are you – poor, sick, old ere your time –
Nearer one whit your own sublime
Than we who never have turned a rhyme?
   Sing, riding's a joy! For me, I ride.

VIII

And you, great sculptor – so, you gave
A score of years to Art, her slave,
And that's your Venus, whence we turn
To yonder girl that fords the burn!
   You acquiesce, and shall I repine?
What, man of music, you grown grey
With notes and nothing else to say,
Is this your sole praise from a friend,
'Greatly his opera's strains intend,
But in music we know how fashions end!'
   I gave my youth; but we ride, in fine.

IX

Who knows what's fit for us? Had fate
Proposed bliss here should sublimate
My being – had I signed the bond –
Still one must lead some life beyond,
   Have a bliss to die with, dim-descried.
This foot once planted on the goal,
This glory-garland round my soul,
Could I descry such? Try and test!
I sink back shuddering from the quest.
Earth being so good, would heaven seem best?
   Now, heaven and she are beyond this ride.

X

And yet – she has not spoke so long!
What if heaven be that, fair and strong
At life's best, with our eyes upturned
Whither life's flower is first discerned,
   We, fixed so, ever should so abide?

What if we still ride on, we two
With life for ever old yet new,
Changed not in kind but in degree,
The instant made eternity, –
And heaven just prove that I and she
   Ride, ride together, for ever ride?

THE PIED PIPER OF HAMELIN

A CHILD'S STORY

I

HAMELIN Town's in Brunswick,
 By famous Hanover city;
The river Weser, deep and wide,
Washes its wall on the southern side;
A pleasanter spot you never spied;
 But, when begins my ditty,
Almost five hundred years ago,
To see the townsfolk suffer so
 From vermin, was a pity.

II

 Rats!
They fought the dogs and killed the cats,
 And bit the babies in the cradles,
And ate the cheeses out of the vats,
 And licked the soup from the cooks' own ladles,
Split open the kegs of salted sprats,
Made nests inside men's Sunday hats,
And even spoiled the women's chats
  By drowning their speaking
  With shrieking and squeaking
In fifty different sharps and flats.

III

At last the people in a body
 To the Town Hall came flocking:
''Tis clear,' cried they, 'our Mayor's a noddy;
 And as for our Corporation – shocking

To think we buy gowns lined with ermine
For dolts that can't or won't determine
What's best to rid us of our vermin!
You hope, because you're old and obese,
To find in the furry civic robe ease?
Rouse up, sirs! Give your brains a racking
To find the remedy we're lacking,
Or, sure as fate, we'll send you packing!'
At this the Mayor and Corporation
Quaked with a mighty consternation.

IV

An hour they sat in council,
   At length the Mayor broke silence:
'For a guilder I'd my ermine gown sell,
   I wish I were a mile hence!
It's easy to bid one rack one's brain –
I'm sure my poor head aches again,
I've scratched it so, and all in vain.
Oh for a trap, a trap, a trap!'
Just as he said this, what should hap
At the chamber door but a gentle tap?
'Bless us,' cried the Mayor, 'what's that?'
(With the Corporation as he sat,
Looking little though wondrous fat;
Nor brighter was his eye, nor moister
Than a too-long-opened oyster,
Save when at noon his paunch grew mutinous
For a plate of turtle green and glutinous)
'Only a scraping of shoes on the mat?
Anything like the sound of a rat
Makes my heart go pit-a-pat!'

V

'Come in!' – the Mayor cried, looking bigger.
And in did come the strangest figure!
His queer long coat from heel to head
Was half of yellow and half of red,
And he himself was tall and thin,
With sharp blue eyes, each like a pin,
And light loose hair, yet swarthy skin,
No tuft on cheek nor beard on chin,
But lips where smiles went out and in;
There was no guessing his kith and kin:
And nobody could enough admire
The tall man and his quaint attire.
Quoth one: 'It's as my great-grandsire,
Starting up at the Trump of Doom's tone,
Had walked this way from his painted tombstone!'

VI

He advanced to the council-table:
And, 'Please your honours,' said he, 'I'm able,
By means of a secret charm, to draw
    All creatures living beneath the sun,
    That creep or swim or fly or run,
After me so as you never saw!
And I chiefly use my charm
On creatures that do people harm,
The mole and toad and newt and viper;
And people call me the Pied Piper.'
(And here they noticed round his neck
    A scarf of red and yellow stripe,
To match with his coat of the self-same cheque;
    And at the scarf's end hung a pipe;

And his fingers, they noticed, were ever straying
As if impatient to be playing
Upon this pipe, as low it dangled
Over his vesture so old-fangled.)
'Yet,' said he, 'poor piper as I am,
In Tartary I freed the Cham,
   Last June, from his huge swarms of gnats;
I eased in Asia the Nizam
   Of a monstrous brood of vampyre-bats:
And as for what your brain bewilders,
   If I can rid your town of rats
Will you give me a thousand guilders?'
'One? fifty thousand!' – was the exclamation
Of the astonished Mayor and Corporation.

VII

Into the street the Piper stept,
   Smiling first a little smile,
As if he knew what magic slept
   In his quiet pipe the while;
Then, like a musical adept,
To blow the pipe his lips he wrinkled,
And green and blue his sharp eyes twinkled,
Like a candle-flame where salt is sprinkled;
And ere three shrill notes the pipe uttered,
You heard as if an army muttered;
And the muttering grew to a grumbling;
And the grumbling grew to a mighty rumbling;
And out of the houses the rats came tumbling.
Great rats, small rats, lean rats, brawny rats,
Brown rats, black rats, grey rats, tawny rats,

Grave old plodders, gay young friskers,
    Fathers, mothers, uncles, cousins,
Cocking tails and pricking whiskers,
    Families by tens and dozens,
Brothers, sisters, husbands, wives —
Followed the Piper for their lives.
From street to street he piped advancing,
And step for step they followed dancing,
Until they came to the river Weser,
    Wherein all plunged and perished!
— Save one who, stout as Julius Caesar,
Swam across and lived to carry
    (As he, the manuscript he cherished)
To Rat-land home his commentary:
Which was, 'At the first shrill notes of the pipe,
I heard a sound as of scraping tripe,
And putting apples, wondrous ripe,
Into a cider-press's gripe:
And a moving away of pickle-tub-boards,
And a leaving ajar of conserve-cupboards,
And a drawing the corks of train-oil-flasks,
And a breaking the hoops of butter-casks:
And it seemed as if a voice
    (Sweeter far than bý harp or bý psaltery
Is breathed) called out, "Oh rats, rejoice!
    The world is grown to one vast drysaltery!
So munch on, crunch on, take your nuncheon,
Breakfast, supper, dinner, luncheon!"
And just as a bulky sugar-puncheon,
All ready staved, like a great sun shone
Glorious scarce an inch before me,
Just as methought it said, "Come, bore me!"
— I found the Weser rolling o'er me.'

VIII

You should have heard the Hamelin people
Ringing the bells till they rocked the steeple.
'Go,' cried the Mayor, 'and get long poles,
Poke out the nests and block up the holes!
Consult with carpenters and builders,
And leave in our town not even a trace
Of the rats!' – when suddenly, up the face
Of the Piper perked in the market-place,
With a, 'First, if you please, my thousand guilders!'

IX

A thousand guilders! The Mayor looked blue;
So did the Corporation too.
For council dinners made rare havoc
With Claret, Moselle, Vin-de-Grave, Hock;
And half the money would replenish
Their cellar's biggest butt with Rhenish.
To pay this sum to a wandering fellow
With a gipsy coat of red and yellow!
'Beside,' quoth the Mayor with a knowing wink,
'Our business was done at the river's brink;
We saw with our eyes the vermin sink,
And what's dead can't come to life, I think.
So, friend, we're not the folks to shrink
From the duty of giving you something for drink,
And a matter of money to put in your poke;
But as for the guilders, what we spoke
Of them, as you very well know, was in joke.
Beside, our losses have made us thrifty.
A thousand guilders! Come, take fifty!'

X

The Piper's face fell, and he cried
'No trifling! I can't wait, beside!
I've promised to visit by dinnertime
Bagdat, and accept the prime
Of the Head-Cook's pottage, all he's rich in,
For having left, in the Caliph's kitchen,
Of a nest of scorpions no survivor:
With him I proved no bargain-driver,
With you, don't think I'll bate a stiver!
And folks who put me in a passion
May find me pipe after another fashion.'

XI

'How?' cried the Mayor, 'd'ye think I brook
Being worse treated than a Cook?
Insulted by a lazy ribald
With idle pipe and vesture piebald?
You threaten us, fellow? Do your worst,
Blow your pipe there till you burst!'

XII

Once more he stept into the street
    And to his lips again
  Laid his long pipe of smooth straight cane;
And ere he blew three notes (such sweet
Soft notes as yet musician's cunning
    Never gave the enraptured air)
There was a rustling that seemed like a bustling
Of merry crowds justling at pitching and hustling,
Small feet were pattering, wooden shoes clattering,

Little hands clapping and little tongues chattering,
And, like fowls in a farm-yard when barley is scattering
Out came the children running.
All the little boys and girls,
With rosy cheeks and flaxen curls,
And sparkling eyes and teeth like pearls,
Tripping and skipping, ran merrily after
The wonderful music with shouting and laughter.

XIII

The Mayor was dumb, and the Council stood
As if they were changed into blocks of wood,
Unable to move a step, or cry
To the children merrily skipping by,
– Could only follow with the eye
That joyous crowd at the Piper's back.
But how the Mayor was on the rack,
And the wretched Council's bosoms beat,
As the Piper turned from the High Street
To where the Weser rolled its waters
Right in the way of their sons and daughters!
However he turned from South to West,
And to Koppelberg Hill his steps addressed,
And after him the children pressed;
Great was the joy in every breast.
'He never can cross that mighty top!
He's forced to let the piping drop,
And we shall see our children stop!'
When, lo, as they reached the mountainside,
A wondrous portal opened wide,
As if a cavern was suddenly hollowed;
And the Pipe advanced and the children followed,

And when all were in to the very last,
The door in the mountain-side shut fast.
Did I say, all? No! One was lame,
   And could not dance the whole of the way;
And in after years, if you would blame
   His sadness, he was used to say, —
'It's dull in our town since my playmates left!
I can't forget that I'm bereft
Of all the pleasant sights they see,
Which the Piper also promised me.
For he led us, he said, to a joyous land,
Joining the town and just at hand,
Where waters gushed and fruit-trees grew
And flowers put forth a fairer hue,
And everything was strange and new;
The sparrows were brighter than peacocks here,
And their dogs outran our fallow deer,
And honey-bees had lost their stings,
And horses were born with eagles' wings:
And just as I became assured
My lame foot would be speedily cured,
The music stopped and I stood still,
And found myself outside the hill,
Left alone against my will,
To go now limping as before,
And never hear of that country more!'

XIV

Alas, alas for Hamelin!
   There came into many a burgher's pate
   A text which says that heaven's gate
   Opes to the rich at as easy rate

As the needle's eye takes a camel in!
The Mayor sent East, West, North and South,
To offer the Piper, by word of mouth,
　　Wherever it was men's lot to find him,
Silver and gold to his heart's content,
If he'd only return the way he went,
　　And bring the children behind him.
But when they saw 'twas a lost endeavour,
And Piper and dancers were gone for ever,
They made a decree that lawyers never
　　Should think their records dated duly
If, after the day of the month and year,
These words did not as well appear,
　　'And so long after what happened here
On the Twenty-second of July,
Thirteen hundred and seventy-six:'
And the better in memory to fix
The place of the children's last retreat,
They called it, the Pied Piper's Street –
Where any one playing on pipe or tabor
Was sure for the future to lose his labour.
Nor suffered they hostelry or tavern
　　To shock with mirth a street so solemn;
But opposite the place of the cavern
　　They wrote the story on a column,
And on the great church-window painted
The same, to make the world acquainted
How their children were stolen away,
And there it stands to this very day.
And I must not omit to say
That in Transylvania there's a tribe
Of alien people who ascribe
The outlandish ways and dress

On which their neighbours lay such stress,
To their fathers and mothers having risen
Out of some subterraneous prison
Into which they were trepanned
Long time ago in a mighty band
Out of Hamelin town in Brunswick land,
But how or why, they don't understand.

XV

So, Willy, let me and you be wipers
Of scores out with all men – especially pipers!
And, whether they pipe us free fróm rats or fróm mice,
If we've promised them aught, let us keep our promise!

A GRAMMARIAN'S FUNERAL

TIME: SHORTLY AFTER THE REVIVAL OF
LEARNING IN EUROPE

LET us begin and carry up this corpse,
 Singing together.
Leave we the common crofts, the vulgar thorpes
 Each in its tether
Sleeping safe on the bosom of the plain,
 Cared-for till cock-crow:
Look out if yonder be not day again
 Rimming the rock-row!
That's the appropriate country; there, man's thought,
 Rarer, intenser,
Self-gathered for an outbreak, as it ought,
 Chafes in the censer.
Leave we the unlettered plain its herd and crop;
 Seek we sepulture
On a tall mountain, citied to the top,
 Crowded with culture!
All the peaks soar, but one the rest excels;
 Clouds overcome it;
No! yonder sparkle is the citadel's
 Circling its summit.
Thither our path lies; wind we up the heights:
 Wait ye the warning?
Our low life was the level's and the night's;
 He's for the morning.
Step to a tune, square chests, erect each head,
 'Ware the beholders!

This is our master, famous, calm and dead,
    Borne on our shoulders.

Sleep, crop and herd! sleep, darkling thorpe and croft,
    Safe from the weather!
He, whom we convoy to his grave aloft,
    Singing together,
He was a man born with thy face and throat,
    Lyric Apollo!
Long he lived nameless: how should spring take note
    Winter would follow?
Till lo, the little touch, and youth was gone!
    Cramped and diminished,
Moaned he, 'New measures, other feet anon!
    My dance is finished?'
No, that's the world's way: (keep the mountain-side,
    Make for the city!)
He knew the signal, and stepped on with pride
    Over men's pity;
Left play for work, and grappled with the world
    Bent on escaping:
'What's in the scroll,' quoth he, 'thou keepest furled?
    Show me their shaping,
Theirs who most studied man, the bard and sage, —
    Give!' – So, he gowned him,
Straight got by heart that book to its last page:
    Learned, we found him.
Yea, but we found him bald too, eyes like lead,
    Accents uncertain:
'Time to taste life,' another would have said,
    'Up with the curtain!'
This man said rather, 'Actual life comes next?
    Patience a moment!

Grant I have mastered learning's crabbed text,
 Still there's the comment.
Let me know all! Prate not of most or least,
 Painful or easy!
Even to the crumbs I'd fain eat up the feast,
 Ay, nor feel queasy.'
Oh, such a life as he resolved to live,
 When he had learned it,
When he had gathered all books had to give!
 Sooner, he spurned it.
Image the whole, then execute the parts —
 Fancy the fabric
Quite, ere you build, ere steel strike fire from quartz,
 Ere mortar dab brick!

(Here's the town-gate reached: there's the market-place
 Gaping before us.)
Yea, this in him was the peculiar grace
 (Hearten our chorus!)
That before living he'd learn how to live —
 No end to learning:
Earn the means first — God surely will contrive
 Use for our earning.
Others mistrust and say, 'But time escapes:
 Live now or never!'
He said, 'What's time? Leave Now for dogs and apes!
 Man has Forever.'
Back to his book then: deeper drooped his head:
 Calculus racked him:
Leaden before, his eyes grew dross of lead:
 Tussis attacked him.
'Now, master, take a little rest!' — not he!
 (Caution redoubled,

110

Step two abreast, the way winds narrowly!)
    Not a whit troubled
Back to his studies, fresher than at first,
    Fierce as a dragon
He (soul-hydroptic with a sacred thirst)
    Sucked at the flagon.
Oh, if we draw a circle premature,
    Heedless of far gain,
Greedy for quick returns of profit, sure
    Bad is our bargain!
Was it not great? did not he throw on God,
    (He loves the burthen) –
God's task to make the heavenly period
    Perfect the earthen?
Did not he magnify the mind, show clear
    Just what it all meant?
He would not discount life, as fools do here,
    Paid by instalment.
He ventured neck or nothing – heaven's success
    Found, or earth's failure:
'Wilt thou trust death or not?' He answered 'Yes:
    Hence with life's pale lure!'
That low man seeks a little thing to do,
    Sees it and does it:
This high man, with a great thing to pursue,
    Dies ere he knows it.
That low man goes on adding one to one,
    His hundred's soon hit:
This high man, aiming at a million,
    Misses an unit.
That, has the world here – should he need the next,
    Let the world mind him!

This, throws himself on God, and unperplexed
    Seeking shall find him.
So, with the throttling hands of death at strife,
    Ground he at grammar;
Still, thro' the rattle, parts of speech were rife:
    While he could stammer
He settled *Hoti's* business – let it be! –
    Properly based *Oun* –
Gave us the doctrine of the enclitic *De*,
    Dead from the waist down.
Well, here's the platform, here's the proper place:
    Hail to your purlieus,
All ye highfliers of the feathered race,
    Swallows and curlews!
Here's the top-peak; the multitude below
    Live, for they can, there:
This man decided not to Live but Know –
    Bury this man there?
Here – here's his place, where meteors shoot, clouds form,
    Lightnings are loosened,
Stars come and go! Let joy break with the storm,
    Peace let the dew send!
Lofty designs must close in like effects:
    Loftily lying,
Leave him – still loftier than the world suspects,
    Living and dying.

THE STATUE AND THE BUST

THERE'S a palace in Florence, the world knows well,
And a statue watches it from the square,
And this story of both do our townsmen tell.

Ages ago, a lady there,
At the farthest window facing the East
Asked, 'Who rides by with the royal air?'

The bridesmaids' prattle around her ceased;
She leaned forth, one on either hand;
They saw how the blush of the bride increased —

They felt by its beats her heart expand —
As one at each ear and both in a breath
Whispered, 'The Great-Duke Ferdinand.'

That self-same instant, underneath,
The Duke rode past in his idle way,
Empty and fine like a swordless sheath.

Gay he rode, with a friend as gay,
Till he threw his head back — 'Who is she?'
— 'A bride the Riccardi brings home to-day.'

Hair in heaps lay heavily
Over a pale brow spirit-pure —
Carved like the heart of a coal-black tree,

Crisped like a war-steed's encolure —
And vainly sought to dissemble her eyes
Of the blackest black our eyes endure.

And lo, a blade for a knight's emprise
Filled the fine empty sheath of a man, —
The Duke grew straightway brave and wise.

He looked at her, as a lover can;
She looked at him, as one who awakes:
The past was a sleep, and her life began.

Now, love so ordered for both their sakes,
A feast was held that selfsame night
In the pile which the mighty shadow makes.

(For Via Larga is three-parts light,
But the palace overshadows one,
Because of a crime which may God requite!

To Florence and God the wrong was done,
Through the first republic's murder there
By Cosimo and his cursed son.)

The Duke (with the statue's face in the square)
Turned in the midst of his multitude
At the bright approach of the bridal pair.

Face to face the lovers stood
A single minute and no more,
While the bridegroom bent as a man subdued —

Bowed till his bonnet brushed the floor —
For the Duke on the lady a kiss conferred,
As the courtly custom was of yore.

In a minute can lovers exchange a word?
If a word did pass, which I do not think,
Only one out of the thousand heard.

That was the bridegroom. At day's brink
He and his bride were alone at last
In a bedchamber by a taper's blink.

Calmly he said that her lot was cast,
That the door she had passed was shut on her
Till the final catafalk repassed.

The world meanwhile, its noise and stir,
Through a certain window facing the East,
She could watch like a convent's chronicler.

Since passing the door might lead to a feast,
And a feast might lead to so much beside,
He, of many evils, chose the least.

'Freely I choose too,' said the bride –
'Your window and its world suffice,'
Replied the tongue, while the heart replied –

'If I spend the night with that devil twice,
May his window serve as my loop of hell
Whence a damned soul looks on paradise!

'I fly to the Duke who loves me well,
Sit by his side and laugh at sorrow
Ere I count another ave-bell.

''Tis only the coat of a page to borrow,
And tie my hair in a horse-boy's trim,
And I save my soul – but not to-morrow' –

(She checked herself and her eye grew dim)
'My father tarries to bless my state:
I must keep it one day more for him.

'Is one day more so long to wait?
Moreover the Duke rides past, I know;
We shall see each other, sure as fate.'

She turned on her side and slept. Just so!
So we resolve on a thing and sleep:
So did the lady, ages ago.

That night the Duke said, 'Dear or cheap
As the cost of this cup of bliss may prove
To body or soul, I will drain it deep.'

And on the morrow, bold with love,
He beckoned the bridegroom (close on call,
As his duty bade, by the Duke's alcove)

And smiled ' 'Twas a very funeral,
Your lady will think, this feast of ours, —
A shame to efface, whate'er befall!

'What if we break from the Arno bowers,
And try if Petraja, cool and green,
Cure last night's fault with this morning's flowers?'

The bridegroom, not a thought to be seen
On his steady brow and quiet mouth,
Said, 'Too much favour for me so mean!

'But, alas! my lady leaves the South;
Each wind that comes from the Apennine
Is a menace to her tender youth:

'Nor a way exists, the wise opine,
If she quits her palace twice this year,
To avert the flower of life's decline.'

116

Quoth the Duke, 'A sage and a kindly fear.
Moreover Petraja is cold this spring:
Be our feast to-night as usual here!'

And then to himself – 'Which night shall bring
Thy bride to her lover's embraces, fool –
Or I am the fool, and thou art the king!

'Yet my passion must wait a night, nor cool –
For to-night the Envoy arrives from France
Whose heart I unlock with thyself, my tool.

'I need thee still and might miss perchance,
To-day is not wholly lost, beside,
With its hope of my lady's countenance:

'For I ride – what should I do but ride?
And passing her palace, if I list,
May glance at its window – well betide!'

So said, so done: nor the lady missed
One ray that broke from the ardent brow,
Nor a curl of the lips where the spirit kissed.

Be sure that each renewed the vow,
No morrow's sun should arise and set
And leave them as it left them now.

But next day passed, and next day yet,
With still fresh cause to wait one day more
Ere each leaped over the parapet.

And still, as love's brief morning wore,
With a gentle start, half smile, half sigh,
They found love not as it seemed before.

117

They thought it would work infallibly,
But not in despite of heaven and earth:
The rose would blow when the storm passed by.

Meantime they could profit in winter's dearth
By store of fruits that supplant the rose:
The world and its ways have a certain worth:

And to press a point while these oppose
Were simple policy; better wait:
We lose no friends and we gain no foes.

Meantime, worse fates than a lover's fate,
Who daily may ride and pass and look
Where his lady watches behind the grate!

And she – she watched the square like a book
Holding one picture and only one,
Which daily to find she undertook:

When the picture was reached the book was done,
And she turned from the picture at night to scheme
Of tearing it out for herself next sun.

So weeks grew months, years; gleam by gleam
The glory dropped from their youth and love,
And both perceived they had dreamed a dream;

Which hovered as dreams do, still above:
But who can take a dream for a truth?
Oh, hide our eyes from the next remove!

One day, as the lady saw her youth
Depart, and the silver thread that streaked
Her hair, and, worn by the serpent's tooth,

118

The brow so puckered, the chin so peaked, —
And wondered who the woman was,
Hollow-eyed and haggard-cheeked,

Fronting her silent in the glass —
'Summon here,' she suddenly said,
'Before the rest of my old self pass,

'Him, the Carver, a hand to aid,
Who fashions the clay no love will change,
And fixes a beauty never to fade.

'Let Robbia's craft so apt and strange
Arrest the remains of young and fair,
And rivet them while the seasons range.

'Make me a face on the window there,
Waiting as ever, mute the while,
My love to pass below in the square!

'And let me think that it may beguile
Dreary days which the dead must spend
Down in their darkness under the aisle,

'To say, "What matters it at the end?
I did no more while my heart was warm
Than does that image, my pale-faced friend."

'Where is the use of the lip's red charm,
The heaven of hair, the pride of the brow,
And the blood that blues the inside arm —

'Unless we turn, as the soul knows how,
The earthly gift to an end divine?
A lady of clay is as good, I trow.'

But long ere Robbia's cornice, fine,
With flowers and fruits which leaves enlace,
Was set where now is the empty shrine –

(And, leaning out of a bright blue space,
As a ghost might lean from a chink of sky,
The passionate pale lady's face –

Eyeing ever, with earnest eye
And quick-turned neck at its breathless stretch,
Some one who ever is passing by –)

The Duke had sighed like the simplest wretch
In Florence, 'Youth – my dream escapes!
Will its record stay?' And he bade them fetch

Some subtle moulder of brazen shapes –
'Can the soul, the will, die out of a man
Ere his body find the grave that gapes?

'John of Douay shall effect my plan,
Set me on horseback here aloft,
Alive, as the crafty sculptor can,

'In the very square I have crossed so oft:
That men may admire, when future suns
Shall touch the eyes to a purpose soft,

'While the mouth and the brow stay brave in bronze –
Admire and say, "When he was alive
How he would take his pleasure once!"

'And it shall go hard but I contrive
To listen the while, and laugh in my tomb
At idleness which aspires to strive.'

* * *

So! While these wait the trump of doom.
How do their spirits pass, I wonder,
Nights and days in the narrow room?

Still, I suppose, they sit and ponder
What a gift life was, ages ago,
Six steps out of the chapel yonder.

Only they see not God, I know,
Nor all that chivalry of his,
The soldier-saints who, row on row,

Burn upward each to his point of bliss –
Since, the end of life being manifest,
He had burned his way thro' the world to this.

I hear you reproach, 'But delay was best,
For their end was a crime.' – Oh, a crime will do
As well, I reply, to serve for a test,

As a virtue golden through and through,
Sufficient to vindicate itself
And prove its worth at a moment's view!

Must a game be played for the sake of pelf?
Where a button goes, 'twere an epigram
To offer the stamp of the very Guelph.

The true has no value beyond the sham:
As well the counter as coin, I submit,
When your table's a hat, and your prize a dram.

Stake your counter as boldly every whit,
Venture as warily, use the same skill,
Do your best, whether winning or losing it,

If you choose to play! – is my principle.
Let a man contend to the uttermost
For his life's set prize, be it what it will!

The counter our lovers staked was lost
As surely as if it were lawful coin:
And the sin I impute to each frustrate ghost

Is – the unlit lamp and the ungirt loin,
Though the end in sight was a vice, I say.
You of the virtue (we issue join)
How strive you? *De te, fabula!*

PORPHYRIA'S LOVER

The rain set early in to-night,
  The sullen wind was soon awake,
It tore the elm-tops down for spite,
  And did its worst to vex the lake:
  I listened with heart fit to break.
When glided in Porphyria; straight
  She shut the cold out and the storm,
And kneeled and made the cheerless grate
  Blaze up, and all the cottage warm;
  Which done, she rose, and from her form
Withdrew the dripping cloak and shawl,
  And laid her soiled gloves by, untied
Her hat and let the damp hair fall,
  And, last, she sat down by my side
  And called me. When no voice replied,
She put my arm about her waist,
  And made her smooth white shoulder bare,
And all her yellow hair displaced,
  And, stooping, made my cheek lie there,
  And spread, o'er all, her yellow hair,
Murmuring how she loved me – she
  Too weak, for all her heart's endeavour,
To set its struggling passion free
  From pride, and vainer ties dissever,
  And give herself to me for ever.
But passion sometimes would prevail,
  Nor could to-night's gay feast restrain
A sudden thought of one so pale
  For love of her, and all in vain:
  So, she was come through wind and rain.

Be sure I looked up at her eyes
   Happy and proud; at last I knew
Porphyria worshipped me; surprise
   Made my heart swell, and still it grew
   While I debated what to do.
That moment she was mine, mine, fair,
   Perfectly pure and good: I found
A thing to do, and all her hair
   In one long yellow string I wound
   Three times her little throat around,
And strangled her. No pain felt she;
   I am quite sure she felt no pain.
As a shut bud that holds a bee,
   I warily oped her lids: again
   Laughed the blue eyes without a stain.
And I untightened next the tress
   About her neck; her cheek once more
Blushed bright beneath my burning kiss:
   I propped her head up as before,
   Only, this time my shoulder bore
Her head, which droops upon it still:
   The smiling rosy little head,
So glad it has its utmost will,
   That all it scorned at once is fled,
   And I, its love, am gained instead!
Porphyria's love: she guessed not how
   Her darling one wish would be heard.
And thus we sit together now,
   And all night long we have not stirred,
   And yet God has not said a word!

'CHILDE ROLAND TO THE DARK TOWER CAME'

(See Edgar's song in 'LEAR')

I

MY first thought was, he lied in every word,
   That hoary cripple, with malicious eye
   Askance to watch the working of his lie
On mine, and mouth scarce able to afford
Suppression of the glee, that pursed and scored
   Its edge, at one more victim gained thereby.

II

What else should he be set for, with his staff?
   What, save to waylay with his lies, ensnare
   All travellers who might find him posted there,
And ask the road? I guessed what skull-like laugh
Would break, what crutch 'gin write my epitaph
   For pastime in the dusty thoroughfare,

III

If at his counsel I should turn aside
   Into that ominous tract which, all agree,
   Hides the Dark Tower. Yet acquiescingly
I did turn as he pointed: neither pride
Nor hope rekindling at the end descried,
   So much as gladness that some end might be.

IV

For, what with my whole world-wide wandering,
  What with my search drawn out thro' years, my hope
  Dwindled into a ghost not fit to cope
With that obstreperous joy success would bring,
I hardly tried now to rebuke the spring
  My heart made, finding failure in its scope.

V

As when a sick man very near to death
  Seems dead indeed, and feels begin and end
  The tears and takes the farewell of each friend,
And hears one bid the other go, draw breath
Freelier outside ('since all is o'er,' he saith,
  'And the blow fallen no grieving can amend:')

VI

While some discuss if near the other graves
  Be room enough for this, and when a day
  Suits best for carrying the corpse away,
With care about the banners, scarves and staves:
And still the man hears all, and only craves
  He may not shame such tender love and stay.

VII

Thus, I had so long suffered in this quest,
  Heard failure prophesied so oft, been writ
  So many times among 'The Band' – to wit,
The knights who to the Dark Tower's search addressed
Their steps – that just to fail as they, seemed best,
  And all the doubt was now – should I be fit?

VIII

So, quiet as despair, I turned from him,
  That hateful cripple, out of his highway
  Into the path he pointed. All the day
Had been a dreary one at best, and dim
Was settling to its close, yet shot one grim
  Red leer to see the plain catch its estray.

IX

For mark! no sooner was I fairly found
  Pledged to the plain, after a pace or two,
  Than, pausing to throw backward a last view
O'er the safe road, 'twas gone; grey plain all round:
Nothing but plain to the horizon's bound.
  I might go on; nought else remained to do.

X

So, on I went. I think I never saw
  Such starved ignoble nature; nothing throve:
  For flowers – as well expect a cedar grove!
But cockle, spurge, according to their law
Might propagate their kind, with none to awe,
  You'd think; a burr had been a treasure-trove.

XI

No! penury, inertness and grimace,
  In some strange sort, were the land's portion. 'See
  Or shut your eyes,' said Nature peevishly,
'It nothing skills: I cannot help my case:
'Tis the Last Judgement's fire must cure this place,
  Calcine its clods and set my prisoners free.'

XII

If there pushed any ragged thistle-stalk
    Above its mates, the head was chopped; the bents
    Were jealous else. What made those holes and rents
In the dock's harsh swarth leaves, bruised as to baulk
All hope of greenness? 'tis a brute must walk
    Pashing their life out, with a brute's intents.

XIII

As for the grass, it grew as scant as hair
    In leprosy; thin dry blades pricked the mud
    Which underneath looked kneaded up with blood.
One stiff blind horse, his every bone a-stare,
Stood stupefied, however he came there:
    Thrust out past service from the devil's stud!

XIV

Alive? he might be dead for aught I know,
    With that red gaunt and colloped neck a-strain,
    And shut eyes underneath the rusty mane;
Seldom went such grotesqueness with such woe;
I never saw a brute I hated so;
    He must be wicked to deserve such pain.

XV

I shut my eyes and turned them on my heart.
    As a man calls for wine before he fights,
    I asked one draught of earlier, happier sights,
Ere fitly I could hope to play my part.
Think first, fight afterwards — the soldier's art:
    One taste of the old time sets all to rights.

XVI

Not it! I fancied Cuthbert's reddening face
  Beneath its garniture of curly gold,
  Dear fellow, till I almost felt him fold
An arm in mine to fix me to the place,
That way he used. Alas, one night's disgrace!
  Out went my heart's new fire and left it cold.

XVII

Giles then, the soul of honour – there he stands
  Frank as ten years ago when knighted first.
  What honest man should dare (he said) he durst.
Good – but the scene shifts – faugh! what hangman hands
Pin to his breast a parchment? His own bands
  Read it. Poor traitor, spit upon and curst!

XVIII

Better this present than a past like that;
  Back therefore to my darkening path again!
  No sound, no sight as far as eye could strain.
Will the night send a howlet or a bat?
I asked: when something on the dismal flat
  Came to arrest my thoughts and change their train.

XIX

A sudden little river crossed my path
  As unexpected as a serpent comes.
  No sluggish tide congenial to the glooms;
This, as it frothed by, might have been a bath
For the fiend's glowing hoof – to see the wrath
  Of its black eddy bespate with flakes and spumes.

XX

So pretty yet so spiteful! All along,
  Low scrubby alders kneeled down over it;
  Drenched willows flung them headlong in a fit
Of mute despair, a suicidal throng;
The river which had done them all the wrong,
  Whate'er that was, rolled by, deterred no whit.

XXI

Which, while I forded, – good saints, how I feared
  To set my foot upon a dead man's cheek,
  Each step, or feel the spear I thrust to seek
For hollows, tangled in his hair or beard!
– It may have been a water-rat I speared,
  But, ugh! it sounded like a baby's shriek.

XXII

Glad was I when I reached the other bank.
  Now for a better country. Vain presage!
  Who were the strugglers, what war did they wage,
Whose savage trample thus could pad the dank
Soil to a plash? Toads in a poisoned tank,
  Or wild cats in a red-hot iron cage –

XXIII

The fight must so have seemed in that fell cirque.
  What penned them there, with all the plain to choose?
  No foot-print leading to that horrid mews,
None out of it. Mad brewage set to work
Their brains, no doubt, like galley-slaves the Turk
  Pits for his pastime, Christians against Jews.

XXIV

And more than that – a furlong on – why, there!
  What bad use was that engine for, that wheel,
  Or brake, not wheel – that harrow fit to reel
Men's bodies out like silk? with all the air
Of Tophet's tool, on earth left unaware,
  Or brought to sharpen its rusty teeth of steel.

XXV

Then came a bit of stubbed ground, once a wood,
  Next a marsh, it would seem, and now mere earth
  Desperate and done with; (so a fool finds mirth,
Makes a thing and then mars it, till his mood
Changes and off he goes!) within a rood –
  Bog, clay and rubble, sand and stark black dearth.

XXVI

Now blotches rankling, coloured gay and grim,
  Now patches where some leanness of the soil's
  Broke into moss or substances like boils;
Then came some palsied oak, a cleft in him
Like a distorted mouth that splits its rim
  Gaping at death, and dies while it recoils.

XXVII

And just as far as ever from the end!
  Nought in the distance but the evening, nought
  To point my footstep further! At the thought,
A great black bird, Apollyon's bosom-friend,
Sailed past, nor beat his wide wing dragon-penned
  That brushed my cap – perchance the guide I sought.

XXVIII

For, looking up, aware I somehow grew,
   'Spite of the dusk, the plain had given place
   All round to mountains – with such name to grace
Mere ugly heights and heaps now stolen in view.
How thus they had surprised me, – solve it, you!
   How to get from them was no clearer case.

XXIX

Yet half I seemed to recognize some trick
   Of mischief happened to me, God knows when –
   In a bad dream perhaps. Here ended, then,
Progress this way. When, in the very nick
Of giving up, one time more, came a click
   As·when a trap shuts – you're inside the den!

XXX

Burningly it came on me all at once,
   This was the place! those two hills on the right,
   Crouched like two bulls locked horn in horn in fight;
While to the left, a tall scalped mountain . . . Dunce,
Dotard, a-dozing at the very nonce,
   After a life spent training for the sight!

XXXI

What in the midst lay but the Tower itself?
   The round squat turret, blind as the fool's heart,
   Built of brown stone, without a counterpart
In the whole world. The tempest's mocking elf
Points to the shipman thus the unseen shelf
   He strikes on, only when the timbers start.

XXXII

Not see? because of night perhaps? – why, day
  Came back again for that! before it left,
  The dying sunset kindled through a cleft:
The hills, like giants at a hunting, lay,
Chin upon hand, to see the game at bay, –
  'Now stab and end the creature – to the heft!'

XXXIII

Not hear? when noise was everywhere! it tolled
  Increasing like a bell. Names in my ears
  Of all the lost adventurers my peers, –
How such a one was wrong, and such was bold,
And such was fortunate, yet each of old
  Lost, lost! one moment knelled the woe of years.

XXXIV

There they stood, ranged along the hill-sides, met
  To view the last of me, a living frame
  For one more picture! in a sheet of flame
I saw them and I knew them all. And yet
Dauntless the slug-horn to my lips I set,
  And blew. *'Childe Roland to the Dark Tower came.'*

CHRISTMAS EVE

OUT of the little chapel I burst
  Into the fresh night-air again.
Five minutes full, I waited first
  In the doorway, to escape the rain
That drove in gusts down the common's centre
  At the edge of which the chapel stands,
Before I plucked up heart to enter.
  Heaven knows how many sorts of hands
Reached past me, groping for the latch
Of the inner door that hung on catch
More obstinate the more they fumbled,
  Till, giving way at last with a scold
Of the crazy hinge, in squeezed or tumbled
  One sheep more to the rest in fold,
And left me irresolute, standing sentry
In the sheepfold's lath-and-plaster entry,
Six feet long by three feet wide,
Partitioned off from the vast inside –
  I blocked up half of it at least.
No remedy; the rain kept driving.
  They eyed me much as some wild beast,
That congregation, still arriving,
Some of them by the main road, white
A long way past me into the night,
Skirting the common, then diverging;
Not a few suddenly emerging
From the common's self thro' the paling-gaps,
– They house in the gravel-pits perhaps,

Where the road stops short with its safeguard border
Of lamps, as tired of such disorder; –
But the most turned in yet more abruptly
From a certain squalid knot of alleys,
Where the town's bad blood once slept corruptly,
Which now the little chapel rallies
And leads into day again, – its priestliness
Lending itself to hide their beastliness
So cleverly (thanks in part to the mason),
And putting so cheery a whitewashed face on
Those neophytes too much in lack of it,
That, where you cross the common as I did,
And meet the party thus presided,
'Mount Zion' with Love-lane at the back of it,
They front you as little disconcerted
As, bound for the hills, her fate averted,
And her wicked people made to mind him,
Lot might have marched with Gomorrah behind him.

II

Well, from the road, the lanes or the common,
In came the flock: the fat weary woman,
Panting and bewildered, down-clapping
Her umbrella with a mighty report,
Grounded it by me, wry and flapping,
A wreck of whalebones; then, with a snort,
Like a startled horse, at the interloper
(Who humbly knew himself improper,
But could not shrink up small enough)
– Round to the door, and in, – the gruff
Hinge's invariable scold

135

Making my very blood run cold.
Prompt in the wake of her, up-pattered
On broken clogs, the many-tattered
Little old-faced peaking sister-turned-mother
Of the sickly babe she tried to smother
Somehow up, with its spotted face,
From the cold, on her breast, the one warm place;
She too must stop, wring the poor ends dry
Of a draggled shawl, and add thereby
Her tribute to the door-mat, sopping
Already from my own clothes' dropping,
Which yet she seemed to grudge I should stand on:
    Then, stooping down to take off her pattens,
She bore them defiantly, in each hand one,
Planted together before her breast
And its babe, as good as a lance in rest.
    Close on her heels, the dingy satins
Of a female something, past me flitted,
    With lips as much too white, as a streak
    Lay far too red on each hollow cheek;
And it seemed the very door-hinge pitied
All that was left of a woman once,
Holding at least its tongue for the nonce.
Then a tall yellow man, like the Penitent Thief,
With his jaw bound up in a handkerchief,
And eyelids screwed together tight,
Led himself in by some inner light.
And, except from him, from each that entered,
    I got the same interrogation –
'What, you the alien, you have ventured
    To take with us, the elect, your station?
A carer for none of it, a Gallio!' –
    Thus, plain as print, I read the glance

At a common prey, in each countenance
  As of huntsman giving his hounds the tallyho.
And, when the door's cry drowned their wonder,
  The draught, it always sent in shutting,
Made the flame of the single tallow candle
In the cracked square lantern I stood under,
  Shoot its blue lip at me, rebutting
As it were, the luckless cause of scandal:
I verily fancied the zealous light
(In the chapel's secret, too!) for spite
Would shudder itself clean off the wick,
With the airs of a Saint John's Candlestick.
There was no standing it much longer.
'Good folks,' thought I, as resolve grew stronger,
'This way you perform the Grand-Inquisitor
When the weather sends you a chance visitor?
You are the men, and wisdom shall die with you,
And none of the old Seven Churches vie with you!
But still, despite the pretty perfection
  To which you carry your trick of exclusiveness,
And, taking God's word under wise protection,
  Correct its tendency to diffusiveness,
And bid one reach it over hot ploughshares, –
  Still, as I say, though you've found salvation,
If I should choose to cry, as now, "Shares!" –
  See if the best of you bars me my ration!
I prefer, if you please, for my expounder
Of the laws of the feast, the feast's own Founder;
Mine's the same right with your poorest and sickliest
  Supposing I don the marriage vestiment:
  So, shut your mouth and open your Testament,
And carve me my portion at your quickliest!'

Accordingly, as a shoemaker's lad
   With wizened face in want of soap,
     And wet apron wound round his waist like a rope,
(After stopping outside, for his cough was bad,
To get the fit over, poor gentle creature,
And so avoid disturbing the preacher)
– Passed in, I sent my elbow spikewise
At the shutting door, and entered likewise,
Received the hinge's accustomed greeting,
   And crossed the threshold's magic pentacle,
   And found myself in full conventicle,
– To wit, in Zion Chapel Meeting,
On the Christmas-Eve of 'Forty-nine,
   Which, calling its flock to their special clover,
   Found all assembled and one sheep over,
Whose lot, as the weather pleased, was mine.

III

I very soon had enough of it.
   The hot smell and the human noises,
And my neighbour's coat, the greasy cuff of it,
   Were a pebble-stone that a child's hand poises,
Compared with the pig-of-lead-like pressure
   Of the preaching man's immense stupidity,
As he poured his doctrine forth, full measure,
   To meet his audience's avidity.
You needed not the wit of the Sibyl
   To guess the cause of it all, in a twinkling:
   No sooner our friend had got an inkling
Of treasure hid in the Holy Bible,
(Whene'er 'twas the thought first struck him,
How death, at unawares, might duck him
Deeper than the grave, and quench

The gin-shop's light in hell's grim drench)
Than he handled it so, in fine irreverence,
  As to hug the book of books to pieces:
And, a patchwork of chapters and texts in severance,
  Not improved by the private dog's-ears and creases,
Having clothed his own soul with, he'd fain see equipt yours,—
So tossed you again your Holy Scriptures.
And you picked them up, in a sense, no doubt:
  Nay, had but a single face of my neighbours
  Appeared to suspect that the preacher's labours
Were help which the world could be saved without,
'Tis odds but I might have borne in quiet
A qualm or two at my spiritual diet,
Or (who can tell?) perchance even mustered
  Somewhat to urge in behalf of the sermon:
But the flock sat on, divinely flustered.
  Sniffing, methought, its dew of Hermon
With such content in every snuffle,
As the devil inside us loves to ruffle.
My old fat woman purred with pleasure,
  And thumb round thumb went twirling faster,
While she, to his periods keeping measure,
  Maternally devoured the pastor.
The man with the handkerchief untied it,
Showed us a horrible wen inside it,
Gave his eyelids yet another screwing,
And rocked himself as the woman was doing.
The shoemaker's lad, discreetly choking,
Kept down his cough. 'Twas too provoking!
My gorge rose at the nonsense and stuff of it;
  So, saying like Eve when she plucked the apple,
  'I wanted a taste, and now there's enough of it,'
I flung out of the little chapel.

IV

There was a lull in the rain, a lull
   In the wind too; the moon was risen,
And would have shone out pure and full,
   But for the ramparted cloud-prison,
Block on block built up in the West,
For what purpose the wind knows best,
Who changes his mind continually.
And the empty other half of the sky
Seemed in its silence as if it knew
What, any moment, might look through
A chance gap in that fortress massy: –
   Through its fissures you got hints
   Of the flying moon, by the shifting tints,
Now, a dull lion-colour, now, brassy
Burning to yellow, and whitest yellow,
Like furnace-smoke just ere flames bellow,
All a-simmer with intense strain
To let her through, – then blank again,
At the hope of her appearance failing.
Just by the chapel, a break in the railing
Shows a narrow path directly across;
'Tis ever dry walking there, on the moss –
Besides, you go gently all the way uphill.
   I stooped under and soon felt better;
My head grew lighter, my limbs more supple,
   As I walked on, glad to have slipt the fetter.
My mind was full of the scene I had left,
   That placid flock, that pastor vociferant,
   – How this outside was pure and different!
The sermon, now – what a mingled weft
Of good and ill! Were either less,
   Its fellow had coloured the whole distinctly;

But alas for the excellent earnestness,
  And the truths, quite true if stated succinctly,
But as surely false, in their quaint presentment,
However to pastor and flock's contentment!
Say rather, such truths looked false to your eyes,
  With his provings and parallels twisted and twined,
Till how could you know them, grown double their size
  In the natural fog of the good man's mind,
Like yonder spots of our roadside lamps,
Haloed about with the common's damps?
Truth remains true, the fault's in the prover;
  The zeal was good, and the aspiration;
And yet, and yet, fifty times over,
  Pharaoh received no demonstration,
By his Baker's dreams of Baskets Three,
Of the doctrine of the Trinity, –
Although, as our preacher thus embellished it,
Apparently his hearers relished it
With so unfeigned a gust – who knows if
They did not prefer our friend to Joseph?
But so it is everywhere, one way with all of them!
  These people have really felt, no doubt,
A something, the motion they style the Call of them;
  And this is their method of bringing about,
By a mechanism of words and tones,
(So many texts in so many groans)
A sort of reviving and reproducing,
  More or less perfectly, (who can tell?)
The mood itself, which strengthens by using;
  And how that happens, I understand well.
A tune was born in my head last week,
Out of the thump-thump and shriek-shriek
  Of the train, as I came by it, up from Manchester;

And when, next week, I take it back again,
My head will sing to the engine's clack again,
    While it only makes my neighbour's haunches stir,
– Finding no dormant musical sprout
In him, as in me, to be jolted out.
'Tis the taught already that profits by teaching;
He gets no more from the railway's preaching
    Than, from this preacher who does the rail's office, I:
Whom therefore the flock cast a jealous eye on.
Still, why paint over their door 'Mount Zion',
    To which all flesh shall come, saith the prophecy?

V

But wherefore be harsh on a single case?
    After how many modes, this Christmas-Eve,
Does the self-same weary thing take place?
    The same endeavour to make you believe,
And with much the same effect, no more:
    Each method abundantly convincing,
As I say, to those convinced before,
    But scarce to be swallowed without wincing
By the not-as-yet-convinced. For me,
I have my own church equally:
And in this church my faith sprang first!
    (I said, as I reached the rising ground,
And the wind began again, with a burst
    Of rain in my face, and a glad rebound
From the heart beneath, as if, God speeding me,
I entered his church-door, nature leading me)
– In youth I looked to these very skies,
And probing their immensities,

I found God there, his visible power;
  Yet felt in my heart, amid all its sense
  Of the power, an equal evidence
That his love, there too, was the nobler dower.
For the loving worm within its clod,
Were diviner than a loveless god
Amid his worlds, I will dare to say.
  You know what I mean: God's all, man's nought:
  But also, God, whose pleasure brought
Man into being, stands away
  As it were a handbreadth off, to give
Room for the newly-made to live,
And look at him from a place apart,
And use his gifts of brain and heart,
Given, indeed, but to keep for ever.
Who speaks of man, then, must not sever
Man's very elements from man,
Saying, 'But all is God's' – whose plan
Was to create man and then leave him
Able, his own word saith, to grieve him,
But able to glorify him too,
As a mere machine could never do,
That prayed or praised, all unaware
Of its fitness for aught but praise and prayer,
Made perfect as a thing of course.
Man, therefore, stands on his own stock
Of love and power as a pin-point rock:
And, looking to God who ordained divorce
Of the rock from his boundless continent,
Sees, in his power made evident,
Only excess by a million-fold
O'er power God gave man in the mould.
For, note: man's hand, first formed to carry

143

A few pounds' weight, when taught to marry
Its strength with an engine's, lifts a mountain,
  – Advancing in power by one degree;
  And why count steps through eternity?
But love is the ever-springing fountain:
Man may enlarge or narrow his bed
For the water's play, but the water-head –
How can he multiply or reduce it?
  As easy create it, as cause it to cease;
He may profit by it, or abuse it,
  But 'tis not a thing to bear increase
As power does: be love less or more
  In the heart of man, he keeps it shut
  Or opes it wide, as he pleases, but
Love's sum remains what it was before.
So, gazing up, in my youth, at love
As seen through power, ever above
All modes which make it manifest,
My soul brought all to a single test –
That he, the Eternal First and Last,
Who, in his power, had so surpassed
All man conceives of what is might, –
Whose wisdom, too, showed infinite,
– Would prove as infinitely good;
Would never, (my soul understood,)
With power to work all love desires,
Bestow e'en less than man requires;
That he who endlessly was teaching,
Above my spirit's utmost reaching,
What love can do in the leaf or stone,
(So that to master this alone,
This done in the stone or leaf for me,
I must go on learning endlessly)

144

Would never need that I, in turn,
  Should point him out defect unheeded,
And show that God had yet to learn
  What the meanest human creature needed,
– Not life, to wit, for a few short years,
Tracking his way through doubts and fears,
While the stupid earth on which I stay
  Suffers no change, but passive adds
  Its myriad years to myriads,
Though I, he gave it to, decay,
Seeing death come and choose about me,
And my dearest ones depart without me.
No: love which, on earth, amid all the shows of it,
  Has ever been seen the sole good of life in it,
The love, ever growing there, spite of the strife in it,
  Shall arise, made perfect, from death's repose of it.
And I shall behold thee, face to face,
O God, and in thy light retrace
How in all I loved here, still wast thou!
Whom pressing to, then, as I fain would now,
I shall find as able to satiate
  The love, thy gift, as my spirit's wonder
Thou art able to quicken and sublimate,
  With this sky of thine, that I now walk under,
And glory in thee for, as I gaze
Thus, thus! Oh, let men keep their ways
Of seeking thee in a narrow shrine –
Be this my way! And this *is* mine!

VI

For lo, what think you? suddenly
The rain and the wind ceased, and the sky

Received at once the full fruition
Of the moon's consummate apparition.
The black cloud-barricade was riven,
Ruined beneath her feet, and driven
Deep in the West; while, bare and breathless,
  North and South and East lay ready
For a glorious thing that, dauntless, deathless,
  Sprang across them and stood steady.
'Twas a moon-rainbow, vast and perfect,
From heaven to heaven extending, perfect
As the mother-moon's self, full in face.
It rose, distinctly at the base
  With its seven proper colours chorded,
Which still, in the rising, were compressed,
Until at last they coalesced,
  And supreme the spectral creature lorded
In a triumph of whitest white, –
  Above which intervened the night.
But above night too, like only the next,
  The second of a wondrous sequence,
  Reaching in rare and rarer frequence,
Till the heaven of heavens were circumflexed,
Another rainbow rose, a mightier,
Fainter, flushier and flightier, –
Rapture dying along its verge.
Oh, whose foot shall I see emerge,
Whose, from the straining topmost dark,
On to the keystone of that arc?

VII

This sight was shown me, there and then, –
Me, one out of a world of men,

Singled forth, as the chance might hap
To another if, in a thunderclap
Where I heard noise and you saw flame,
Some one man knew God called his name.
For me, I think I said, 'Appear!
Good were it to be ever here.
If thou wilt, let me build to thee
Service-tabernacles three,
Where, forever in thy presence,
In ecstatic acquiescence,
Far alike from thriftless learning
And ignorance's undiscerning,
I may worship and remain!'
   Thus at the show above me, gazing
With upturned eyes, I felt my brain
   Glutted with the glory, blazing
Throughout its whole mass, over and under
Until at length it burst asunder
And out of it bodily there streamed,
The too-much glory, as it seemed,
Passing from out me to the ground,
Then palely serpentining round
Into the dark with mazy error.

VIII

All at once I looked up with terror.
He was there.
He Himself with His human air.
On the narrow pathway, just before.
I saw the back of Him, no more –
He had left the chapel, then, as I.
I forgot all about the sky.
No face: only the sight

147

Of a sweepy garment, vast and white,
With a hem that I could recognize.
I felt terror, no surprise;
My mind filled with the cataract,
At one bound of the mighty fact.
I remember, He did say

Doubtless that, to this world's end,
Where two or three should meet and pray,

He would be in the midst, their friend;
Certainly He was there with them!

And my pulses leaped for joy

Of the golden thought without alloy,
That I saw His very vesture's hem.
Then rushed the blood back, cold and clear,
With a fresh enhancing shiver of fear;
And I hastened, cried out while I pressed
To the salvation of the Vest,
But not so, Lord! It cannot be
That Thou, indeed, art leaving me –
Me, that have despised Thy friends!
Did my heart make no amends?
Thou art the love of God – above
His power, didst hear me place His love,
And that was leaving the world for Thee.'
Therefore Thou must not turn from me
As I had chosen the other part!
Folly and pride o'ercame my heart.
Our best is bad, nor bears Thy test;
Still, it should be our very best.
I thought it best that Thou, the Spirit,

Be worshipped in spirit and in truth,
And in beauty, as even we require it –

Not in the forms burlesque, uncouth,

I left but now, as scarcely fitted
For Thee: I knew not what I pitied.
But, all I felt there, right or wrong,
    What is it to Thee, who curest sinning?
Am I not weak as Thou art strong?
    I have looked to Thee from the beginning,
Straight up to Thee through all the world
Which, like an idle scroll, lay furled
To nothingness on either side:
And since the time Thou wast descried,
Spite of the weak heart, so have I
Lived ever, and so fain would die,
Living and dying, Thee before!
But if Thou leavest me —

IX

                    Less or more,
I suppose that I spoke thus.
When, — have mercy, Lord, on us!
The whole face turned upon me full.
    And I spread myself beneath it,
    As when the bleacher spreads, to seethe it
In the cleansing sun, his wool, —
Steeps in the flood of noontide whiteness
    Some defiled, discoloured web —
So lay I, saturate with brightness.
    And when the flood appeared to ebb,
Lo, I was walking, light and swift,
    With my senses settling fast and steadying,
But my body caught up in the whirl and drift
    Of the Vesture's amplitude, still eddying
On, just before me, still to be followed,
    As it carried me after with its motion:

What shall I say? – as a path were hollowed
   And a man went weltering through the ocean,
Sucked along in the flying wake
Of the luminous water-snake.
Darkness and cold were cloven, as through
I passed, upborne yet walking too.
And I turned to myself at intervals, –
'So He said, so it befalls.
God who registers the cup
   Of mere cold water, for His sake
To a disciple rendered up,
   Disdains not His own thirst to slake
At the poorest love was ever offered:
And because my heart I proffered,
With true love trembling at the brim,
He suffers me to follow Him
For ever, my own way, – dispensed
From seeking to be influenced
By all the less immediate ways
   That earth, in worships manifold,
Adopts to reach, by prayer and praise,
   The garment's hem, which, lo, I hold!'

X

And so we crossed the world and stopped.
   For where am I, in city or plain,
   Since I am 'ware of the world again?
And what is this that rises propped
With pillars of prodigious girth?
Is it really on the earth,
This miraculous Dome of God?
Has the angel's measuring-rod

Which numbered cubits, gem from gem,
'Twixt the gates of the New Jerusalem,
Meted it out, – and what he meted,
Have the sons of men completed?
– Binding, ever as He bade,
Columns in the colonnade
With arms wide open to embrace
The entry of the human race
To the breast of . . . what is it, yon building,
Ablaze in front, all paint and gilding,
With marble for brick, and stone of price
For garniture of the edifice?
Now I see; it is no dream;
It stands there and it does not seem;
For ever, in pictures, thus it looks,
And thus I have read of it in books
Often in England, leagues away,
And wondered how these fountains play,
Growing up eternally
Each to a musical water-tree,
Whose blossoms drop, a glittering boon,
Before my eyes, in the light of the moon,
To the granite lavers underneath.
Liar and dreamer in your teeth!
I, the sinner that speak to you,
Was in Rome this night, and stood, and knew
Both this and more. For see, for see,
The dark is rent, mine eye is free
To pierce the crust of the outer wall,
And I view inside, and all there, all,
As the swarming hollow of a hive,
The whole Basilica alive!
Men in the chancel, body and nave,

Men on the pillars' architrave,
Men on the statues, men on the tombs
With popes and kings in their porphyry wombs,
All famishing in expectation
Of the main-altar's consummation.
For see, for see, the rapturous moment
Approaches, and earth's best endowment
Blends with heaven's; the taper-fires
Pant up, the winding brazen spires
Heave loftier yet the baldachin;
The incense-gaspings, long kept in,
Suspire in clouds; the organ blatant
Holds his breath and grovels latent,
As if God's hushing finger grazed him,
(Like Behemoth when He praised him)
At the silver bell's shrill tinkling,
Quick cold drops of terror sprinkling
On the sudden pavement strewed
With faces of the multitude.
Earth breaks up, time drops away,
In flows heaven, with its new day
Of endless life, when He who trod,
Very man and very God,
This earth in weakness, shame and pain,
Dying the death whose signs remain
Up yonder on the accursed tree, –
Shall come again, no more to be
Of captivity the thrall,
But the one God, All in all,
King of kings, Lord of lords,
As His servant John received the words,
'I died, and live for evermore!'

XI

Yet I was left outside the door.
Why sit I here on the threshold-stone
Left till He return, alone
Save for the garment's extreme fold
Abandoned still to bless my hold?
My reason, to my doubt, replied,
As if a book were opened wide,
And at a certain page I traced
Every record undefaced,
Added by successive years, –
The harvestings of truth's stray ears
Singly gleaned, and in one sheaf
Bound together for belief.
Yes, I said – that He will go
And sit with these in turn, I know.
Their faith's heart beats, though her head swims
Too giddily to guide her limbs,
Disabled by their palsy-stroke
From propping mine. Though Rome's gross yoke
Drops off, no more to be endured,
Her teaching is not so obscured
By errors and perversities,
That no truth shines athwart the lies:
And He, whose eye detects a spark
Even where, to man's, the whole seems dark,
May well see flame where each beholder
Acknowledges the embers smoulder.
But I, a mere man, fear to quit
The clue God gave me as most fit
To guide my footsteps through life's maze,
Because Himself discerns all ways

Open to reach him: I, a man
Able to mark where faith began
To swerve aside, till from its summit
Judgement drops her damning plummet,
Pronouncing such a fatal space
Departed from the founder's base:
He will not bid me enter too,
But rather sit, as now I do,
Awaiting His return outside.
— 'Twas thus my reason straight replied
And joyously I turned, and pressed
The garment's skirt upon my breast,
Until, afresh its light suffusing me,
My heart cried — What has been abusing me
That I should wait here lonely and coldly,
Instead of rising, entering boldly,
Baring truth's face, and letting drift
Her veils of lies as they choose to shift?
Do these men praise Him? I will raise
My voice up to their point of praise!
I see the error; but above
The scope of error, see the love. —
Oh, love of those first Christian days!
— Fanned so soon into a blaze,
From the spark preserved by the trampled sect,
That the antique sovereign Intellect
Which then sat ruling in the world,
Like a change in dreams, was hurled
From the throne he reigned upon:
You looked up and he was gone.
Gone, his glory of the pen!
— Love, with Greece and Rome in ken,
Bade her scribes abhor the trick

Of poetry and rhetoric,
And exult with hearts set free,
In blessed imbecility
Scrawled, perchance, on some torn sheet
Leaving Sallust incomplete.
Gone, his pride of sculptor, painter!
– Love, while able to acquaint her
While the thousand statues yet
Fresh from chisel, pictures wet
From brush, she saw on every side,
Chose rather with an infant's pride
To frame those portents which impart
Such unction to true Christian Art.
Gone, music too! The air was stirred
By happy wings: Terpander's bird
(That, when the cold came, fled away)
Would tarry not the wintry day, –
As more-enduring sculpture must,
Till filthy saints rebuked the gust
With which they chanced to get a sight
Of some dear naked Aphrodite
They glanced a thought above the toes of,
By breaking zealously her nose off.
Love, surely, from that music's lingering,
Might have filched her organ-fingering,
Nor chosen rather to set prayings
To hog-grunts, praises to horse-neighings.
Love was the startling thing, the new:
Love was the all-sufficient too;
And seeing that, you see the rest:
As a babe can find its mother's breast
As well in darkness as in light,
Love shut our eyes, and all seemed right.

True, the world's eyes are open now:
— Less need for me to disallow
Some few that keep Love's zone unbuckled,
Peevish as ever to be suckled,
Lulled by the same old baby-prattle
With intermixture of the rattle,
When she would have them creep, stand steady
Upon their feet, or walk already,
Not to speak of trying to climb.
I will be wise another time,
And not desire a wall between us,
    When next I see a church-roof cover
So many species of one genus,
    All with foreheads bearing *lover*
Written above the earnest eyes of them;
    All with breasts that beat for beauty,
Whether sublimed, to the surprise of them,
    In noble daring, steadfast duty,
The heroic in passion, or in action, —
Or, lowered for sense's satisfaction,
To the mere outside of human creatures,
Mere perfect form and faultless features.
What? with all Rome here, whence to levy
    Such contributions to their appetite,
With women and men in a gorgeous bevy,
    They take, as it were, a padlock, clap it tight
On their southern eyes, restrained from feeding.
On the glories of their ancient reading,
On the beauties of their modern singing,
On the wonders of the builder's bringing,
On the majesties of Art around them, —
    And, all these loves, late struggling incessant,

When faith has at last united and bound them,
    They offer up to God for a present?
Why, I will, on the whole, be rather proud of it, —
    And, only taking the act in reference
To the other recipients who might have allowed it,
    I will rejoice that God had the preference.

XII

So I summed up my new resolves:
    Too much love there can never be.
And where the intellect devolves
    Its function on love exclusively,
I, a man who possesses both,
Will accept the provision, nothing loth,
— Will feast my love, then depart elsewhere,
That my intellect may find its share.
And ponder, O soul, the while thou departest,
And see thou applaud the great heart of the artist,
Who, examining the capabilities
    Of the block of marble he has to fashion
    Into a type of thought or passion, —
Not always, using obvious facilities,
Shapes it, as any artist can,
Into a perfect symmetrical man,
Complete from head to foot of the life-size,
Such as old Adam stood in his wife's eyes, —
But, now and then, bravely aspires to consummate
A Colossus by no means so easy to come at,
And uses the whole of his block for the bust,
    Leaving the mind of the public to finish it,
Since cut it ruefully short he must:

On the face alone he expends his devotion,
   He rather would mar than resolve to diminish it,
— Saying, 'Applaud me for this grand notion
Of what a face may be! As for completing it
   In breast and body and limbs, do that, you!'
All hail! I fancy how, happily meeting it,
   A trunk and legs would perfect the statue,
Could man carve so as to answer volition.
   And how much nobler than petty cavils,
   Were a hope to find, in my spirit-travels,
Some artist of another ambition,
Who having a block to carve, no bigger,
   Has spent his power on the opposite quest,
   And believed to begin at the feet was best —
For so may I see, ere I die, the whole figure!

XIII

No sooner said than out in the night!
My heart beat lighter and more light:
And still, as before, I was walking swift,
   With my senses settling fast and steadying,
But my body caught up in the whirl and drift
   Of the Vesture's amplitude, still eddying
On just before me, still to be followed,
   As it carried me after with its motion,
— What shall I say? — as a path were hollowed,
   And a man went weltering through the ocean,
Sucked along in the flying wake
Of the luminous water-snake.

XIV

Alone! I am left alone once more —
  (Save for the garment's extreme fold
  Abandoned still to bless my hold)
Alone, beside the entrance-door
Of a sort of temple, — perhaps a college,
— Like nothing I ever saw before
At home in England, to my knowledge.
The tall old quaint irregular town!
  It may be . . . though which, I can't affirm . . . any
  Of the famous middle-age towns of Germany;
And this flight of stairs where I sit down,
Is it Halle, Weimar, Cassel, Frankfort
Or Göttingen, I have to thank for't?
It may be Göttingen, — most likely.
Through the open door I catch obliquely
Glimpses of a lecture-hall;
  And not a bad assembly neither,
Ranged decent and symmetrical
  On benches, waiting what's to see there;
Which, holding still by the Vesture's hem,
I also resolve to see with them,
Cautious this time how I suffer to slip
The chance of joining in fellowship
With any that call themselves His friends;
  As these folks do, I have a notion.
  But hist — a buzzing and emotion!
All settle themselves, the while ascends
By the creaking rail to the lecture-desk,
  Step by step, deliberate
  Because of his cranium's over-freight,
Three parts sublime to one grotesque,

If I have proved an accurate guesser,
The hawk-nosed high-cheek-boned Professor,
I felt at once as if there ran
A shoot of love from my heart to the man —
That sallow virgin-minded studious
   Martyr to mild enthusiasm,
As he uttered a kind of cough-preludious
   That woke my sympathetic spasm,
(Beside some spitting that made me sorry)
And stood, surveying his auditory
With a wan pure look, well nigh celestial, —
   Those blue eyes had survived so much!
   While, under the foot they could not smutch,
Lay all the fleshly and the bestial.
Over he bowed, and arranged his notes,
Till the auditory's clearing of throats
Was done with, died into a silence;
   And, when each glance was upward sent,
   Each bearded mouth composed intent,
And a pin might be heard drop half a mile hence, —
He pushed back higher his spectacles,
Let the eye stream out like lamps from cells,
And giving his head of hair — a hake
   Of undressed tow, for colour and quantity —
One rapid and impatient shake,
   (As our own Young England adjusts a jaunty tie
When about to impart, on mature digestion,
Some thrilling view of the surplice-question)
— The Professor's grave voice, sweet though hoarse,
Broke into his Christmas-Eve discourse.

XV

And he began it by observing
    How reason dictated that men
Should rectify the natural swerving,
    By a reversion, now and then,
To the well-heads of knowledge, few
And far away, whence rolling grew
The life-stream wide whereat we drink,
Commingled, as we needs must think,
With waters alien to the source;
To do which, aimed this eve's discourse;
Since, where could be a fitter time
For tracing backward to its prime
This Christianity, this lake,
This reservoir, whereat we slake,
From one or other bank, our thirst?
So, he proposed inquiring first
Into the various sources whence
    This Myth of Christ is derivable;
Demanding from the evidence,
    (Since plainly no such life was liveable)
How these phenomena should class?
Whether 'twere best opine Christ was,
Or never was at all, or whether
He was and was not, both together —
It matters little for the name,
So the idea be left the same.
Only, for practical purpose' sake,
'Twas obviously as well to take
The popular story, – understanding
    How the ineptitude of the time,
And the penman's prejudice, expanding
    Fact into fable fit for the clime,

Had, by slow and sure degrees, translated it
   Into this myth, this Individuum, –
Which, when reason had strained and abated it
   Of foreign matter, left, for residuum,
A Man! – a right true man, however,
Whose work was worthy a man's endeavour:
Work, that gave warrant almost sufficient
   To his disciples, for rather believing
He was just omnipotent and omniscient,
   As it gives to us, for as frankly receiving
His word, their tradition, – which, though it meant
Something entirely different
From all that those who only heard it,
In their simplicity thought and averred it,
Had yet a meaning quite as respectable:
For, among other doctrines delectable,
Was he not surely the first to insist on
   The natural sovereignty of our race? –
   Here the lecturer came to a pausing-place.
And while his cough, like a drouthy piston,
Tried to dislodge the husk that grew to him,
I seized the occasion of bidding adieu to him,
The Vesture still within my hand.

XVI

I could interpret its command.
This time He would not bid me enter
The exhausted air-bell of the Critic.
Truth's atmosphere may grow mephitic
When Papist struggles with Dissenter,
Impregnating its pristine clarity,
– One, by his daily fare's vulgarity,
Its gust of broken meat and garlic;

– One, by his soul's too-much presuming
To turn the frankincense's fuming
   And vapours of the candle starlike
Into the cloud her wings she buoys on.
   Each, that thus sets the pure air seething,
   May poison it for healthy breathing –
But the Critic leaves no air to poison;
Pumps out with ruthless ingenuity
Atom by atom, and leaves you – vacuity.
Thus much of Christ does he reject?
And what retain? His intellect?
What is it I must reverence duly?
Poor intellect for worship, truly,
Which tells me simply what was told
   (If mere morality, bereft
   Of the God in Christ, be all that's left)
Elsewhere by voices manifold;
With this advantage, that the stater
   Made nowise the important stumble
   Of adding, he, the sage and humble,
Was also one with the Creator.
You urge Christ's followers' simplicity:
   But how does shifting blame, evade it?
Have wisdom's words no more felicity?
   The stumbling-block, his speech – who laid it?
How comes it that for one found able
To sift the truth of it from fable,
Millions believe it to the letter?
Christ's goodness, then – does that fare better?
Strange goodness, which upon the score
   Of being goodness, the mere due
Of man to fellow-man, much more
   To God, – should take another view

Of its possessor's privilege,
And bid him rule his race! You pledge
Your fealty to such rule? What, all –
From heavenly John and Attic Paul,
And that brave weather-battered Peter,
Whose stout faith only stood completer
For buffets, sinning to be pardoned,
As, more his hands hauled nets, they hardened, –
All, down to you, the man of men,
Professing here at Göttingen,
Compose Christ's flock! They, you and I,
Are sheep of a good man! And why?
The goodness, – how did he acquire it?
Was it self-gained, did God inspire it?
Choose which; then tell me, on what ground
Should its possessor dare propound
His claim to rise o'er us an inch?
  Were goodness all some man's invention,
  Who arbitrarily made mention
What we should follow, and whence flinch, –
What qualities might take the style
  Of right and wrong, – and had such guessing
  Met with as general acquiescing
As graced the alphabet erewhile,
When A got leave an Ox to be,
No Camel (quoth the Jews) like G, –
For thus inventing thing and title
Worship were that man's fit requital.
But if the common conscience must
Be ultimately judge, adjust
Its apt name to each quality
Already known, – I would decree

Worship for such mere demonstration
  And simple work of nomenclature,
  Only the day I praised, not nature,
But Harvey, for the circulation.
I would praise such a Christ, with pride
And joy, that he, as none beside,
Had taught us how to keep the mind
God gave him, as God gave his kind,
Freer than they from fleshly taint:
I would call such a Christ our Saint,
As I declare our Poet, him
Whose insight makes all others dim:
A thousand poets pried at life,
And only one amid the strife
Rose to be Shakespeare: each shall take
His crown, I'd say, for the world's sake –
Though some objected – 'Had we seen
The heart and head of each, what screen
Was broken there to give them light,
While in ourselves it shuts the sight,
We should no more admire, perchance,
That these found truth out at a glance,
Than marvel how the bat discerns
Some pitch-dark cavern's fifty turns,
Led by a finer tact, a gift
He boasts, which other birds must shift
Without, and grope as best they can.'
No, freely I would praise the man, –
Nor one whit more, if he contended
That gift of his, from God descended.
Ah friend, what gift of man's does not?
No nearer something, by a jot,

Rise an infinity of nothings
   Than one: take Euclid for your teacher:
Distinguish kinds: do crownings, clothings,
   Make that creator which was creature?
Multiply gifts upon man's head,
And what, when all's done, shall be said
But – the more gifted he, I ween!
   That one's made Christ, this other, Pilate,
And this might be all that has been, –
   So what is there to frown or smile at?
What is left for us, save, in growth
Of soul, to rise up, far past both,
From the gift looking to the giver,
And from the cistern to the river,
And from the finite to infinity,
And from man's dust to God's divinity?

XVII

Take all in a word: the truth in God's breast
Lies trace for trace upon ours impressed:
Though He is so bright and we so dim,
We are made in His image to witness Him:
And were no eye in us to tell,
   Instructed by no inner sense,
The light of heaven from the dark of hell,
   That light would want its evidence, –
Though justice, good and truth were still
Divine, if, by some demon's will,
Hatred and wrong had been proclaimed
Law through the worlds, and right misnamed.
No mere exposition of morality
Made or in part or in totality,

Should win you to give it worship, therefore:
And, if no better proof you will care for,
— Whom do you count the worst man upon earth?
  Be sure, he knows, in his conscience, more
Of what right is, than arrives at birth
  In the best man's acts that we bow before:
This last knows better — true, but my fact is,
'Tis one thing to know, and another to practise.
And thence I conclude that the real God-function
Is to furnish a motive and injunction
For practising what we know already.
And such an injunction and such a motive
As the God in Christ, do you waive, and 'heady,
High-minded,' hang your tablet-votive
Outside the fane on a finger-post?
Morality to the uttermost,
Supreme in Christ as we all confess,
Why need we prove would avail no jot
To make Him God, if God He were not?
What is the point where Himself lays stress?
Does the precept run 'Believe in good,
In justice, truth, now understood
For the first time?' — or, 'Believe in me,
Who lived and died, yet essentially
Am Lord of Life?' Whoever can take
The same to his heart and for mere love's sake
Conceive of the love, — that man obtains
A new truth; no conviction gains
Of an old one only, made intense
By a fresh appeal to his faded sense.

XVIII

Can it be that He stays inside?
   Is the Vesture left me to commune with?
   Could my soul find aught to sing in tune with
Even at this lecture, if she tried?
Oh, let me at lowest sympathize
With the lurking drop of blood that lies
In the desiccated brain's white roots
Without throb for Christ's attributes,
As the lecturer makes his special boast!
If love's dead there, it has left a ghost.
Admire we, how from heart to brain
   (Though to say so strike the doctors dumb)
One instinct rises and falls again,
   Restoring the equilibrium.
And how when the Critic had done his best,
And the pearl of price, at reason's test,
Lay dust and ashes levigable
On the Professor's lecture-table, –
When we looked for the inference and monition
That our faith, reduced to such condition,
Be swept forthwith to its natural dust-hole, –
   He bids us, when we least expect it,
Take back our faith, – if it be not just whole,
   Yet a pearl indeed, as his tests affect it,
Which fact pays damage done rewardingly,
So, prize we our dust and ashes accordingly!
'Go home and venerate the myth
I thus have experimented with –
This man, continue to adore him
Rather than all who went before him,
And all who ever followed after!' –
   Surely for this I may praise you, my brother!

Will you take the praise in tears or laughter?
   That's one point gained: can I compass another?
Unlearned love was safe from spurning –
Can't we respect your loveless learning?
Let us at least give learning honour!
What laurels had we showered upon her,
Girding her loins up to perturb
Our theory of the Middle Verb;
Or Turk-like brandishing a scimitar
O'er anapaests in comic-trimeter;
Or curing the halt and maimed 'Iketides',
While we lounged on at our indebted ease:
Instead of which, a tricksy demon
Sets her at Titus or Philemon!
When ignorance wags his ears of leather
And hates God's word, 'tis altogether;
Nor leaves he his congenial thistles
To go and browse on Paul's Epistles.
– And you, the audience, who might ravage
The world wide, enviably savage,
Nor heed the cry of the retriever,
More than Herr Heine (before his fever), –
I do not tell a lie so arrant
   As say my passion's wings are furled up,
And, without plainest heavenly warrant,
   I were ready and glad to give the world up –
But still, when you rub brow meticulous,
   And ponder the profit of turning holy
   If not for God's, for your own sake solely,
– God forbid I should find you ridiculous!
Deduce from this lecture all that eases you,
Nay, call yourselves, if the calling pleases you,
'Christians', – abhor the deist's pravity, –

Go on, you shall no more move my gravity
Than, when I see boys ride a-cockhorse,
I find it in my heart to embarrass them
By hinting that their stick's a mock horse,
And they really carry what they say carries them.

XIX

So sat I talking with my mind.
   I did not long to leave the door
   And find a new church, as before,
But rather was quiet and inclined
To prolong and enjoy the gentle resting
From further tracking and trying and testing.
This tolerance is a genial mood!
(Said I, and a little pause ensued.)
One trims the bark 'twist shoal and shelf,
   And sees, each side, the good effects of it,
A value for religion's self,
   A carelessness about the sects of it.
Let me enjoy my own conviction,
   Not watch my neighbour's faith with fretfulness,
Still spying there some dereliction
   Of truth, perversity, forgetfulness!
Better a mild indifferentism,
   Teaching that both our faiths (though duller
His shine through a dull spirit's prism)
   Originally had one colour!
Better pursue a pilgrimage
   Through ancient and through modern times
   To many peoples, various climes,
Where I may see saint, savage, sage
Fuse their respective creeds in one
Before the general Father's throne!

XX

— 'Twas the horrible storm began afresh!
The black night caught me in his mesh,
Whirled me up, and flung me prone.
I was left on the college-step alone.
I looked, and far there, ever fleeting
Far, far away, the receding gesture,
And looming of the lessening Vesture! —
Swept forward from my stupid hand,
While I watched my foolish heart expand
In the lazy glow of benevolence,
  O'er the various modes of man's belief.
I sprang up with fear's vehemence.

  Needs must there be one way, our chief
Best way of worship: let me strive
To find it, and when found, contrive
My fellows also take their share!
This constitutes my earthly care:
God's is above it and distinct.
For I, a man, with men am linked
And not a brute with brutes; no gain
That I experience, must remain
Unshared: but should my best endeavour
To share it, fail — subsisteth ever
God's care above, and I exult
That God, by God's own ways occult,
May — doth, I will believe — bring back
All wanderers to a single track.
Meantime, I can but testify
God's care for me — no more, can I —
It is but for myself I know;
  The world rolls witnessing around me
  Only to leave me as it found me;

Men cry there, but my ear is slow;
Their races flourish or decay
– What boots it, while yon lucid way
Loaded with stars divides the vault?
But soon my soul repairs its fault
When, sharpening sense's hebetude,
She turns on my own life! So viewed,
No mere mote's-breadth but teems immense
With witnessings of providence:
And woe to me if when I look
Upon that record, the sole book
Unsealed to me, I take no heed
Of any warning that I read!
Have I been sure, this Christmas-Eve,
God's own hand did the rainbow weave,
Whereby the truth from heaven slid
Into my soul? – I cannot bid
The world admit He stooped to heal
My soul, as if in a thunder-peal
Where one heard noise, and one saw flame,
I only knew He named my name:
But what is the world to me, for sorrow
Or joy in its censure, when to-morrow
It drops the remark, with just-turned head
Then, on again, 'That man is dead'?
Yes, but for me – my name called, – drawn
As a conscript's lot from the lap's black yawn,
He has dipt into on a battle-dawn:
Bid out of life by a nod, a glance, –
Stumbling, mute-mazed, at nature's chance, –
With a rapid finger circled round,
Fixed to the first poor inch of ground
To fight from, where his foot was found;

Whose ear but a minute since lay free
To the wide camp's buzz and gossipry –
Summoned, a solitary man
To end his life where his life began,
From the safe glad rear, to the dreadful van!
Soul of mine, hadst thou caught and held
By the hem of the Vesture! –

XXI

     And I caught
At the flying robe, and unrepelled
 Was lapped again in its folds full-fraught
With warmth and wonder and delight,
God's mercy being infinite.
For scarce had the words escaped my tongue,
When, at a passionate bound, I sprung,
Out of the wandering world of rain,
Into the little chapel again.

XXII

How else was I found there, bolt upright
 On my bench, as if I had never left it?
– Never flung out on the common at night,
 Nor met the storm and wedge-like cleft it,
Seen the raree-show of Peter's successor,
Or the laboratory of the Professor!
For the Vision, that was true, I wist,
True as that heaven and earth exist.
There sat my friend, the yellow and tall,
 With his neck and its wen in the selfsame place;
Yet my nearest neighbour's cheek showed gall.
 She had slid away a contemptuous space:

And the old fat woman, late so placable,
Eyed me with symptoms, hardly mistakable,
Of her milk of kindness turning rancid.
In short, a spectator might have fancied
That I had nodded, betrayed by slumber,
Yet kept my seat, a warning ghastly,
Through the heads of the sermon, nine in number,
And woke up now at the tenth and lastly.
But again, could such disgrace have happened?
　　Each friend at my elbow had surely nudged it;
And, as for the sermon, where did my nap end?
　　Unless I heard it, could I have judged it?
Could I report as I do at the close,
First, the preacher speaks through his nose:
Second, his gesture is too emphatic:
　　Thirdly, to waive what's pedagogic,
　　The subject-matter itself lacks logic:
Fourthly, the English is ungrammatic.
Great news! the preacher is found no Pascal,
Whom, if I pleased, I might to the task call
Of making square to a finite eye
The circle of infinity,
And find so all-but-just-succeeding!
Great news! the sermon proves no reading
Where bee-like in the flowers I bury me,
Like Taylor's the immortal Jeremy!
And now that I know the very worst of him,
What was it I thought to obtain at first of him?
Ha! Is God mocked, as He asks?
Shall I take on me to change his tasks,
And dare, despatched to a river-head
　　For a simple draught of the element,

Neglect the thing for which He sent,
    And return with another thing instead? —
Saying, 'Because the water found
Welling up from underground,
Is mingled with the taints of earth,
While thou, I know, dost laugh at dearth,
And couldst, at wink or word, convulse
The world with the leap of a river-pulse, —
Therefore I turned from the oozings muddy,
    And bring Thee a chalice I found, instead:
See the brave veins in the breccia ruddy!
    One would suppose that the marble bled.
What matters the water? A hope I have nursed:
The waterless cup will quench my thirst.'
— Better have knelt at the poorest stream
    That trickles in pain from the straitest rift!
    For the less or the more is all God's gift,
Who blocks up or breaks wide the granite-seam.
And here, is there water or not, to drink?
    I then, in ignorance and weakness,
Taking God's help, have attained to think
    My heart does best to receive in meekness
That mode of worship, as most to His mind,
Where earthly aids being cast behind,
His All in All appears serene
With the thinnest human veil between,
Letting the mystic lamps, the seven,
    The many motions of his spirit,
Pass, as they list, to earth from heaven.
    For the preacher's merit or demerit,
It were to be wished the flaws were fewer
    In the earthen vessel, holding treasure

Which lies as safe in a golden ewer;
   But the main thing is, does it hold good measure?
Heaven soon sets right all other matters! —
   Ask, else, these ruins of humanity,
This flesh worn out to rags and tatters,
   This soul at struggle with insanity,
Who thence take comfort — can I doubt? —
Which an empire gained, were a loss without.
May it be mine! And let us hope
That no worse blessing befall the Pope,
Turned sick at last of to-day's buffoonery,
   Of posturings and petticoatings,
   Beside his Bourbon bully's gloatings
In the bloody orgies of drunk poltroonery!
Nor may the Professor forego its peace
   At Göttingen presently, when, in the dusk
Of his life, if his cough, as I fear, should increase,
   Prophesied of by that horrible husk —
When thicker and thicker the darkness fills
The world through his misty spectacles,
And he gropes for something more substantial
   Than a fable, myth or personification, —
May Christ do for him what no mere man shall,
   And stand confessed as the God of salvation!
Meantime, in the still recurring fear
   Lest myself, at unawares, be found,
   While attacking the choice of my neighbours round,
With none of my own made — I choose here!
The giving out of the hymn reclaims me;
I have done: and if any blames me,
Thinking that merely to touch in brevity
   The topics I dwell on, were unlawful, —
   Or worse, that I trench, with undue levity,

On the bounds of the holy and the awful, —
I praise the heart, and pity the head of him,
And refer myself to THEE, instead of him,
Who head and heart alike discernest,
 Looking below light speech we utter,
 When frothy spume and frequent sputter
Prove that the soul's depths boil in earnest!
May truth shine out, stand ever before us!
I put up pencil and join chorus
To Hepzibah Tune, without further apology,
 The last five verses of the third section
 Of the seventeenth hymn of Whitfield's Collection,
To conclude with the doxology.

ARTEMIS PROLOGIZES

I AM a goddess of the ambrosial courts,
And save by Here, Queen of Pride, surpassed
By none whose temples whiten this the world.
Through heaven I roll my lucid moon along;
I shed in hell o'er my pale people peace;
On earth I, caring for the creatures, guard
Each pregnant yellow wolf and fox-bitch sleek,
And every feathered mother's callow brood,
And all that love green haunts and loneliness.
Of men, the chaste adore me, hanging crowns
Of poppies red to blackness, bell and stem,
Upon my image at Athenai here;
And this dead Youth, Asclepios bends above,
Was dearest to me. He, my buskined step
To follow through the wild-wood leafy ways,
And chase the panting stag, or swift with darts
Stop the swift ounce, or lay the leopard low,
Neglected homage to another god:
Whence Aphrodite, by no midnight smoke
Of tapers lulled, in jealousy despatched
A noisome lust that, as the gadbee stings,
Possessed his stepdame Phaidra for himself
The son of Theseus her great absent spouse.
Hippolutos exclaiming in his rage
Against the fury of the Queen, she judged
Life insupportable; and, pricked at heart
An Amazonian stranger's race should dare
To scorn her, perished by the murderous cord:
Yet, ere she perished, blasted in a scroll

The fame of him her swerving made not swerve.
And Theseus, read, returning, and believed,
And exiled, in the blindness of his wrath,
The man without a crime who, last as first,
Loyal, divulged not to his sire the truth.
Now Theseus from Poseidon had obtained
That of his wishes should be granted three,
And one he imprecated straight – 'Alive
May ne'er Hippolutos reach other lands!'
Poseidon heard, ai ai! And scarce the prince
Had stepped into the fixed boots of the car
That give the feet a stay against the strength
Of the Henetian horses, and around
His body flung the rein, and urged their speed
Along the rocks and shingles of the shore,
When from the gaping wave a monster flung
His obscene body in the coursers' path.
These, mad with terror, as the sea-bull sprawled
Wallowing about their feet, lost care of him
That reared them; and the master-chariot-pole
Snapping beneath their plunges like a reed,
Hippolutos, whose feet were trammelled fast,
Was yet dragged forward by the circling rein
Which either hand directed; nor they quenched
The frenzy of their flight before each trace,
Wheel-spoke and splinter of the woeful car,
Each boulder-stone, sharp stub and spiny shell,
Huge fish-bone wrecked and wreathed amid the sands
On that detested beach, was bright with blood
And morsels of his flesh: then fell the steeds
Head foremost, crashing in their mooned fronts,
Shivering with sweat, each white eye horror-fixed.
His people, who had witnessed all afar,

Bore back the ruins of Hippolutos.
But when his sire, too swoln with pride, rejoiced
(Indomitable as a man foredoomed)
That vast Poseidon had fulfilled his prayer,
I, in a flood of glory visible,
Stood o'er my dying votary and, deed
By deed, revealed, as all took place, the truth.
Then Theseus lay the woefullest of men,
And worthily; but ere the death-veils hid
His face, the murdered prince full pardon breathed
To his rash sire. Whereat Athenai wails.

   So I, who ne'er forsake my votaries,
Lest in the cross-way none the honey-cake
Should tender, nor pour out the dog's hot life;
Lest at my fane the priests disconsolate
Should dress my image with some faded poor
Few crowns, made favours of, nor dare object
Such slackness to my worshippers who turn
Elsewhere the trusting heart and loaded hand,
As they had climbed Olumpos to report
Of Artemis and nowhere found her throne –
I interposed: and, this eventful night, –
(While round the funeral pyre the populace
Stood with fierce light on their black robes which bound
Each sobbing head, while yet their hair they clipped
O'er the dead body of their withered prince,
And, in his palace, Theseus prostrated
On the cold hearth, his brow cold as the slab
'Twas bruised on, groaned away the heavy grief –
As the pyre fell, and down the cross logs crashed
Sending a crowd of sparkles through the night,
And the gay fire, elate with mastery,
Towered like a serpent o'er the clotted jars

Of wine, dissolving oils and frankincense,
And splendid gums like gold), – my potency
Conveyed the perished man to my retreat
In the thrice-venerable forest here.
And this white-bearded sage who squeezes now
The berried plant, is Phoibos' son of fame,
Asclepios, whom my radiant brother taught
The doctrine of each herb and flower and root,
To know their secret'st virtue and express
The saving soul of all: who so has soothed
With lavers the torn brow and murdered cheeks,
Composed the hair and brought its gloss again,
And called the red bloom to the pale skin back,
And laid the strips and jagged ends of flesh
Even once more, and slacked the sinew's knot
Of every tortured limb – that now he lies
As if mere sleep possessed him underneath
These interwoven oaks and pines. Oh cheer,
Divine presenter of the healing rod,
Thy snake, with ardent throat and lulling eye,
Twines his lithe spires around! I say, much cheer!
Proceed thou with thy wisest pharmacies!
And ye, white crowd of woodland sister-nymphs,
Ply, as the sage directs, these buds and leaves
That strew the turf around the twain! While I
Await, in fitting silence, the event.

AN EPISTLE

CONTAINING THE STRANGE MEDICAL EXPERIENCE
OF KARSHISH, THE ARAB PHYSICIAN

KARSHISH, the picker-up of learning's crumbs,
The not-incurious in God's handiwork
(This man's-flesh He hath admirably made,
Blown like a bubble, kneaded like a paste,
To coop up and keep down on earth a space
That puff of vapour from his mouth, man's soul)
— To Abib, all-sagacious in our art,
Breeder in me of what poor skill I boast,
Like me inquisitive how pricks and cracks
Befall the flesh through too much stress and strain,
Whereby the wily vapour fain would slip
Back and rejoin its source before the term, —
And aptest in contrivance (under God)
To baffle it by deftly stopping such: —
The vagrant Scholar to his Sage at home
Sends greeting (health and knowledge, fame with peace)
Three samples of true snakestone — rarer still,
One of the other sort, the melon-shaped,
(But fitter, pounded fine, for charms than drugs)
And writeth now the twenty-second time.

My journeyings were brought to Jericho:
Thus I resume. Who studious in our art
Shall count a little labour unrepaid?
I have shed sweat enough, left flesh and bone
On many a flinty furlong of this land.
Also, the country-side is all on fire

With rumours of a marching hitherward:
Some say Vespasian cometh, some, his son.
A black lynx snarled and pricked a tufted ear;
Lust of my blood inflamed his yellow balls:
I cried and threw my staff and he was gone.
Twice have the robbers stripped and beaten me,
And once a town declared me for a spy;
But at the end, I reached Jerusalem,
Since this poor covert where I pass the night,
This Bethany, lies scarce the distance thence
A man with plague-sores at the third degree
Runs till he drops down dead. Thou laughest here!
'Sooth, it elates me, thus reposed and safe,
To void the stuffing of my travel-scrip
And share with thee whatever Jewry yields.
A viscid choler is observable
In tertians, I was nearly bold to say;
And falling-sickness hath a happier cure
Than our school wots of: there's a spider here
Weaves no web, watches on the ledge of tombs,
Sprinkled with mottles on an ash-grey back;
Take five and drop them . . . but who knows his mind,
The Syrian runagate I trust this to?
His service payeth me a sublimate
Blown up his nose to help the ailing eye.
Best wait: I reach Jerusalem at morn,
There set in order my experiences,
Gather what most deserves, and give thee all —
Or I might add, Judaea's gum-tragacanth
Scales off in purer flakes, shines clearer-grained,
Cracks 'twixt the pestle and the porphyry,
In fine exceeds our produce. Scalp-disease
Confounds me, crossing so with leprosy —

Thou hadst admired one sort I gained at Zoar —
But zeal outruns discretion. Here I end.

    Yet stay: my Syrian blinketh gratefully,
Protesteth his devotion is my price —
Suppose I write what harms not, though he steal?
I half resolve to tell thee, yet I blush,
What set me off a-writing first of all.
An itch I had, a sting to write, a tang!
For, be it this town's barrenness — or else
The Man had something in the look of him —
His case has struck me far more than 'tis worth.
So, pardon if — (lest presently I lose
In the great press of novelty at hand
The care and pains this somehow stole from me)
I bid thee take the thing while fresh in mind,
Almost in sight — for, wilt thou have the truth?
The very man is gone from me but now,
Whose ailment is the subject of discourse.
Thus then, and let thy better wit help all!

    'Tis but a case of mania — subinduced
By epilepsy, at the turning-point
Of trance prolonged unduly some three days:
When, by the exhibition of some drug
Or spell, exorcization, stroke of art
Unknown to me and which 'twere well to know,
The evil thing out-breaking all at once
Left the man whole and sound of body indeed, —
But, flinging (so to speak) life's gates too wide,
Making a clear house of it too suddenly,
The first conceit that entered might inscribe
Whatever it was minded on the wall

So plainly at that vantage, as it were,
(First come, first served) that nothing subsequent
Attaineth to erase those fancy-scrawls
The just-returned and new-established soul
Hath gotten now so thoroughly by heart
That henceforth she will read or these or none.
And first – the man's own firm conviction rests
That he was dead (in fact they buried him)
– That he was dead and then restored to life
By a Nazarene physician of his tribe:
– 'Sayeth, the same bade 'Rise,' and he did rise.
'Such cases are diurnal,' thou wilt cry.
Not so this figment! – not, that such a fume,
Instead of giving way to time and health,
Should eat itself into the life of life,
As saffron tingeth flesh, blood, bones and all!
For see, how he takes up the after-life.
The man – it is one Lazarus a Jew,
Sanguine, proportioned, fifty years of age,
The body's habit wholly laudable,
As much, indeed, beyond the common health
As he were made and put aside to show.
Think, could we penetrate by any drug
And bathe the wearied soul and worried flesh,
And bring it clear and fair, by three days' sleep!
Whence has the man the balm that brightens all?
This grown man eyes the world now like a child.
Some elders of his tribe, I should premise,
Led in their friend, obedient as a sheep,
To bear my inquisition. While they spoke,
Now sharply, now with sorrow, – told the case, –
He listened not except I spoke to him,
But folded his two hands and let them talk,

Watching the flies that buzzed: and yet no fool.
And that's a sample how his years must go.
Look, if a beggar, in fixed middle-life,
Should find a treasure, – can he use the same
With straitened habits and with tastes starved small,
And take at once to his impoverished brain
The sudden element that changes things,
That sets the undreamed-of rapture at his hand
And puts the cheap old joy in the scorned dust?
Is he not such an one as moves to mirth –
Warily parsimonious, when no need,
Wasteful as drunkenness at undue times?
All prudent counsel as to what befits
The golden mean, is lost on such an one:
The man's fantastic will is the man's law.
So here – we call the treasure knowledge, say,
Increased beyond the fleshly faculty –
Heaven opened to a soul while yet on earth,
Earth forced on a soul's use while seeing heaven:
The man is witless of the size, the sum,
The value in proportion of all things,
Or whether it be little or be much.
Discourse to him of prodigious armaments
Assembled to besiege his city now,
And of the passing of a mule with gourds –
'Tis one! Then take it on the other side,
Speak of some trifling fact, – he will gaze rapt
With stupor at its very littleness,
(Far as I see) as if in that indeed
He caught prodigious import, whole results;
And so will turn to us the bystanders
In ever the same stupor (note this point)
That we too see not with his opened eyes.

Wonder and doubt come wrongly into play,
Preposterously, at cross purposes.
Should his child sicken unto death, – why, look
For scarce abatement of his cheerfulness,
Or pretermission of the daily craft!
While a word, gesture, glance from that same child
At play or in the school or laid asleep,
Will startle him to an agony of fear,
Exasperation, just as like. Demand
The reason why – ' 'tis but a word,' object –
'A gesture' – he regards thee as our lord
Who lived there in the pyramid alone,
Looked at us (dost thou mind?) when, being young,
We both would unadvisedly recite
Some charm's beginning, from that book of his,
Able to bid the sun throb wide and burst
All into stars, as suns grown old are wont.
Thou and the child have each a veil alike
Thrown o'er your heads, from under which ye both
Stretch your blind hands and trifle with a match
Over a mine of Greek fire, did ye know!
He holds on firmly to some thread of life –
(It is the life to lead perforcedly)
Which runs across some vast distracting orb
Of glory on either side that meagre thread,
Which, conscious of, he must not enter yet –
The spiritual life around the earthly life:
The law of that is known to him as this,
His heart and brain move there, his feet stay here.
So is the man perplext with impulses
Sudden to start off crosswise, not straight on,
Proclaiming what is right and wrong across,
And not along, this black thread through the blaze –

'It should be' baulked by 'here it cannot be.'
And oft the man's soul springs into his face
As if he saw again and heard again
His sage that bade him 'Rise' and he did rise.
Something, a word, a tick o' the blood within
Admonishes: then back he sinks at once
To ashes, who was very fire before,
In sedulous recurrence to his trade
Whereby he earneth him the daily bread;
And studiously the humbler for that pride.
Professedly the faultier that he knows
God's secret, while he holds the thread of life.
Indeed the especial marking of the man
Is prone submission to the heavenly will –
Seeing it, what it is, and why it is.
'Sayeth, he will wait patient to the last
For that same death which must restore his being
To equilibrium, body loosening soul
Divorced even now by premature full growth:
He will live, nay, it pleaseth him to live
So long as God please, and just how God please.
He even seeketh not to please God more
(Which meaneth, otherwise) than as God please.
Hence, I perceive not he affects to preach
The doctrine of his sect whate'er it be,
Make proselytes as madmen thirst to do:
How can he give his neighbour the real ground,
His own conviction? Ardent as he is –
Call his great truth a lie, why, still the old
'Be it as God please' reassureth him.
I probed the sore as thy disciple should:
'How, beast,' said I, 'this stolid carelessness
Sufficeth thee, when Rome is on her march

To stamp out like a little spark thy town,
Thy tribe, thy crazy tale and thee at once?'
He merely looked with his large eyes on me.
The man is apathetic, you deduce?
Contrariwise, he loves both old and young,
Able and weak, affects the very brutes
And birds – how say I? flowers of the field –
As a wise workman recognizes tools
In a master's workshop, loving what they make.
Thus is the man as harmless as a lamb:
Only impatient, let him do his best,
At ignorance and carelessness and sin –
An indignation which is promptly curbed:
As when in certain travel I have feigned
To be an ignoramus in our art
According to some preconceived design,
And happed to hear the land's practitioners
Steeped in conceit sublimed by ignorance,
Prattle fantastically on disease,
Its cause and cure – and I must hold my peace!

Thou wilt object – Why have I not ere this
Sought out the sage himself, the Nazarene
Who wrought this cure, inquiring at the source,
Conferring with the frankness that befits?
Alas! it grieveth me, the learned leech
Perished in a tumult many years ago,
Accused, – our learning's fate, – of wizardry,
Rebellion, to the setting up a rule
And creed prodigious as described to me.
His death, which happened when the earthquake fell
(Prefiguring, as soon appeared, the loss
To occult learning in our lord the sage

Who lived there in the pyramid alone)
Was wrought by the mad people — that's their wont!
On vain recourse, as I conjecture it,
To his tried virtue, for miraculous help —
How could he stop the earthquake? That's their way!
The other imputations must be lies:
But take one, though I loathe to give it thee,
In mere respect for any good man's fame.
(And after all, our patient Lazarus
Is stark mad; should we count on what he says?
Perhaps not: though in writing to a leech
'Tis well to keep back nothing of a case.)
This man so cured regards the curer, then,
As — God forgive me! who but God himself,
Creator and sustainer of the world,
That came and dwelt in flesh on it awhile!
— 'Sayeth that such an one was born and lived,
Taught, healed the sick, broke bread at his own house,
Then died, with Lazarus by, for aught I know,
And yet was . . . what I said nor choose repeat,
And must have so avouched himself, in fact,
In hearing of this very Lazarus
Who saith — but why all this of what he saith?
Why write of trivial matters, things of price
Calling at every moment for remark?
I noticed on the margin of a pool
Blue-flowering borage, the Aleppo sort,
Aboundeth, very nitrous. It is strange!

Thy pardon for this long and tedious case,
Which, now that I review it, needs must seem
Unduly dwelt on, prolixly set forth!
Nor I myself discern in what is writ

Good cause for the peculiar interest
And awe indeed this man has touched me with.
Perhaps the journey's end, the weariness
Had wrought upon me first. I met him thus:
I crossed a ridge of short sharp broken hills
Like an old lion's cheek teeth. Out there came
A moon made like a face with certain spots
Multiform, manifold and menacing:
Then a wind rose behind me. So we met
In this old sleepy town at unaware,
The man and I. I send thee what is writ.
Regard it as a chance, a matter risked
To this ambiguous Syrian – he may lose,
Or steal, or give it thee with equal good.
Jerusalem's repose shall make amends
For time this letter wastes, thy time and mine;
Till when, once more thy pardon and farewell!

The very God! think, Abib; dost thou think?
So, the All-Great, were the All-Loving too –
So, through the thunder comes a human voice
Saying, 'O heart I made, a heart beats here!
Face, my hands fashioned, see it in myself!
Thou hast no power nor mayst conceive of mine,
But love I gave thee, with myself to love,
And thou must love me who have died for thee!'
The madman saith He said so: it is strange.

JOHANNES AGRICOLA IN
MEDITATION

THERE'S heaven above, and night by night
 I look right through its gorgeous roof;
No suns and moons though e'er so bright
 Avail to stop me; splendour-proof
 I keep the broods of stars aloof:
For I intend to get to God,
 For 'tis to God I speed so fast,
For in God's breast, my own abode,
 Those shoals of dazzling glory, passed,
 I lay my spirit down at last.
I lie where I have always lain,
 God smiles as he has always smiled;
Ere suns and moons could wax and wane,
 Ere stars were thundergirt, or piled
 The heavens, God thought on me his child;
Ordained a life for me, arrayed
 Its circumstances every one
To the minutest; ay, God said
 This head this hand should rest upon
 Thus, ere he fashioned star or sun.
And having thus created me,
 Thus rooted me, he bade me grow,
Guiltless for ever, like a tree
 That buds and blooms, nor seeks to know
 The law by which it prospers so:
But sure that thought and word and deed
 All go to swell his love for me,

Me, made because that love had need
   Of something irreversibly
   Pledged solely its content to be.
Yes, yes, a tree which must ascend,
   No poison-gourd foredoomed to stoop!
I have God's warrant, could I blend
   All hideous sins, as in a cup,
   To drink the mingled venoms up;
Secure my nature will convert
   The draught to blossoming gladness fast:
While sweet dews turn to the gourd's hurt,
   And bloat, and while they bloat it, blast,
   As from the first its lot was cast.
For as I lie, smiled on, full-fed
   By unexhausted power to bless,
I gaze below on hell's fierce bed,
   And those its waves of flame oppress,
   Swarming in ghastly wretchedness;
Whose life on earth aspired to be
   One altar-smoke, so pure! – to win
If not love like God's love for me,
   At least to keep his anger in;
   And all their striving turned to sin.
Priest, doctor, hermit, monk grown white
   With prayer, the broken-hearted nun,
The martyr, the wan acolyte,
   The incense-swinging child, – undone
   Before God fashioned star or sun!
God, whom I praise; how could I praise,
   If such as I might understand,
Make out and reckon on his ways,
   And bargain for his love, and stand,
   Paying a price, at his right hand?

FRA LIPPO LIPPI

[Florentine painter, 1412–69]

I AM poor brother Lippo, by your leave!
You need not clap your torches to my face.
Zooks, what's to blame? you think you see a monk!
What, 'tis past midnight, and you go the rounds,
And here you catch me at an alley's end
Where sportive ladies leave their doors ajar?
The Carmine's my cloister: hunt it up,
Do, – harry out, if you must show your zeal,
Whatever rat, there, haps on his wrong hole,
And nip each softling of a wee white mouse,
Weke, weke, that's crept to keep him company!
Aha, you know your betters! Then, you'll take
Your hand away that's fiddling on my throat,
And please to know me likewise. Who am I?
Why, one, sir, who is lodging with a friend
Three streets off – he's a certain . . . how d'ye call?
Master – a . . . Cosimo of the Medici,
I' the house that caps the corner. Boh! you were best!
Remember and tell me, the day you're hanged,
How you affected such a gullet's-gripe!
But you, sir, it concerns you that your knaves
Pick up a manner nor discredit you:
Zooks, are we pilchards, that they sweep the streets
And count fair prize what comes into their net?
He's Judas to a tittle, that man is!
Just such a face! Why, sir, you make amends.
Lord, I'm not angry! Bid your hangdogs go
Drink out this quarter-florin to the health

Of the munificent House that harbours me
(And many more beside, lads! more beside!)
And all's come square again. I'd like his face —
His, elbowing on his comrade in the door
With the pike and lantern, — for the slave that holds
John Baptist's head a-dangle by the hair
With one hand ('Look you, now,' as who should say)
And his weapon in the other, yet unwiped!
It's not your chance to have a bit of chalk,
A wood-coal or the like? or you should see!
Yes, I'm the painter, since you style me so.
What, brother Lippo's doings, up and down,
You know them and they take you? like enough!
I saw the proper twinkle in your eye —
'Tell you, I liked your looks at very first.
Let's sit and set things straight now, hip to haunch.
Here's spring come, and the nights one makes up bands
To roam the town and sing out carnival,
And I've been three weeks shut within my mew,
A-painting for the great man, saints and saints
And saints again. I could not paint all night —
Ouf! I leaned out of window for fresh air.
There came a hurry of feet and little feet,
A sweep of lute-strings, laughs, and whifts of song, —
Flower o' the broom,
Take away love, and our earth is a tomb!
Flower o' the quince,
I let Lisa go, and what good in life since?
Flower o' the thyme — and so on. Round they went.
Scarce had they turned the corner when a titter
Like the skipping of rabbits by moonlight, — three slim
     shapes,
And a face that looked up . . . zooks, sir, flesh and blood,

That's all I'm made of! Into shreds it went,
Curtain and counterpane and coverlet,
All the bed-furniture – a dozen knots,
There was a ladder! Down I let myself,
Hands and feet, scrambling somehow, and so dropped,
And after them. I came up with the fun
Hard by Saint Laurence, hail fellow, well met, –
Flower o' the rose,
If I've been merry, what matter who knows?
And so as I was stealing back again
To get to bed and have a bit of sleep
Ere I rise up to-morrow and go work
On Jerome knocking at his poor old breast
With his great round stone to subdue the flesh,
You snap me of the sudden. Ah, I see!
Though your eye twinkles still, you shake your head –
Mine's shaved – a monk, you say – the sting's in that!
If Master Cosimo announced himself,
Mum's the word naturally; but a monk!
Come, what am I a beast for? tell us, now!
I was a baby when my mother died
And father died and left me in the street.
I starved there, God knows how, a year or two
On fig-skins, melon-parings, rinds and shucks,
Refuse and rubbish. One fine frosty day,
My stomach being empty as your hat,
The wind doubled me up and down I went.
Old Aunt Lapaccia trussed me with one hand,
(Its fellow was a stinger as I knew)
And so along the wall, over the bridge,
By the straight cut to the convent. Six words there,
While I stood munching my first bread that month:
'So, boy, you're minded,' quoth the good fat father

Wiping his own mouth, 'twas refection-time, —
'To quit this very miserable world?
Will you renounce' . . . 'the mouthful of bread?' thought
   I;
By no means! Brief, they made a monk of me;
I did renounce the world, its pride and greed,
Palace, farm, villa, shop and banking-house,
Trash, such as these poor devils of Medici
Have given their hearts to — all at eight years old.
Well, sir, I found in time, you may be sure,
'Twas not for nothing — the good bellyful,
The warm serge and the rope that goes all round,
Add day-long blessed idleness beside!
'Let's see what the urchin's fit for' — that came next.
Not overmuch their way, I must confess.
Such a to-do! They tried me with their books:
Lord, they'd have taught me Latin in pure waste!
Flower o' the clove,
All the Latin I construe is, 'amo' I love!
But, mind you, when a boy starves in the streets
Eight years together, as my fortune was,
Watching folk's faces to know who will fling
The bit of half-stripped grape-bunch he desires,
And who will curse or kick him for his pains, —
Which gentleman processional and fine,
Holding a candle to the Sacrament,
Will wink and let him lift a plate and catch
The droppings of the wax to sell again,
Or holla for the Eight and have him whipped, —
How say I? — nay, which dog bites, which lets drop
His bone from the heap of offal in the street, —
Why, soul and sense of him grow sharp alike,
He learns the look of things, and none the less

For admonition from the hunger-pinch.
I had a store of such remarks, be sure,
Which, after I found leisure, turned to use.
I drew men's faces on my copy-books,
Scrawled them within the antiphonary's marge.
Joined legs and arms to the long music-notes,
Found eyes and nose and chin for A's and B's,
And made a string of pictures of the world
Betwixt the ins and outs of verb and noun,
On the wall, the bench, the door. The monks looked
    black.
'Nay,' quoth the Prior, 'turn him out, d'ye say?
In no wise. Lose a crow and catch a lark.
What if at last we get our man of parts,
We Carmelites, like those Camaldolese
And Preaching Friars, to do our church up fine
And put the front on it that ought to be!'
And hereupon he bade me daub away.
Thank you! my head being crammed, the walls a blank,
Never was such prompt disemburdening.
First, every sort of monk, the black and white,
I drew them, fat and lean: then, folk at church,
From good old gossips waiting to confess
Their cribs of barrel-droppings, candle-ends, —
To the breathless fellow at the altar-foot,
Fresh from his murder, safe and sitting there
With the little children round him in a row
Of admiration, half for his beard and half
For that white anger of his victim's son
Shaking a fist at him with one fierce arm,
Signing himself with the other because of Christ
(Whose sad face on the cross sees only this
After the passion of a thousand years)

Till some poor girl, her apron o'er her head,
(Which the intense eyes looked through) came at eve
On tiptoe, said a word, dropped in a loaf,
Her pair of earrings and a bunch of flowers
(The brute took growling), prayed, and so was gone.
I painted all, then cried "Tis ask and have;
Choose, for more's ready!' – laid the ladder flat,
And showed my covered bit of cloister-wall.
The monks closed in a circle and praised loud
Till checked, taught what to see and not to see,
Being simple bodies, – 'That's the very man!
Look at the boy who stoops to pat the dog!
That woman's like the Prior's niece who comes
To care about his asthma: it's the life!'
But there my triumph's straw-fire flared and funked;
Their betters took their turn to see and say:
The Prior and the learned pulled a face
And stopped all that in no time. 'How? what's here?
Quite from the mark of painting, bless us all!
Faces, arms, legs and bodies like the true
As much as pea and pea! it's devil's-game!
Your business is not to catch men with show,
With homage to the perishable clay,
But lift them over it, ignore it all,
Make them forget there's such a thing as flesh.
Your business is to paint the souls of men –
Man's soul, and it's a fire, smoke . . . no, it's not . . .
It's vapour done up like a new-born babe –
(In that shape when you die it leaves your mouth)
It's . . . well, what matters talking, it's the soul!
Give us no more of body than shows soul!
Here's Giotto, with his Saint a-praising God,
That sets us praising, – why not stop with him?

Why put all thoughts of praise out of our head
With wonder at lines, colours, and what not?
Paint the soul, never mind the legs and arms!
Rub all out, try at it a second time.
Oh, that white smallish female with the breasts,
She's just my niece . . . Herodias, I would say, –
Who went and danced and got men's heads cut off!
Have it all out!' Now, is this sense, I ask?
A fine way to paint soul, by painting body
So ill, the eye can't stop there, must go further
And can't fare worse! Thus, yellow does for white
When what you put for yellow's simply black,
And any sort of meaning looks intense
When all beside itself means and looks nought.
Why can't a painter lift each foot in turn,
Left foot and right foot, go a double step,
Make his flesh liker and his soul more like,
Both in their order? Take the prettiest face,
The Prior's niece . . . patron-saint – is it so pretty
You can't discover if it means hope, fear,
Sorrow or joy? won't beauty go with these?
Suppose I've made her eyes all right and blue,
Can't I take breath and try to add life's flash,
And then add soul and heighten them three-fold?
Or say there's beauty with no soul at all –
(I never saw it – put the case the same –)
If you get simple beauty and nought else,
You get about the best thing God invents:
That's somewhat: and you'll find the soul you have
    missed,
Within yourself, when you return him thanks.
'Rub all out!' Well, well, there's my life, in short,
And so the thing has gone on ever since.

I'm grown a man no doubt, I've broken bounds:
You should not take a fellow eight years old
And make him swear to never kiss the girls.
I'm my own master, paint now as I please —
Having a friend, you see, in the Corner-house!
Lord, it's fast holding by the rings in front —
Those great rings serve more purposes than just
To plant a flag in, or tie up a horse!
And yet the old schooling sticks, the old grave eyes
Are peeping o'er my shoulder as I work,
The heads shake still — 'It's art's decline, my son!
You're not of the true painters, great and old;
Brother Angelico's the man, you'll find;
Brother Lorenzo stands his single peer:
Fag on at flesh, you'll never make the third!'
Flower o' the pine,
You keep your mistr . . . manners, and I'll stick to mine!
I'm not the third, then: bless us, they must know!
Don't you think they're the likeliest to know,
They with their Latin? So, I swallow my rage,
Clench my teeth, suck my lips in tight, and paint
To please them — sometimes do and sometimes don't;
For, doing most, there's pretty sure to come
A turn, some warm eve finds me at my saints —
A laugh, a cry, the business of the world —
(*Flower o' the peach,*
Death for us all, and his own life for each!)
And my whole soul revolves, the cup runs over,
The world and life's too big to pass for a dream,
And I do these wild things in sheer despite,
And play the fooleries you catch me at,
In pure rage! The old mill-horse, out at grass
After hard years, throws up his stiff heels so,

Although the miller does not preach to him
The only good of grass is to make chaff.
What would men have? Do they like grass or no —
May they or mayn't they? all I want's the thing
Settled for ever one way. As it is,
You tell too many lies and hurt yourself:
You don't like what you only like too much,
You do like what, if given you at your word,
You find abundantly detestable.
For me, I think I speak as I was taught;
I always see the garden and God there
A-making man's wife: and, my lesson learned,
The value and significance of flesh,
I can't unlearn ten minutes afterwards,

    You understand me: I'm a beast, I know.
But see, now — why, I see as certainly
As that the morning-star's about to shine,
What will hap some day. We've a youngster here
Comes to our convent, studies what I do,
Slouches and stares and lets no atom drop:
His name is Guidi — he'll not mind the monks —
They call him Hulking Tom, he lets them talk —
He picks my practice up — he'll paint apace,
I hope so — though I never live so long,
I know what's sure to follow. You be judge!
You speak no Latin more than I, belike;
However, you're my man, you've seen the world
— The beauty and the wonder and the power,
The shapes of things, their colours, lights and shades,
Changes, surprises, — and God made it all!
— For what? Do you feel thankful, ay or no,
For this fair town's face, yonder river's line,

The mountain round it and the sky above,
Much more the figures of man, woman, child,
These are the frame to? What's it all about?
To be passed over, despised? or dwelt upon,
Wondered at? oh, this last of course! – you say.
But why not do as well as say, – paint these
Just as they are, careless what comes of it?
God's works – paint anyone, and count it crime
To let a truth slip. Don't object, 'His works
Are here already; nature is complete:
Suppose your reproduce her – (which you can't)
There's no advantage! you must beat her, then.'
For, don't you mark? we're made so that we love
First when we see them painted, things we have passed
Perhaps a hundred times nor cared to see;
And so they are better, painted – better to us,
Which is the same thing. Art was given for that;
God uses us to help each other so,
Lending our minds out. Have you noticed, now,
Your cullion's hanging face? A bit of chalk,
And trust me but you should, though! How much more,
If I drew higher things with the same truth!
That were to take the Prior's pulpit-place,
Interpret God to all of you! Oh, oh,
It makes me mad to see what men shall do
And we in our graves! This world's no blot for us,
Nor blank; it means intensely, and means good:
To find its meaning is my meat and drink.
'Ay, but you don't so instigate to prayer!'
Strikes in the Prior: 'when your meaning's plain
It does not say to folk – remember matins,
Or, mind you fast next Friday!' Why, for this
What need of art at all? A skull and bones,

Two bits of stick nailed crosswise, or, what's best,
A bell to chime the hour with, does as well.
I painted a Saint Laurence six months since
At Prato, splashed the fresco in fine style:
'How looks my painting, now the scaffold's down?'
I ask a brother: 'Hugely,' he returns –
'Already not one phiz of your three slaves
Who turn the Deacon off his toasted side,
But's scratched and prodded to our heart's content,
The pious people have so eased their own
With coming to say prayers there in a rage:
We get on fast to see the bricks beneath.
Expect another job this time next year,
For pity and religion grow i' the crowd –
Your painting serves its purpose!' Hang the fools!

    – That is – you'll not mistake an idle word
Spoke in a huff by a poor monk, God wot,
Tasting the air this spicy night which turns
The unaccustomed head like Chianti wine!
Oh, the church knows! don't misreport me, now!
It's natural a poor monk out of bounds
Should have his apt word to excuse himself:
And hearken how I plot to make amends.
I have bethought me: I shall paint a piece
. . . There's for you! Give me six months, then go, see
Something in Sant' Ambrogio's! Bless the nuns!
They want a cast o' my office. I shall paint
God in the midst, Madonna and her babe,
Ringed by a bowery flowery angel-brood,
Lilies and vestments and white faces, sweet
As puff on puff of grated orris-root
When ladies crowd to Church at midsummer.

And then i' the front, of course a saint or two —
Saint John, because he saves the Florentines,
Saint Ambrose, who puts down in black and white
The convent's friends and gives them a long day,
And Job, I must have him there past mistake,
The man of Uz (and Us without the z,
Painters who need his patience). Well, all these
Secured at their devotion, up shall come
Out of a corner when you least expect,
As one by a dark stair into a great light,
Music and talking, who but Lippo! I! —
Mazed, motionless and moonstruck — I'm the man!
Back I shrink — what is this I see and hear?
I, caught up with my monk's-things by mistake,
My old serge gown and rope that goes all round,
I, in this presence, this pure company!
Where's a hole, where's a corner for escape?
Then steps a sweet angelic slip of a thing
Forward, puts out a soft palm — 'Not so fast!'
— Addresses the celestial presence, 'nay —
He made you and devised you, after all,
Though he's none of you! Could Saint John there
    draw —
His camel-hair make up a painting-brush?
We come to brother Lippo for all that,
Iste perfecit opus!' So, all smile —
I shuffle sideways with my blushing face
Under the cover of a hundred wings
Thrown like a spread of kirtles when you're gay
And play hot cockles, all the doors being shut,
Till, wholly unexpected, in there pops
The hothead husband! Thus I scuttle off
To some safe bench behind, not letting go

The palm of her, the little lily thing
That spoke the good word for me in the nick,
Like the Prior's niece . . . Saint Lucy, I would say.
And so all's saved for me, and for the church
A pretty picture gained. Go, six months hence!
Your hand, sir, and good-bye: no lights, no lights!
The street's hushed, and I know my own way back,
Don't fear me! There's the grey beginning. Zooks!

ANDREA DEL SARTO

(CALLED 'THE FAULTLESS PAINTER')

BUT do not let us quarrel any more,
No, my Lucrezia; bear with me for once:
Sit down and all shall happen as you wish.
You turn your face, but does it bring your heart?
I'll work then for your friend's friend, never fear,
Treat his own subject after his own way,
Fix his own time, accept too his own price,
And shut the money into this small hand
When next it takes mine. Will it? tenderly?
Oh, I'll content him, – but to-morrow, Love!
I often am much wearier than you think,
This evening more than usual, and it seems
As if – forgive now – should you let me sit
Here by the window with your hand in mine
And look a half-hour forth on Fiesole,
Both of one mind, as married people use,
Quietly, quietly the evening through,
I might get up to-morrow to my work
Cheerful and fresh as ever. Let us try.
To-morrow, how you shall be glad for this!
Your soft hand is a woman of itself,
And mine the man's bared breast she curls inside.
Don't count the time lost, neither; you must serve
For each of the five pictures we require:
It saves a model. So! keep looking so –
My serpentining beauty, rounds on rounds!
– How could you ever prick those perfect ears,
Even to put the pearl there! oh, so sweet –

My face, my moon, my everybody's moon,
Which everybody looks on and calls his,
And, I suppose, is looked on by in turn,
While she looks — no one's: very dear, no less.
You smile? why, there's my picture ready made,
There's what we painters call our harmony!
A common greyness silvers everything, —
All in a twilight, you and I alike
— You, at the point of your first pride in me
(That's gone you know), — but I, at every point;
My youth, my hope, my art, being all toned down
To yonder sober pleasant Fiesole.
There's the bell clinking from the chapel-top;
That length of convent-wall across the way
Holds the trees safer, huddled more inside;
The last monk leaves the garden; days decrease,
And autumn grows, autumn in everything.
Eh? the whole seems to fall into a shape
As if I saw alike my work and self
And all that I was born to be and do,
A twilight-piece. Love, we are in God's hand.
How strange now, looks the life he makes us lead;
So free we seem, so fettered fast we are!
I feel he laid the fetter: let it lie!
This chamber for example — turn your head —
All that's behind us! You don't understand
Nor care to understand about my art,
But you can hear at least when people speak:
And that cartoon, the second from the door
— It is the thing, Love! so such things should be —
Behold Madonna! — I am bold to say.
I can do with my pencil what I know,
What I see, what at bottom of my heart

I wish for, if I ever wish so deep –
Do easily, too – when I say, perfectly,
I do not boast, perhaps: yourself are judge,
Who listened to the Legate's talk last week,
And just as much they used to say in France.
At any rate 'tis easy, all of it!
No sketches first, no studies, that's long past:
I do what many dream of, all their lives,
– Dream? strive to do, and agonize to do,
And fail in doing. I could count twenty such
On twice your fingers, and not leave this town,
Who strive – you don't know how the others strive
To paint a little thing like that you smeared
Carelessly passing with your robes afloat, –
Yet do much less, so much less, Someone says,
(I know his name, no matter) – so much less!
Well, less is more, Lucrezia: I am judged.
There burns a truer light of God in them,
In their vexed beating stuffed and stopped-up brain,
Heart, or whate'er else, than goes on to prompt
This low-pulsed forthright craftsman's hand of mine.
Their works drop groundward, but themselves, I know,
Reach many a time a heaven that's shut to me,
Enter and take their place there sure enough,
Though they come back and cannot tell the world.
My works are nearer heaven, but I sit here.
The sudden flood of these men! at a word –
Praise them, it boils, or blame them, it boils too.
I, painting from myself and to myself,
Know what I do, am unmoved by men's blame
Or their praise either. Somebody remarks
Morello's outline there is wrongly traced,
His hue mistaken; what of that? or else,

Rightly traced and well ordered; what of that?
Speak as they please, what does the mountain care?
Ah, but a man's reach should exceed his grasp,
Or what's a heaven for? All is silver-grey
Placid and perfect with my art: the worse!
I know both what I want and what might gain,
And yet how profitless to know, to sigh
'Had I been two, another and myself,
Our head would have o'erlooked the world!' No doubt.
Yonder's a work now, of that famous youth
The Urbinate who died five years ago.
('Tis copied, George Vasari sent it me.)
Well, I can fancy how he did it all,
Pouring his soul, with kings and popes to see,
Reaching, that heaven might so replenish him,
Above and through his art – for it gives way;
That arm is wrongly put – and there again –
A fault to pardon in the drawing's lines,
Its body, so to speak: its soul is right,
He means right – that, a child may understand.
Still, what an arm! and I could alter it:
But all the play, the insight and the stretch –
Out of me, out of me! And wherefore out?
Had you enjoined them on me, given me soul,
We might have risen to Rafael, I and you!
Nay, Love, you did give all I asked, I think –
More than I merit, yes, by many times.
But had you – oh, with the same perfect brow
And perfect eyes, and more than perfect mouth,
And the low voice my soul hears, as a bird
The fowler's pipe, and follows to the snare –
Had you, with these the same, but brought a mind!
Some women do so. Had the mouth there urged

'God and the glory! never care for gain.
The present by the future, what is that?
Live for fame, side by side with Angelo!
Rafael is waiting: up to God, all three!'
I might have done it for you. So it seems:
Perhaps not. All is as God over-rules.
Beside, incentives come from the soul's self;
The rest avail not. Why do I need you?
What wife had Rafael, or has Angelo?
In this world, who can do a thing, will not;
And who would do it, cannot, I perceive:
Yet the will's somewhat – somewhat, too, the power –
And thus we half-men struggle. At the end,
God, I conclude, compensates, punishes.
'Tis safer for me, if the award be strict,
That I am something underrated here,
Poor this long while, despised, to speak the truth.
I dared not, do you know, leave home all day,
For fear of chancing on the Paris lords.
The best is when they pass and look aside;
But they speak sometimes; I must bear it all.
Well may they speak! That Francis, that first time,
And that long festal year at Fontainebleau!
I surely then could sometimes leave the ground,
Put on the glory, Rafael's daily wear,
In that humane great monarch's golden look, –
One finger in his beard or twisted curl
Over his mouth's good mark that made the smile,
One arm about my shoulder, round my neck,
The jingle of his gold chain in my ear,
I painting proudly with his breath on me,
All his court round him, seeing with his eyes,
Such frank French eyes, and such a fire of souls

Profuse, my hand kept plying by those hearts, —
And, best of all, this, this, this face beyond,
This in the background, waiting on my work,
To crown the issue with a last reward!
A good time, was it not, my kingly days?
And had you not grown restless . . . but I know —
'Tis done and past; 'twas right, my instinct said;
Too live the life grew, golden and not grey,
And I'm the weak-eyed bat no sun should tempt
Out of the grange whose four walls make his world.
How could it end in any other way?
You called me, and I came home to your heart.
The triumph was — to reach and stay there; since
I reached it ere the triumph, what is lost?
Let my hands frame your face in your hair's gold,
You beautiful Lucrezia that are mine!
'Rafael did this, Andrea painted that;
The Roman's is the better when you pray,
But still the other's Virgin was his wife — '
Men will excuse me. I am glad to judge
Both pictures in your presence; clearer grows
My better fortune, I resolve to think.
For, do you know, Lucrezia, as God lives,
Said one day Angelo, his very self,
To Rafael . . . I have known it all these years . . .
(When the young man was flaming out his thoughts
Upon a palace-wall for Rome to see,
Too lifted up in heart because of it)
'Friend, there's a certain sorry little scrub
Goes up and down our Florence, none cares how,
Who, were he set to plan and execute
As you are, pricked on by your popes and kings,
Would bring the sweat into that brow of yours!'

To Rafael's! – And indeed the arm is wrong.
I hardly dare ... yet, only you to see,
Give the chalk here – quick, thus the line should go!
Ay, but the soul! he's Rafael! rub it out!
Still, all I care for, if he spoke the truth,
What he? why, who but Michel Angelo?
(Do you forget already words like those?)
If really there was such a chance, so lost, –
Is, whether you're – not grateful – but more pleased.
Well, let me think so. And you smile indeed!
This hour has been an hour! Another smile?
If you would sit thus by me every night
I should work better, do you comprehend?
I mean that I should earn more, give you more.
See, it is settled dusk now; there's a star;
Morello's gone, the watch-lights show the wall,
The cue-owls speak the name we call them by.
Come from the window, love, – come in, at last,
Inside the melancholy little house
We built to be so gay with. God is just.
King Francis may forgive me: oft at nights
When I look up from painting, eyes tired out,
The walls become illumined, brick from brick
Distinct, instead of mortar, fierce bright gold,
That gold of his I did cement them with!
Let us but love each other. Must you go?
That Cousin here again? he waits outside?
Must see you – you, and not with me? Those loans?
More gaming debts to pay? you smiled for that?
Well, let smiles buy me! have you more to spend?
While hand and eye and something of a heart
Are left me, work's my ware, and what's it worth?
I'll pay my fancy. Only let me sit

The grey remainder of the evening out,
Idle, you call it, and muse perfectly
How I could paint, were I but back in France,
One picture, just one more – the Virgin's face
Not yours this time! I want you at my side
To hear them – that is, Michel Angelo –
Judge all I do and tell you of its worth.
Will you? To-morrow, satisfy your friend.
I take the subjects for his corridor,
Finish the portrait out of hand – there, there,
And throw him in another thing or two
If he demurs; the whole should prove enough
To pay for this same Cousin's freak. Beside,
What's better and what's all I care about,
Get you the thirteen scudi for the ruff!
Love, does that please you? Ah, but what does he,
The Cousin! what does he to please you more?

I am grown peaceful as old age to-night.
I regret little, I would change still less.
Since there my past life lies, why alter it?
The very wrong to Francis! – it is true
I took his coin, was tempted and complied,
And built this house and sinned, and all is said.
My father and my mother died of want.
Well, had I riches of my own? you see
How one gets rich! Let each one bear his lot.
They were born poor, lived poor, and poor they died:
And I have laboured somewhat in my time
And not been paid profusely. Some good son
Paint my two hundred pictures – let him try!
No doubt, there's something strikes a balance. Yes,
You loved me quite enough, it seems to-night.

This must suffice me here. What would one have?
In heaven, perhaps, new chances, one more chance —
Four great walls in the New Jerusalem,
Meted on each side by the angel's reed,
For Leonard, Rafael, Angelo and me
To cover — the three first without a wife,
While I have mine! So — still they overcome
Because there's still Lucrezia, — as I choose.

Again the Cousin's whistle! Go, my Love.

THE BISHOP ORDERS HIS TOMB
AT SAINT PRAXED'S CHURCH

ROME, 15—

VANITY, saith the preacher, vanity!
Draw round my bed: is Anselm keeping back?
Nephews – sons mine . . . ah God, I know not! Well –
She, men would have to be your mother once,
Old Gandolf envied me, so fair she was!
What's done is done, and she is dead beside,
Dead long ago, and I am Bishop since,
And as she died so must we die ourselves,
And thence ye may perceive the world's a dream.
Life, how and what is it? As here I lie
In this state-chamber, dying by degrees,
Hours and long hours in the dead night, I ask
'Do I live, am I dead?' Peace, peace seems all.
Saint Praxed's ever was the church for peace;
And so, about this tomb of mine. I fought
With tooth and nail to save my niche, ye know:
– Old Gandolf cozened me, despite my care;
Shrewd was that snatch from out the corner South
He graced his carrion with, God curse the same!
Yet still my niche is not so cramped but thence
One sees the pulpit o' the epistle-side,
And somewhat of the choir, those silent seats,
And up into the aery dome where live
The angels, and a sunbeam's sure to lurk:
And I shall fill my slab of basalt there,
And 'neath my tabernacle take my rest,
With those nine columns round me, two and two,

216

The odd one at my feet where Anselm stands:
Peach-blossom marble all, the rare, the ripe
As fresh-poured red wine of a mighty pulse.
– Old Gandolf with his paltry onion-stone,
Put me where I may look at him! True peach,
Rosy and flawless: how I earned the prize!
Draw close: that conflagration of my church
– What then? So much was saved if aught were missed!
My sons, ye would not be my death? Go dig
The white-grape vineyard where the oil-press stood,
Drop water gently till the surface sink,
And if ye find . . . Ah God, I know not, I! . . .
Bedded in store of rotten fig-leaves soft,
And corded up in a tight olive-frail,
Some lump, ah God, of *lapis lazuli*,
Big as a Jew's head cut off at the nape,
Blue as a vein o'er the Madonna's breast . . .
Sons, all have I bequeathed you, villas, all,
That brave Frascati villa with its bath,
So, let the blue lump poise between my knees,
Like God the Father's globe on both his hands
Ye worship in the Jesu Church so gay,
For Gandolf shall not choose but see and burst!
Swift as a weaver's shuttle fleet our years:
Man goeth to the grave, and where is he?
Did I say basalt for my slab, sons? Black –
'Twas ever antique-black I meant! How else
Shall ye contrast my frieze to come beneath?
The bas-relief in bronze ye promised me,
Those Pans and Nymphs ye wot of, and perchance
Some tripod, thyrsus, with a vase or so,
The Saviour at his sermon on the mount,
Saint Praxed in a glory, and one Pan

Ready to twitch the Nymph's last garment off,
And Moses with the tables . . . but I know
Ye mark me not! What do they whisper thee,
Child of my bowels, Anselm? Ah, ye hope
To revel down my villas while I gasp
Bricked o'er with beggar's mouldy travertine
Which Gandolf from his tomb-top chuckles at!
Nay, boys, ye love me – all of jasper, then!
'Tis jasper ye stand pledged to, lest I grieve.
My bath must needs be left behind, alas!
One block, pure green as a pistachio-nut,
There's plenty jasper somewhere in the world –
And have I not Saint Praxed's ear to pray
Horses for ye, and brown Greek manuscripts,
And mistresses with great smooth marbly limbs?
– That's if ye carve my epitaph aright,
Choice Latin, picked phrase, Tully's every word,
No gaudy ware like Gandolf's second line –
Tully, my masters? Ulpian serves his need!
And then how I shall lie through centuries,
And hear the blessed mutter of the mass,
And see God made and eaten all day long,
And feel the steady candle-flame, and taste
Good strong thick stupefying incense-smoke!
For as I lie here, hours of the dead night,
Dying in state and by such slow degrees,
I fold my arms as if they clasped a crook,
And stretch my feet forth straight as stone can point,
And let the bedclothes, for a mortcloth, drop
Into great laps and folds of sculptor's-work:
And as yon tapers dwindle, and strange thoughts
Grow, with a certain humming in my ears,
About the life before I lived this life,

And this life too, popes, cardinals and priests,
Saint Praxed at his sermon on the mount,
Your tall pale mother with her talking eyes,
And new-found agate urns as fresh as day,
And marble's language, Latin pure, discreet,
– Aha, ELUCESCEBAT quoth our friend?
No Tully, said I, Ulpian at the best!
Evil and brief hath been my pilgrimage.
All *lapis*, all, sons! Else I give the Pope
My villas! Will ye ever eat my heart?
Ever your eyes were as a lizard's quick,
They glitter like your mother's for my soul,
Or ye would heighten my impoverished frieze,
Piece out its starved design, and fill my vase
With grapes, and add a vizor and a Term,
And to the tripod ye would tie a lynx
That in his struggle throws the thyrsus down,
To comfort me on my entablature
Whereon I am to lie till I must ask
'Do I live, am I dead?' There, leave me, there!
For ye have stabbed me with ingratitude
To death – ye wish it – God, ye wish it! Stone –
Gritstone, a-crumble! Clammy squares which sweat
As if the corpse they keep were oozing through –
And no more *lapis* to delight the world!
Well go! I bless ye. Fewer tapers there,
But in a row: and, going, turn your backs
– Ay, like departing altar-ministrants,
And leave me in my church, the church for peace,
That I may watch at leisure if he leers –
Old Gandolf, at me, from his onion-stone,
As still he envied me, so fair she was!

No more wine? then we'll push back chairs and talk.
A final glass for me, though: cool, i' faith!
We ought to have our Abbey back, you see.
It's different, preaching in basilicas,
And doing duty in some masterpiece
Like this of brother Pugin's, bless his heart!
I doubt if they're half baked, those chalk rosettes,
Ciphers and stucco-twiddlings everywhere;
It's just like breathing in a lime-kiln: eh?
These hot long ceremonies of our church
Cost us a little – oh, they pay the price,
You take me – amply pay it! Now, we'll talk.

So, you despise me, Mr Gigadibs.
No deprecation, – nay, I beg you, sir!
Beside 'tis our engagement: don't you know,
I promised, if you'd watch a dinner out,
We'd see truth dawn together? – truth that peeps
Over the glasses' edge when dinner's done,
And body gets its sop and holds its noise
And leaves soul free a little. Now's the time:
Truth's break of day! You do despise me then.
And if I say, 'despise me,' – never fear!
I know you do not in a certain sense –
Not in my arm-chair, for example: here,
I well imagine you respect my place
(*Status*, *entourage*, worldly circumstance)
Quite to its value – very much indeed:
– Are up to the protesting eyes of you

In pride at being seated here for once –
You'll turn it to such capital account!
When somebody, through years and years to come,
Hints of the bishop, – names me – that's enough:
'Blougram? I knew him' – (into it you slide)
'Dined with him once, a Corpus Christi Day,
All alone, we two; he's a clever man:
And after dinner, – why, the wine you know, –
Oh, there was wine, and good! – what with the wine . . .
'Faith, we began upon all sorts of talk!
He's no bad fellow, Blougram; he had seen
Something of mine he relished, some review:
He's quite above their humbug in his heart,
Half-said as much, indeed – the thing's his trade.
I warrant, Blougram's sceptical at times:
How otherwise? I liked him, I confess!'
Che che, my dear sir, as we say at Rome,
Don't you protest now! It's fair give and take;
You have had your turn and spoken your home-truths:
The hand's mine now, and here you follow suit.

Thus much conceded, still the first fact stays –
You do despise me; your ideal of life
Is not the bishop's: you would not be I.
You would like better to be Goethe, now,
Or Buonaparte, or, bless me, lower still,
Count D'Orsay, – so you did what you preferred,
Spoke as you thought, and, as you cannot help,
Believed or disbelieved, no matter what,
So long as on that point, whate'er it was,
You loosed your mind, were whole and sole yourself.
– That, my ideal never can include,
Upon that element of truth and worth

221

Never be based! for say they make me Pope —
(They can't – suppose it for our argument!)
Why, there I'm at my tether's end, I've reached
My height, and not a height which pleases you:
An unbelieving Pope won't do, you say.
It's like those eerie stories nurses tell,
Of how some actor on a stage played Death,
With pasteboard crown, sham orb and tinselled dart,
And called himself the monarch of the world;
Then, going in the tire-room afterward,
Because the play was done, to shift himself,
Got touched upon the sleeve familiarly,
The moment he had shut the closet door,
By Death himself. Thus God might touch a Pope
At unawares, ask what his baubles mean,
And whose part he presumed to play just now.
Best be yourself, imperial, plain and true!

So, drawing comfortable breath again,
You weigh and find, whatever more or less
I boast of my ideal realized
Is nothing in the balance when opposed
To your ideal, your grand simple life,
Of which you will not realize one jot.
I am much, you are nothing; you would be all,
I would be merely much: you beat me there.

No, friend, you do not beat me: hearken why!
The common problem, yours, mine, every one's,
Is – not to fancy what were fair in life
Provided it could be, – but, finding first
What may be, then find how to make it fair

Up to our means: a very different thing!
No abstract intellectual plan of life
Quite irrespective of life's plainest laws,
But one, a man, who is man and nothing more,
May lead within a world which (by your leave)
Is Rome or London, not Fool's-paradise.
Embellish Rome, idealize away,
Make paradise of London if you can,
You're welcome, nay, you're wise.

                            A simile!
We mortals cross the ocean of this world
Each in his average cabin of a life;
The best's not big, the worst yields elbow-room.
Now for our six months' voyage – how prepare?
You come on shipboard with a landsman's list
Of things he calls convenient: so they are!
An India screen is pretty furniture,
A piano-forte is a fine resource,
All Balzac's novels occupy one shelf,
The new edition fifty volumes long;
And little Greek books, with the funny type
They get up well at Leipsic, fill the next:
Go on! slabbed marble, what a bath it makes!
And Parma's pride, the Jerome, let us add!
'Twere pleasant could Correggio's fleeting glow
Hang full in face of one where'er one roams,
Since he more than the others brings with him
Italy's self, – the marvellous Modenese! –
Yet was not on your list before, perhaps.
– Alas, friend, here's the agent . . . is't the name?
The captain, or whoever's master here –
You see him screw his face up; what's his cry

Ere you set foot on shipboard? 'Six feet square!'
If you won't understand what six feet mean,
Compute and purchase stores accordingly –
And if, in pique because he overhauls
Your Jerome, piano, bath, you come on board
Bare – why, you cut a figure at the first
While sympathetic landsmen see you off;
Not afterward, when long ere half seas over,
You peep up from your utterly naked boards
Into some snug and well-appointed berth,
Like mine for instance (try the cooler jug –
Put back the other, but don't jog the ice!)
And mortified you mutter 'Well and good;
He sits enjoying his sea-furniture;
'Tis stout and proper, and there's store of it:
Though I've the better notion, all agree,
Of fitting rooms up. Hang the carpenter,
Neat ship-shape fixings and contrivances –
I would have brought my Jerome, frame and all!'
And meantime you bring nothing: never mind –
You've proved your artist-nature: what you don't
You might bring, so despise me, as I say.

Now come, let's backward to the starting-place.
See my way: we're two college friends, suppose.
Prepare together for our voyage, then;
Each note and check the other in his work, –
Here's mine, a bishop's outfit; criticize!
What's wrong? why won't you be a bishop too?

Why first, you don't believe, you don't and can't,
(Not statedly, that is, and fixedly
And absolutely and exclusively)

In any revelation called divine.
No dogmas nail your faith; and what remains
But say so, like the honest man you are?
First, therefore, overhaul theology!
Nay, I too, not a fool, you please to think,
Must find believing every whit as hard:
And if I do not frankly say as much,
The ugly consequence is clear enough.

　　Now wait, my friend: well, I do not believe —
If you'll accept no faith that is not fixed,
Absolute and exclusive, as you say.
You're wrong — I mean to prove it in due time.
Meanwhile, I know where difficulties lie
I could not, cannot solve, nor ever shall,
So give up hope accordingly to solve —
(To you, and over the wine). Our dogmas then
With both of us, though in unlike degree,
Missing full credence — overboard with them!
I mean to meet you on your own premise:
Good, there go mine in company with yours!

　　And now what are we? unbelievers both,
Calm and complete, determinately fixed
To-day, to-morrow and for ever, pray?
You'll guarantee me that? Not so, I think!
In no wise! all we've gained is, that belief,
As unbelief before, shakes us by fits,
Confounds us like its predecessor. Where's
The gain? how can we guard our unbelief,
Make it bear fruit to us? — the problem here.
Just when we are safest, there's a sunset-touch,
A fancy from a flower-bell, some one's death,

A chorus-ending from Euripides, –
And that's enough for fifty hopes and fears
As old and new at once as nature's self,
To rap and knock and enter in our soul,
Take hands and dance there, a fantastic ring,
Round the ancient idol, on his base again, –
The grand Perhaps! We look on helplessly.
There the old misgivings, crooked questions are –
This good God, – what he could do, if he would,
Would, if he could – then must have done long since:
If so, when, where and how? some way must be, –
Once feel about, and soon or late you hit
Some sense, in which it might be, after all.
Why not, 'The Way, the Truth, the Life?'
                                        – That way
Over the mountain, which who stands upon
Is apt to doubt if it be meant for a road;
While, if he views it from the waste itself,
Up goes the line there, plain from base to brow,
Not vague, mistakeable! what's a break or two
Seen from the unbroken desert either side?
And then (to bring in fresh philosophy)
What if the breaks themselves should prove at last
The most consummate of contrivances
To train a man's eye, teach him what is faith?
And so we stumble at truth's very test!
All we have gained then by our unbelief
Is a life of doubt diversified by faith,
For one of faith diversified by doubt:
We called the chess-board white, – we call it black.

'Well,' you rejoin, 'the end's no worse, at least
We've reason for both colours on the board:

Why not confess then, where I drop the faith
And you the doubt, that I'm as right as you?'

    Because, friend, in the next place, this being so,
And both things even, – faith and unbelief
Left to a man's choice, – we'll proceed a step,
Returning to our image, which I like.

    A man's choice, yes – but a cabin-passenger's –
The man made for the special life o' the world –
Do you forget him? I remember though!
Consult our ship's conditions and you find
One and but one choice suitable to all;
The choice, that you unluckily prefer,
Turning things topsy-turvy – they or it
Going to the ground. Belief or unbelief
Bears upon life, determines its whole course,
Begins at its beginning. See the world
Such as it is, – you made it not, nor I;
I mean to take it as it is, – and you,
Not so you'll take it, – though you get nought else.
I know the special kind of life I like,
What suits the most my idiosyncrasy,
Brings out the best of me and bears me fruit
In power, peace, pleasantness and length of days.
I find that positive belief does this
For me, and unbelief, no whit of this.
– For you, it does, however? – that, we'll try!
'Tis clear, I cannot lead my life, at least,
Induce the world to let me peaceably,
Without declaring at the outset, 'Friends,
I absolutely and peremptorily

Believe!' – I say, faith is my waking life:
One sleeps, indeed, and dreams at intervals,
We know, but waking's the main point with us,
And my provision's for life's waking part.
Accordingly, I use heart, head and hand
All day, I build, scheme, study, and make friends;
And when night overtakes me, down I lie,
Sleep, dream a little, and get done with it,
The sooner the better, to begin afresh.
What's midnight doubt before the dayspring's faith?
You, the philosopher, that disbelieve,
That recognize the night, give dreams their weight –
To be consistent you should keep your bed,
Abstain from healthy acts that prove you man,
For fear you drowse perhaps at unawares!
And certainly at night you'll sleep and dream,
Live through the day and bustle as you please.
And so you live to sleep as I to wake,
To unbelieve as I to still believe?
Well, and the common sense o' the world calls you
Bed-ridden, – and its good things come to me.
Its estimation, which is half the fight,
That's the first-cabin comfort I secure:
The next . . . but you perceive with half an eye!
Come, come, it's best believing, if we may;
You can't but own that!

                    Next, concede again,
If once we choose belief, on all accounts
We can't be too decisive in our faith,
Conclusive and exclusive in its terms,
To suit the world which gives us the good things.
In every man's career are certain points

Whereon he dares not be indifferent;
The world detects him clearly, if he dare,
As baffled at the game, and losing life.
He may care little or he may care much
For riches, honour, pleasure, work, repose,
Since various theories of life and life's
Success are extant which might easily
Comport with either estimate of these;
And whoso chooses wealth or poverty,
Labour or quiet, is not judged a fool
Because his fellow would choose otherwise:
We let him choose upon his own account
So long as he's consistent with his choice.
But certain points, left wholly to himself,
When once a man has arbitrated on,
We say he must succeed there or go hang.
Thus, he should wed the woman he loves most
Or needs most, whatsoe'er the love or need –
For he can't wed twice. Then, he must avouch,
Or follow, at the least, sufficiently,
The form of faith his conscience holds the best,
Whate'er the process of conviction was:
For nothing can compensate his mistake
On such a point, the man himself being judge:
He cannot wed twice, nor twice lose his soul.

Well now, there's one great form of Christian faith
I happened to be born in – which to teach
Was given me as I grew up, on all hands,
As best and readiest means of living by;
The same on examination being proved
The most pronounced moreover, fixed, precise
And absolute form of faith in the whole world –

Accordingly, most potent of all forms
For working on the world. Observe, my friend!
Such as you know me, I am free to say,
In these hard latter days which hamper one,
Myself – by no immoderate exercise
Of intellect and learning, but the tact
To let external forces work for me,
– Bid the street's stones be bread and they are bread;
Bid Peter's creed, or rather, Hildebrand's,
Exalt me o'er my fellows in the world
And make my life an ease and joy and pride;
It does so, – which for me's a great point gained
Who have a soul and body that exact
A comfortable care in many ways.
There's power in me and will to dominate
Which I must exercise, they hurt me else:
In many ways I need mankind's respect,
Obedience, and the love that's born of fear:
While at the same time, there's a taste I have,
A toy of soul, a titillating thing,
Refuses to digest these dainties crude.
The naked life is gross till clothed upon:
I must take what men offer, with a grace
As though I would not, could I help it, take!
An uniform I wear though over-rich –
Something imposed on me, no choice of mine;
No fancy-dress worn for pure fancy's sake
And despicable therefore! now folk kneel
And kiss my hand – of course the Church's hand.
Thus I am made, thus life is best for me,
And thus that it should be I have procured;
And thus it could not be another way,
I venture to imagine.

                              You'll reply,
So far my choice, no doubt, is a success;
But were I made of better elements,
With nobler instincts, purer tastes, like you,
I hardly would account the thing success
Though it did all for me I say.

                              But, friend,
We speak of what is; not of what might be,
And how 'twere better if 'twere otherwise.
I am the man you see here plain enough:
Grant I'm a beast, why, beasts must lead beasts' lives!
Suppose I own at once to tail and claws;
The tailless man exceeds me: but being tailed
I'll lash out lion fashion, and leave apes
To dock their stump and dress their haunches up.
My business is not to remake myself,
But make the absolute best of what God made.
Or – our first simile – though you prove me doomed
To a viler berth still, to the steerage-hole,
The sheep-pen or the pigstye, I should strive
To make what use of each were possible;
And as this cabin gets upholstery,
That hutch should rustle with sufficient straw.
  But, friend, I don't acknowledge quite so fast
I fail of all your manhood's lofty tastes
Enumerated so complacently,
On the mere ground that you forsooth can find
In this particular life I choose to lead
No fit provision for them. Can you not?
Say you, my fault is I address myself
To grosser estimators than should judge?
And that's no way of holding up the soul,

Which, nobler, needs men's praise perhaps, yet knows
One wise man's verdict outweighs all the fools' –
Would like the two, but, forced to choose, takes that.
I pine among my million imbeciles
(You think) aware some dozen men of sense
Eye me and know me, whether I believe
In the last winking Virgin, as I vow,
And am a fool, or disbelieve in her
And am a knave, – approve in neither case,
Withhold their voices though I look their way:
Like Verdi when, at his worst opera's end
(The thing they gave at Florence, – what's its name?)
While the mad houseful's plaudits near outbang
His orchestra of salt-box, tongs and bones,
He looks through all the roaring and the wreaths
Where sits Rossini patient in his stall.

    Nay, friend, I meet you with an answer here –
That even your prime men who appraise their kind
Are men still, catch a wheel within a wheel,
See more in a truth than the truth's simple self,
Confuse themselves. You see lads walk the street
Sixty the minute; what's to note in that?
You see one lad o'erstride a chimney-stack;
Him you must watch – he's sure to fall, yet stands!
Our interest's on the dangerous edge of things.
The honest thief, the tender murderer,
The superstitious atheist, demirep
That loves and saves her soul in new French books –
We watch while these in equilibrium keep
The giddy line midway: one step aside,
They're classed and done with. I, then, keep the line
Before your sages, – just the men to shrink

From the gross weights, coarse scales and labels broad
You offer their refinement. Fool or knave?
Why needs a bishop be a fool or knave
When there's a thousand diamond weights between?
So, I enlist them. Your picked twelve, you'll find,
Profess themselves indignant, scandalized
At thus being held unable to explain
How a superior man who disbelieves
May not believe as well: that's Schelling's way!
It's through my coming in the tail of time,
Nicking the minute with a happy tact.
Had I been born three hundred years ago
They'd say, 'What's strange? Blougram of course
    believes;'
And, seventy years since, 'disbelieves of course.'
But now, 'He may believe; and yet, and yet
How can he?' All eyes turn with interest.
Whereas, step off the line on either side –
You, for example, clever to a fault,
The rough and ready man who write apace,
Read somewhat seldomer, think perhaps even less –
You disbelieve! Who wonders and who cares?
Lord So-and-so – his coat bedropped with wax,
All Peter's chains about his waist, his back
Brave with the needlework of Noodledom –
Believes! Again, who wonders and who cares?
But I, the man of sense and learning too,
The able to think yet act, the this, the that,
I, to believe at this late time of day!
Enough; you see, I need not fear contempt.

  – Except it's yours! Admire me as these may,
You don't. But whom at least do you admire?

Present your own perfection, your ideal,
Your pattern man for a minute – oh, make haste,
Is it Napoleon you would have us grow?
Concede the means; allow his head and hand,
(A large concession, clever as you are)
Good! In our common primal element
Of unbelief (we can't believe, you know –
We're still at that admission, recollect!)
Where do you find – apart from, towering o'er
The secondary temporary aims
Which satisfy the gross taste you despise –
Where do you find his star? – his crazy trust
God knows through what or in what? it's alive
And shines and leads him, and that's all we want.
Have we aught in our sober night shall point
Such ends as his were, and direct the means
Of working out our purpose straight as his,
Nor bring a moment's trouble on success
With after-care to justify the same?
– Be a Napoleon, and yet disbelieve –
Why, the man's mad, friend, take his light away!
What's the vague good o' the world, for which you dare
With comfort to yourself blow millions up?
We neither of us see it! we do see
The blown-up millions – spatter of their brains
And writhing of their bowels and so forth,
In that bewildering entanglement
Of horrible eventualities
Past calculation to the end of time!
Can I mistake for some clear word of God
(Which were my ample warrant for it all)
His puff of hazy instinct, idle talk,
'The State, that's I,' quack-nonsense about crowns,

And (when one beats the man to his last hold)
A vague idea of setting things to rights,
Policing people efficaciously,
More to their profit, most of all to his own;
The whole to end that dismallest of ends
By an Austrian marriage, cant to us the Church,
And resurrection of the old *régime?*
Would I, who hope to live a dozen years,
Fight Austerlitz for reasons such and such?
No: for, concede me but the merest chance
Doubt may be wrong – there's judgement, life to come!
With just that chance, I dare not. Doubt proves right?
This present life is all? – you offer me
Its dozen noisy years, without a chance
That wedding an archduchess, wearing lace,
And getting called by divers new-coined names,
Will drive off ugly thoughts and let me dine,
Sleep, read and chat in quiet as I like!
Therefore I will not.

                Take another case;
Fit up the cabin yet another way.
What say you to the poets? shall we write
Hamlet, Othello – make the world our own,
Without a risk to run of either sort?
I can't! – to put the strongest reason first.
'But try,' you urge, 'the trying shall suffice;
The aim, if reached or not, makes great the life:
Try to be Shakespeare, leave the rest to fate!'
Spare my self-knowledge – there's no fooling me!
If I prefer remaining my poor self,
I say so not in self-dispraise but praise.
If I'm a Shakespeare, let the well alone;
Why should I try to be what now I am?

If I'm no Shakespeare, as too probable, —
His power and consciousness and self-delight
And all we want in common, shall I find —
Trying for ever? while on points of taste
Wherewith, to speak it humbly, he and I
Are dowered alike — I'll ask you, I or he,
Which in our two lives realizes most?
Much, he imagined — somewhat, I possess.
He had the imagination; stick to that!
Let him say, 'In the face of my soul's works
Your world is worthless and I touch it not
Lest I should wrong them' — I'll withdraw my plea.
But does he say so? look upon his life!
Himself, who only can, gives judgement there.
He leaves his towers and gorgeous palaces
To build the trimmest house in Stratford town;
Saves money, spends it, owns the worth of things,
Giulio Romano's pictures, Dowland's lute;
Enjoys a show, respects the puppets, too,
And none more, had he seen its entry once,
Than 'Pandulph, of fair Milan cardinal.'
Why then should I who play that personage,
The very Pandulph Shakespeare's fancy made,
Be told that had the poet chanced to start
From where I stand now (some degree like mine
Being just the goal he ran his race to reach)
He would have run the whole race back, forsooth,
And left being Pandulph, to begin write plays?
Ah, the earth's best can be but the earth's best!
Did Shakespeare live, he could but sit at home
And get himself in dreams the Vatican,
Greek busts, Venetian paintings, Roman walls,
And English books, none equal to his own,

Which I read, bound in gold (he never did).
– Terni's fall, Naples' bay and Gothard's top –
Eh, friend? I could not fancy one of these;
But, as I pour this claret, there they are:
I've gained them – crossed St Gothard last July
With ten mules to the carriage and a bed
Slung inside; is my hap the worse for that?
We want the same things, Shakespeare and myself,
And what I want, I have: he, gifted more,
Could fancy he too had them when he liked,
But not so thoroughly that, if fate allowed,
He would not have them also in my sense.
We play one game; I send the ball aloft
No less adroitly that of fifty strokes
Scarce five go o'er the wall so wide and high
Which sends them back to me: I wish and get.
He struck balls higher and with better skill,
But at a poor fence level with his head,
And hit – his Stratford house, a coat of arms,
Successful dealings in his grain and wool, –
While I receive heaven's incense in my nose
And style myself the cousin of Queen Bess.
Ask him, if this life's all, who wins the game?

Believe – and our whole argument breaks up.
Enthusiasm's the best thing, I repeat;
Only, we can't command it; fire and life
Are all, dead matter's nothing, we agree:
And be it a mad dream or God's very breath,
The fact's the same, – belief's fire, once in us,
Makes of all else mere stuff to show itself:
We penetrate our life with such a glow
As fire lends wood and iron – this turns steel,

That burns to ash – all's one, fire proves its power
For good or ill, since men call flare success.
But paint a fire, it will not therefore burn.
Light one in me, I'll find it food enough!
Why, to be Luther – that's a life to lead,
Incomparably better than my own.
He comes, reclaims God's earth for God, he says,
Sets up God's rule again by simple means,
Re-opens a shut book, and all is done.
He flared out in the flaring of mankind;
Such Luther's luck was: how shall such be mine?
If he succeeded, nothing's left to do:
And if he did not altogether – well,
Strauss is the next advance. All Strauss should be
I might be also. But to what result?
He looks upon no future: Luther did.
What can I gain on the denying side?
Ice makes no conflagration. State the facts,
Read the text right, emancipate the world –
The emancipated world enjoys itself
With scarce a thank-you: Blougram told it first
It could not owe a farthing, – not to him
More than Saint Paul! 'twould press its pay, you think?
Then add there's still that plaguy hundredth chance
Strauss may be wrong. And so a risk is run –
For what gain? not for Luther's, who secured
A real heaven in his heart throughout his life,
Supposing death a little altered things.

'Ay, but since really you lack faith,' you cry,
'You run the same risk really on all sides,
In cool indifference as bold unbelief.
As well be Strauss as swing 'twixt Paul and him.

It's not worth having, such imperfect faith,
No more available to do faith's work
Than unbelief like mine. Whole faith, or none!'

Softly, my friend! I must dispute that point.
Once own the use of faith, I'll find you faith.
We're back on Christian ground. You call for faith:
I show you doubt, to prove that faith exists.
The more of doubt, the stronger faith, I say,
If faith o'ercomes doubt. How I know it does?
By life and man's free will, God gave for that!
To mould life as we choose it, shows our choice:
That's our one act, the previous work's his own.
You criticize the soul? it reared this tree –
This broad life and whatever fruit it bears!
What matter though I doubt at every pore,
Head-doubts, heart-doubts, doubts at my fingers' ends,
Doubts in the trivial work of every day,
Doubts at the very bases of my soul
In the grand moments when she probes herself –
If finally I have a life to show,
The thing I did, brought out in evidence
Against the thing done to me underground
By hell and all its brood, for aught I know?
I say, whence sprang this? shows it faith or doubt?
All's doubt in me; where's break of faith in this?
It is the idea, the feeling and the love,
God means mankind should strive for and show forth
Whatever be the process to that end, –
And not historic knowledge, logic sound,
And metaphysical acumen, sure!
'What think ye of Christ,' friend? when all's done and said,
Like you this Christianity or not?

It may be false, but will you wish it true?
Has it your vote to be so if it can?
Trust you an instinct silenced long ago
That will break silence and enjoin you love
What mortified philosophy is hoarse,
And all in vain, with bidding you despise?
If you desire faith – then you've faith enough:
What else seeks God – nay, what else seek ourselves?
You form a notion of me, we'll suppose,
On hearsay; it's a favourable one:
'But still' (you add), 'there was no such good man,
Because of contradiction in the facts.
One proves, for instance, he was born in Rome,
This Blougram; yet throughout the tales of him
I see he figures as an Englishman.'
Well, the two things are reconcileable.
But would I rather you discovered that,
Subjoining – 'Still, what matter though they be?
Blougram concerns me nought, born here or there.'

Pure faith indeed – you know not what you ask!
Naked belief in God the Omnipotent,
Omniscient, Omnipresent, sears too much
The sense of conscious creatures to be borne.
It were the seeing him, no flesh shall dare.
Some think, Creation's meant to show him forth:
I say it's meant to hide him all it can,
And that's what all the blessed evil's for.
Its use in Time is to environ us,
Our breath, our drop of dew, with shield enough
Against that sight till we can bear its stress.
Under a vertical sun, the exposed brain
And lidless eye and disemprisoned heart

Less certainly would wither up at once
Than mind, confronted with the truth of him.
But time and earth case-harden us to live;
The feeblest sense is trusted most; the child
Feels God a moment, ichors o'er the place,
Plays on and grows to be a man like us.
With me, faith means perpetual unbelief
Kept quiet like the snake 'neath Michael's foot
Who stands calm just because he feels it writhe.
Or, if that's too ambitious, – here's my box –
I need the excitation of a pinch
Threatening the torpor of the inside-nose
Nigh on the imminent sneeze that never comes.
'Leave it in peace' advise the simple folk:
Make it aware of peace by itching-fits,
Say I – let doubt occasion still more faith!

You'll say, once all believed, man, woman, child,
In that dear middle-age these noodles praise.
How you'd exult if I could put you back
Six hundred years, blot out cosmogony,
Geology, ethnology, what not,
(Greek endings, each the little passing-bell
That signifies some faith's about to die),
And set you square with Genesis again, –
When such a traveller told you his last news,
He saw the ark a-top of Ararat
But did not climb there since 'twas getting dusk
And robber-bands infest the mountain's foot!
How should you feel, I ask, in such an age,
How act? As other people felt and did;
With soul more blank than this decanter's knob,
Believe – and yet lie, kill, rob, fornicate
Full in belief's face, like the beast you'd be!

No, when the fight begins within himself,
A man's worth something. God stoops o'er his head,
Satan looks up between his feet – both tug –
He's left, himself, i' the middle: the soul wakes
And grows. Prolong that battle through his life!
Never leave growing till the life to come!
Here, we've got callous to the Virgin's winks
That used to puzzle people wholesomely:
Men have outgrown the shame of being fools.
What are the laws of nature, not to bend
If the Church bid them? – brother Newman asks.
Up with the Immaculate Conception, then –
On to the rack with faith! – is my advice.
Will not that hurry us upon our knees,
Knocking our breasts, 'It can't be – yet it shall!
Who am I, the worm, to argue with my Pope?
Low things confound the high things!' and so forth.
That's better than acquitting God with grace
As some folk do. He's tried – no case is proved,
Philosophy is lenient – he may go!

You'll say, the old system's not so obsolete
But men believe still: ay, but who and where?
King Bomba's lazzaroni foster yet
The sacred flame, so Antonelli writes;
But even of these, what ragamuffin-saint
Believes God watches him continually,
As he believes in fire that it will burn,
Or rain that it will drench him? Break fire's law,
Sin against rain, although the penalty
Be just a singe or soaking? 'No,' he smiles;
'Those laws are laws that can enforce themselves.'

The sum of all is — yes, my doubt is great,
My faith's still greater, then my faith's enough.
I have read much, thought much, experienced much,
Yet would die rather than avow my fear
The Naples liquefaction may be false,
When set to happen by the palace-clock
According to the clouds or dinner-time.
I hear you recommend, I might at least
Eliminate, decrassify my faith
Since I adopt it; keeping what I must
And leaving what I can — such points as this.
I won't — that is, I can't throw one away.
Supposing there's no truth in what I hold
About the need of trial to man's faith,
Still, when you bid me purify the same,
To such a process I discern no end.
Clearing off one excrescence to see two,
There's ever a next in size, now grown as big,
That meets the knife: I cut and cut again!
First cut the Liquefaction, what comes last
But Fichte's clever cut at God himself?
Experimentalize on sacred things!
I trust nor hand nor eye nor heart nor brain
To stop betimes: they all get drunk alike.
The first step, I am master not to take.

You'd find the cutting-process to your taste
As much as leaving growths of lies unpruned,
Nor see more danger in it, — you retort.
Your taste's worth mine; but my taste proves more wise
When we consider that the steadfast hold
On the extreme end of the chain of faith
Gives all the advantage, makes the difference

With the rough purblind mass we seek to rule:
We are their lords, or they are free of us,
Just as we tighten or relax our hold.
So, other matters equal, we'll revert
To the first problem – which, if solved my way
And thrown into the balance, turns the scale –
How we may lead a comfortable life,
How suit our luggage to the cabin's size.

Of course you are remarking all this time
How narrowly and grossly I view life,
Respect the creature-comforts, care to rule
The masses, and regard complacently
'The cabin,' in our old phrase. Well, I do.
I act for, talk for, live for this world now,
As this world prizes action, life and talk:
No prejudice to what next world may prove,
Whose new laws and requirements, my best pledge
To observe then, is that I observe these now,
Shall do hereafter what I do meanwhile.
Let us concede (gratuitously though)
Next life relieves the soul of body, yields
Pure spiritual enjoyment: well, my friend,
Why lose this life i' the meantime, since its use
May be to make the next life more intense?

Do you know, I have often had a dream
(Work it up in your next month's article)
Of man's poor spirit in its progress, still
Losing true life for ever and a day
Through ever trying to be and ever being –
In the evolution of successive spheres –
Before its actual sphere and place of life,
Halfway into the next, which having reached,

It shoots with corresponding foolery
Halfway into the next still, on and off!
As when a traveller, bound from North to South,
Scouts fur in Russia: what's its use in France?
In France spurns flannel: where's its need in Spain?
In Spain drops cloth, too cumbrous for Algiers!
Linen goes next, and last the skin itself,
A superfluity at Timbuctoo.
When, through his journey, was the fool at ease?
I'm at ease now, friend; worldly in this world,
I take and like its way of life; I think
My brothers, who administer the means,
Live better for my comfort – that's good too;
And God, if he pronounce upon such life,
Approves my service, which is better still.
If he keep silence, – why, for you or me
Or that brute beast pulled-up in to-day's 'Times',
What odds is't, save to ourselves, what life we lead?

    You meet me at this issue: you declare, –
All special-pleading done with – truth is truth,
And justifies itself by undreamed ways.
You don't fear but it's better, if we doubt,
To say so, act up to our truth perceived
However feebly. Do then, – act away!
'Tis there I'm on the watch for you. How one acts
Is, both of us agree, our chief concern:
And how you'll act is what I fain would see
If, like the candid person you appear,
You dare to make the most of your life's scheme
As I of mine, live up to its full law
Since there's no higher law that counterchecks.
Put natural religion to the test

You've just demolished the revealed with – quick,
Down to the root of all that checks your will
All prohibition to lie, kill and thieve,
Or even to be an atheistic priest!
Suppose a pricking to incontinence –
Philosophers deduce you chastity
Or shame, from just the fact that at the first
Whoso embraced a woman in the field,
Threw club down and forewent his brains beside,
So, stood a ready victim in the reach
Of any brother savage, club in hand;
Hence saw the use of going out of sight
In wood or cave to prosecute his loves:
I read this in a French book t'other day.
Does law so analysed coerce you much?
Oh, men spin clouds of fuzz where matters end,
But you who reach where the first thread begins,
You'll soon cut that! – which means you can, but won't,
Through certain instincts, blind, unreasoned out,
You dare not set aside, you can't tell why,
But there they are, and so you let them rule.
Then, friend, you seem as much a slave as I,
A liar, conscious coward and hypocrite,
Without the good the slave expects to get,
In case he has a master after all!
You own your instincts? why, what else do I,
Who want, am made for, and must have a God
Ere I can be aught, do aught? – no mere name
Want, but the true thing with what proves its truth,
To wit, a relation from that thing to me,
Touching from head to foot – which touch I feel,
And with it take the rest, this life of ours!
I live my life here; yours you dare not live.

  — Not as I state it, who (you please subjoin)
Disfigure such a life and call it names.
While, to your mind, remains another way
For simple men: knowledge and power have rights,
But ignorance and weakness have rights too
There needs no crucial effort to find truth
If here or there or anywhere about:
We ought to turn each side, try hard and see,
And if we can't, be glad we've earned at least
The right, by one laborious proof the more,
To graze in peace earth's pleasant pasturage.
Men are not angels, neither are they brutes:
Something we may see, all we cannot see.
What need of lying? I say, I see all,
And swear to each detail the most minute
In what I think a Pan's face — you, mere cloud:
I swear I hear him speak and see him wink,
For fear, if once I drop the emphasis,
Mankind may doubt there's any cloud at all.
You take the simple life — ready to see,
Willing to see (for no cloud's worth a face) —
And leaving quiet what no strength can move,
And which, who bids you move? who has the right?
I bid you; but you are God's sheep, not mine:
'*Pastor est tui Dominus.*' You find
In this the pleasant pasture of our life
Much you may eat without the least offence,
Much you don't eat because your maw objects,
Much you would eat but that your fellow-flock
Open great eyes at you and even butt,
And thereupon you like your mates so well
You cannot please yourself, offending them;
Though when they seem exorbitantly sheep,

You weigh your pleasure with their butts and bleats
And strike the balance. Sometimes certain fears
Restrain you, real checks since you find them so;
Sometimes you please yourself and nothing checks:
And thus you graze through life with not one lie,
And like it best.

                But do you, in truth's name?
If so, you beat – which means you are not I –
Who needs must make earth mine and feed my fill
Not simply unbuttoned at, unbickered with,
But motioned to the velvet of the sward
By those obsequious wethers' very selves.
Look at me, sir; my age is double yours:
At yours, I knew beforehand, so enjoyed,
What now I should be – as, permit the word,
I pretty well imagine your whole range
And stretch of tether twenty years to come.
We both have minds and bodies much alike:
In truth's name, don't you want my bishopric,
My daily bread, my influence and my state?
You're young. I'm old; you must be old one day;
Will you find then, as I do hour by hour,
Women their lovers kneel to, who cut curls
From your fat lap-dog's ear to grace a brooch –
Dukes, who petition just to kiss your ring –
With much beside you know or may conceive?
Suppose we die to-night: well, here am I,
Such were my gains, life bore this fruit to me,
While writing all the same my articles
On music, poetry, the fictile vase
Found at Albano, chess, Anacreon's Greek.
But you – the highest honour in your life,

The thing you'll crown yourself with, all your days,
Is – dining here and drinking this last glass
I pour you out in sign of amity
Before we part for ever. Of your power
And social influence, worldly worth in short,
Judge what's my estimation by the fact,
I do not condescend to enjoin, beseech,
Hint secrecy on one of all these words!
You're shrewd and know that should you publish one
The world would brand the lie – my enemies first,
Who'd sneer – 'the bishop's an arch-hypocrite
And knave perhaps, but not so frank a fool.'
Whereas I should not dare for both my ears
Breathe one such syllable, smile one such smile,
Before the chaplain who reflects myself –
My shade's so much more potent than your flesh.
What's your reward, self-abnegating friend?
Stood you confessed of those exceptional
And privileged great natures that dwarf mine –
A zealot with a mad ideal in reach,
A poet just about to print his ode,
A statesman with a scheme to stop this war,
An artist whose religion is his art –
I should have nothing to object: such men
Carry the fire, all things grow warm to them,
Their drugget's worth my purple, they beat me.
But you, – you're just as little those as I –
You, Gigadibs, who, thirty years of age,
Write stately for Blackwood's Magazine,
Believe you see two points in Hamlet's soul
Unseized by the Germans yet – which view you'll print –
Meantime the best you have to show being still
That lively lightsome article we took

Almost for the true Dickens, – what's its name?
'The Slum and Cellar, or Whitechapel life
Limned after dark!' it made me laugh, I know,
And pleased a month, and brought you in ten pounds.
– Success I recognize and compliment,
And therefore give you, if you choose, three words
(The card and pencil-scratch is quite enough)
Which whether here, in Dublin or New York,
Will get you, prompt as at my eyebrow's wink,
Such terms as never you aspired to get
In all our own reviews and some not ours.
Go write your lively sketches! be the first
'Blougram, or The Eccentric Confidence' –
Or better simply say, 'The Outward-bound'.
Why, men as soon would throw it in my teeth
As copy and quote the infamy chalked broad
About me on the church-door opposite.
You will not wait for that experience though,
I fancy, howsoever you decide,
To discontinue – not detesting, not
Defaming, but at least – despising me!

* * *

Over his wine so smiled and talked his hour
Sylvester Blougram, styled *in partibus
Episcopus, nec non* – (the deuce knows what
It's changed to by our novel hierarchy)
With Gigadibs the literary man,
Who played with spoons, explored his plate's design,
And ranged the olive-stones about its edge,
While the great bishop rolled him out his mind.

For Blougram, he believed, say, half he spoke.
The other portion, as he shaped it thus
For argumentatory purposes,

He felt his foe was foolish to dispute.
Some arbitrary accidental thoughts
That crossed his mind, amusing because new,
He chose to represent as fixtures there,
Invariable convictions (such they seemed
Beside his interlocutor's loose cards
Flung daily down, and not the same way twice)
While certain hell-deep instincts, man's weak tongue
Is never bold to utter in their truth
Because styled hell-deep ('tis an old mistake
To place hell at the bottom of the earth)
He ignored these, – not having in readiness
Their nomenclature and philosophy:
He said true things, but called them by wrong names.
'On the whole,' he thought, 'I justify myself
On every point where cavillers like this
Oppugn my life: he tries one kind of fence,
I close, he's worsted, that's enough for him.
He's on the ground: if ground should break away
I take my stand on, there's a firmer yet
Beneath it, both of us may sink and reach.
His ground was over mine and broke the first:
So, let him sit with me this many a year!'

He did not sit five minutes. Just a week
Sufficed his sudden healthy vehemence.
Something had struck him in the 'Outward-bound'
Another way than Blougram's purpose was:
And having bought, not cabin-furniture
But settler's-implements (enough for three)
And started for Australia – there, I hope,
By this time he has tested his first plough,
And studied his last chapter of St John.

ABT VOGLER

(AFTER HE HAS BEEN EXTEMPORIZING UPON THE MUSICAL INSTRUMENT OF HIS INVENTION)

[The Abbé Vogler, 1749–1814]

I

WOULD that the structure brave, the manifold music I
  build,
  Bidding my organ obey, calling its keys to their work,
Claiming each slave of the sound, at a touch, as when
    Solomon willed
  Armies of angels that soar, legions of demons that lurk,
Man, brute, reptile, fly, – alien of end and of aim,
  Adverse, each from the other heaven-high, hell-deep
    removed, –
Should rush into sight at once as he named the ineffable
    Name,
  And pile him a palace straight, to pleasure the princess
    he loved!

II

Would it might tarry like his, the beautiful building of
    mine,
  This which my keys in a crowd pressed and importuned
    to raise!
Ah, one and all, how they helped, would dispart now and
    now combine,
  Zealous to hasten the work, heighten their master his
    praise!

And one would bury his brow with a blind plunge down
    to hell,
  Burrow awhile and build, broad on the roots of things,
Then up again swim into sight, having based me my palace
    well,
  Founded it, fearless of flame, flat on the nether springs.

III

And another would mount and march, like the excellent
    minion he was,
  Ay, another and yet another, one crowd but with many
    a crest,
Raising my rampired walls of gold as transparent as glass,
  Eager to do and die, yield each his place to the rest:
For higher still and higher (as a runner tips with fire,
  When a great illumination surprises a festal night –
Outlining round and round Rome's dome from space to
    spire)
  Up, the pinnacled glory reached, and the pride of my
    soul was in sight.

IV

In sight? Not half! for it seemed, it was certain, to match
    man's birth,
  Nature in turn conceived, obeying an impulse as I;
And the emulous heaven yearned down, made effort to
    reach the earth,
  As the earth had done her best, in my passion, to scale
    the sky;
Novel splendours burst forth, grew familiar and dwelt
    with mine,
  Not a point nor peak but found and fixed its wandering
    star;

Meteor-moons, balls of blaze: and they did not pale nor
    pine,
    For earth had attained to heaven, there was no more
      near nor far.

V

Nay more; for there wanted not who walked in the glare
    and glow,
    Presences plain in the place; or, fresh from the Proto-
      plast,
Furnished for ages to come, when a kindlier wind should
    blow,
    Lured now to begin and live, in a house to their liking
      at last;
Or else the wonderful Dead who have passed through the
    body and gone,
    But were back once more to breathe in an old world
      worth their new:
What never had been, was now; what was, as it shall be
    anon;
    And what is, – shall I say, matched both? for I was made
      perfect too.

VI

All through my keys that gave their sounds to a wish of my
    soul,
    All through my soul that praised as its wish flowed
      visibly forth,
All through music and me! For think, had I painted the
    whole,
    Why, there it had stood, to see, nor the process so
      wonder-worth:

Had I written the same, made verse – still, effect proceeds
from cause,
 Ye know why the forms are fair, ye hear how the tale is
 told;
It is all triumphant art, but art in obedience to laws,
 Painter and poet are proud in the artist-list enrolled:

VII

But here is the finger of God, a flash of the will that can,
 Existent behind all laws, that made them and, lo, they
 are!
And I know not if, save in this, such gift be allowed to man,
 That out of three sounds he frame, not a fourth sound,
 but a star.
Consider it well: each tone of our scale in itself is nought;
 It is everywhere in the world – loud, soft, and all is said:
Give it to me to use! I mix it with two in my thought:
 And, there! Ye have heard and seen: consider and bow
 the head!

VIII

Well, it is gone at last, the palace of music I reared;
 Gone! and the good tears start, the praises that come too
 slow;
For one is assured at first, one scarce can say that he feared,
 That he even gave it a thought, the gone thing was to
 go.
Never to be again! But many more of the kind
 As good, nay, better perchance: is this your comfort to
 me?
To me, who must be saved because I cling with my mind
 To the same, same self, same love, same God: ay, what
 was, shall be.

IX

Therefore to whom turn I but to thee, the ineffable Name?
  Builder and maker, thou, of houses not made with
    hands!
What, have fear of change from thee who art ever the
    same?
  Doubt that thy power can fill the heart that thy power
    expands?
There shall never be one lost good! What was, shall live as
    before;
  The evil is null, is nought, is silence implying sound;
What was good shall be good, with, for evil, so much good
    more;
  On the earth the broken arcs; in the heaven, a perfect
    round.

X

All we have willed or hoped or dreamed of good shall
    exist;
  Not its semblance, but itself; no beauty, nor good, nor
    power
Whose voice has gone forth, but each survives for the
    melodist
  When eternity affirms the conception of an hour.
The high that proved too high, the heroic for earth too
    hard,
  The passion that left the ground to lose itself in the sky,
Are music sent up to God by the lover and the bard;
  Enough that he heard it once: we shall hear it by-and-
    by.

XI

And what is our failure here but a triumph's evidence
    For the fulness of the days? Have we withered or
        agonized?
Why else was the pause prolonged but that singing might
    issue thence?
    Why rushed the discords in but that harmony should be
        prized?
Sorrow is hard to bear, and doubt is slow to clear,
    Each sufferer says his say, his scheme of the weal and
        woe:
But God has a few of us whom he whispers in the ear;
    The rest may reason and welcome: 'tis we musicians
        know.

XII

Well, it is earth with me; silence resumes her reign:
    I will be patient and proud, and soberly acquiesce.
Give me the keys. I feel for the common chord again,
    Sliding by semitones, till I sink to the minor, – yes,
And I blunt it into a ninth, and I stand on alien ground,
    Surveying awhile the heights I rolled from into the
        deep;
Which, hark, I have dared and done, for my resting-place
        is found,
    The C Major of this life: so, now I will try to sleep.

RABBI BEN EZRA

I

Grow old along with me!
The best is yet to be,
The last of life, for which the first was made:
Our times are in His hand
Who saith 'A whole I planned,
Youth shows but half; trust God: see all nor be afraid!'

II

Not that, amassing flowers,
Youth sighed 'Which rose make ours,
Which lily leave and then as best recall?'
Not that, admiring stars,
It yearned 'Nor Jove, nor Mars;
Mine be some figured flame which blends, transcends
them all!'

III

Not for such hopes and fears
Annulling youth's brief years,
Do I remonstrate: folly wide the mark!
Rather I prize the doubt
Low kinds exist without,
Finished and finite clods, untroubled by a spark.

IV

Poor vaunt of life indeed,
Were man but formed to feed
On joy, to solely seek and find and feast:
Such feasting ended, then
As sure an end to men;
Irks care the crop-full bird? Frets doubt the maw-
crammed beast?

V

Rejoice we are allied
To That which doth provide
And not partake, effect and not receive!
A spark disturbs our clod;
Nearer we hold of God
Who gives, than of His tribes that take, I must believe.

VI

Then, welcome each rebuff
That turns earth's smoothness rough,
Each sting that bids nor sit nor stand but go!
Be our joys three-parts pain!
Strive, and hold cheap the strain;
Learn, nor account the pang; dare, never grudge the
throe!

VII

For thence, – a paradox
Which comforts while it mocks, –
Shall life succeed in that it seems to fail:
What I aspired to be,
And was not, comforts me:
A brute I might have been, but would not sink i' the
scale.

VIII

What is he but a brute
Whose flesh has soul to suit,
Whose spirit works lest arms and legs want play?
To man, propose this test –
Thy body at its best
How far can that project thy soul on its lone way?

IX

Yet gifts should prove their use:
I own the Past profuse
Of power each side, perfection every turn:
Eyes, ears took in their dole,
Brain treasured up the whole;
Should not the heart beat once 'How good to live and
learn?'

X

Not once beat 'Praise be Thine!
I see the whole design,
I, who saw power, see now love perfect too:
Perfect I call Thy plan:
Thanks that I was a man!
Maker, remake, complete, – I trust what Thou shalt do!'

XI

For pleasant is this flesh;
Our soul, in its rose-mesh
Pulled ever to the earth, still yearns for rest;
Would we some prize might hold
To match those manifold
Possessions of the brute, – gain most, as we did best!

XII

Let us not always say
    'Spite of this flesh to-day
I strove, made head, gained ground upon the whole!'
    As the bird wings and sings,
    Let us cry 'All good things
Are ours, nor soul helps flesh more, now, than flesh helps
    soul!'

XIII

Therefore I summon age
    To grant youth's heritage,
Life's struggle having so far reached its term:
    Thence shall I pass, approved
    A man, for aye removed
From the developed brute; a god though in the germ.

XIV

And I shall thereupon
    Take rest, ere I be gone
Once more on my adventure brave and new:
    Fearless and unperplexed,
    When I wage battle next,
What weapons to select, what armour to indue.

XV

Youth ended, I shall try
    My gain or loss thereby;
Leave the fire ashes, what survives is gold.
    And I shall weigh the same,
    Give life its praise or blame:
Young, all lay in dispute; I shall know, being old.

XVI

For note, when evening shuts,
A certain moment cuts
The deed off, calls the glory from the grey:
A whisper from the west
Shoots – 'Add this to the rest,
Take it and try its worth: here dies another day.'

XVII

So, still within this life,
Though lifted o'er its strife,
Let me discern, compare, pronounce at last,
'This rage was right i' the main,
That acquiescence vain:
The Future I may face now I have proved the Past.'

XVIII

For more is not reserved
To man, with soul just nerved
To act to-morrow what he learns to-day:
Here, work enough to watch
The Master work, and catch
Hints of the proper craft, tricks of the tool's true play.

XIX

As it was better, youth
Should strive, through acts uncouth,
Toward making, than repose on aught found made:
So, better, age, exempt
From strife, should know, than tempt
Further. Thou waitedest age: wait death nor be afraid!

XX

Enough now, if the Right
And Good and Infinite
Be named here, as thou callest thy hand thine own,
With knowledge absolute,
Subject to no dispute
From fools that crowded youth, nor let thee feel alone.

XXI

Be there, for once and all,
Severed great minds from small,
Announced to each his station in the Past!
Was I, the world arraigned,
Were they, my soul disdained,
Right? Let age speak the truth and give us peace at last!

XXII

Now, who shall arbitrate?
Ten men love what I hate,
Shun what I follow, slight what I receive;
Ten, who in ears and eyes
Match me: we all surmise,
They this thing, and I that: whom shall my soul believe?

XXIII

Not on the vulgar mass
Called 'work', must sentence pass,
Things done, that took the eye and had the price;
O'er which, from level stand,
The low world laid its hand,
Found straightway to its mind, could value in a trice:

XXIV

But all, the world's coarse thumb
And finger failed to plumb,
So passed in making up the main account;
All instincts immature,
All purposes unsure,
That weighed not as his work, yet swelled the man's
amount:

XXV

Thoughts hardly to be packed
Into a narrow act,
Fancies that broke through language and escaped;
All I could never be,
All, men ignored in me,
This, I was worth to God, whose wheel the pitcher shaped.

XXVI

Ay, note that Potter's wheel,
That metaphor! and feel
Why time spins fast, why passive lies our clay, –
Thou, to whom fools propound,
When the wine makes its round,
'Since life fleets, all is change; the Past gone, seize to-day!'

XXVII

Fool! All that is, at all,
Lasts ever, past recall;
Earth changes, but thy soul and God stand sure:
What entered into thee,
That was, is, and shall be:
Time's wheel runs back or stops: Potter and clay endure.

XXVIII

He fixed thee mid this dance
Of plastic circumstance,
This Present, thou, forsooth, wouldst fain arrest:
Machinery just meant
To give thy soul its bent,
Try thee and turn thee forth, sufficiently impressed.

XXIX

What though the earlier grooves
Which ran the laughing loves
Around thy base, no longer pause and press?
What though, about thy rim,
Skull-things in order grim
Grow out, in graver mood, obey the sterner stress?

XXX

Look not thou down but up!
To uses of a cup,
The festal board, lamp's flash and trumpet's peal,
The new wine's foaming flow,
The Master's lips a-glow!
Thou, heaven's consummate cup, what need'st thou
with earth's wheel?

XXXI

But I need, now as then,
Thee, God, who mouldest men;
And since, not even while the whirl was worst,
Did I, – to the wheel of life
With shapes and colours rife,
Bound dizzily, – mistake my end, to slake Thy thirst:

XXXII

So, take and use Thy work:
Amend what flaws may lurk,
What strain o' the stuff, what warpings past the aim!
My times be in Thy hand!
Perfect the cup as planned!
Let age approve of youth, and death complete the same!

CALIBAN UPON SETEBOS; OR, NATURAL THEOLOGY IN THE ISLAND

'Thou thoughtest that I was altogether such a one as thyself.'

['WILL sprawl, now that the heat of day is best,
Flat on his belly in the pit's much mire,
With elbows wide, fists clenched to prop his chin.
And, while he kicks both feet in the cool slush,
And feels about his spine small eft-things course,
Run in and out each arm, and make him laugh:
And while above his head a pompion-plant,
Coating the cave-top as a brow its eye,
Creeps down to touch and tickle hair and beard,
And now a flower drops with a bee inside,
And now a fruit to snap at, catch and crunch, —
He looks out o'er yon sea which sunbeams cross
And recross till they weave a spider-web
(Meshes of fire, some great fish breaks at times)
And talks to his own self, howe'er he please,
Touching that other, whom his dam called God.
Because to talk about Him, vexes — ha,
Could He but know! and time to vex is now,
When talk is safer than in winter-time.
Moreover Prosper and Miranda sleep
In confidence he drudges at their task,
And it is good to cheat the pair, and gibe,
Letting the rank tongue blossom into speech.]

Setebos, Setebos, and Setebos!
'Thinketh, He dwelleth i' the cold o' the moon.

'Thinketh He made it, with the sun to match,
But not the stars; the stars came otherwise;
Only made clouds, winds, meteors, such as that:
Also this isle, what lives and grows thereon,
And snaky sea which rounds and ends the same.

'Thinketh, it came of being ill at ease:
He hated that He cannot change His cold,
Nor cure its ache. 'Hath spied an icy fish
That longed to 'scape the rock-stream where she lived,
And thaw herself within the lukewarm brine
O' the lazy sea her stream thrusts far amid,
A crystal spike 'twixt two warm walls of wave;
Only, she ever sickened, found repulse
At the other kind of water, not her life,
(Green-dense and dim-delicious, bred o' the sun)
Flounced back from bliss she was not born to breathe,
And in her old bounds buried her despair,
Hating and loving warmth alike: so He.

'Thinketh, He made thereat the sun, this isle,
Trees and the fowls here, beast and creeping thing.
Yon otter, sleek-wet, black, lithe as a leech;
Yon auk, one fire-eye in a ball of foam,
That floats and feeds; a certain badger brown
He hath watched hunt with that slant white-wedge eye
By moonlight; and the pie with the long tongue
That pricks deep into oakwarts for a worm,
And says a plain word when she finds her prize,
But will not eat the ants; the ants themselves
That build a wall of seeds and settled stalks
About their hole – He made all these and more,
Made all we see, and us, in spite: how else?

He could not, Himself, make a second self
To be His mate; as well have made Himself:
He would not make what he mislikes or slights,
An eyesore to Him, or not worth His pains:
But did, in envy, listlessness or sport,
Make what Himself would fain, in a manner, be —
Weaker in most points, stronger in a few,
Worthy, and yet mere playthings all the while,
Things He admires and mocks too, - that is it.
Because, so brave, so better though they be,
It nothing skills if He begin to plague.
Look now, I melt a gourd-fruit into mash,
Add honeycomb and pods, I have perceived,
Which bite like finches when they bill and kiss, —
Then, when froth rises bladdery, drink up all,
Quick, quick, till maggots scamper through my brain;
Last, throw me on my back i' the seeded thyme,
And wanton, wishing I were born a bird.
Put case, unable to be what I wish,
I yet could make a live bird out of clay:
Would not I take clay, pinch my Caliban
Able to fly? - for, there, see, he hath wings,
And great comb like the hoopoe's to admire,
And there, a sting to do his foes offence,
There, and I will that he begin to live,
Fly to yon rock-top, nip me off the horns
Of grigs high up that make the merry din,
Saucy through their veined wings, and mind me not.
In which feat, if his leg snapped, brittle clay,
And he lay stupid-like, - why, I should laugh;
And if he, spying me, should fall to weep,
Beseech me to be good, repair his wrong,
Bid his poor leg smart less or grow again, —

Well, as the chance were, this might take or else
Not take my fancy: I might hear his cry,
And give the mankin three sound legs for one,
Or pluck the other off, leave him like an egg,
And lessoned he was mine and merely clay.
Were this no pleasure, lying in the thyme,
Drinking the mash, with brain become alive,
Making and marring clay at will? So He.

'Thinketh, such shows nor right nor wrong in Him,
Nor kind, nor cruel: He is strong and Lord.
'Am strong myself compared to yonder crabs
That march now from the mountain to the sea;
'Let twenty pass, and stone the twenty-first,
Loving not, hating not, just choosing so.
'Say, the first straggler that boasts purple spots
Shall join the file, one pincer twisted off;
'Say, this bruised fellow shall receive a worm,
And two worms he whose nippers end in red;
As it likes me each time, I do: so He.

Well then, 'supposeth He is good i' the main,
Placable if His mind and ways were guessed,
But rougher than His handiwork, be sure!
Oh, He hath made things worthier than Himself,
And envieth that, so helped, such things do more
Than He who made them! What consoles but this?
That they, unless through Him, do nought at all,
And must submit: what other use in things?
'Hath cut a pipe of pithless elder-joint
That, blown through, gives exact the scream o' the jay
When from her wing you twitch the feathers blue:
Sound this, and little birds that hate the jay
Flock within stone's throw, glad their foe is hurt:

Put case such pipe could prattle and boast forsooth
'I catch the birds, I am the crafty thing,
I make the cry my maker cannot make
With his great round mouth; he must blow through mine!'
Would not I smash it with my foot? So He.

But wherefore rough, why cold and ill at ease?
Aha, that is a question! Ask, for that,
What knows, – the something over Setebos
That made Him, or He, may be, found and fought,
Worsted, drove off and did to nothing, perchance.
There may be something quiet o'er His head,
Out of His reach, that feels nor joy nor grief,
Since both derive from weakness in some way.
I joy because the quails come; would not joy
Could I bring quails here when I have a mind:
This Quiet, all it hath a mind to, doth.
'Esteemeth stars the outposts of its couch,
But never spends much thought nor care that way.
It may look up, work up, – the worse for those
It works on! 'Careth but for Setebos
The many-handed as a cuttle-fish,
Who, making Himself feared through what He does,
Looks up, first, and perceives he cannot soar
To what is quiet and hath happy life;
Next looks down here, and out of very spite
Makes this a bauble-world to ape yon real,
These good things to match those as hips do grapes.
'Tis solace making baubles, ay, and sport.
Himself peeped late, eyed Prosper at his books
Careless and lofty, lord now of the isle:
Vexed, 'stitched a book of broad leaves, arrow-shaped,
Wrote thereon, he knows what, prodigious words;

Has peeled a wand and called it by a name;
Weareth at whiles for an enchanter's robe
The eyed skin of a supple oncelot;
And hath an ounce sleeker than youngling mole,
A four-legged serpent he makes cower and couch,
Now snarl, now hold its breath and mind his eye,
And saith she is Miranda and my wife:
'Keeps for his Ariel a tall pouch-bill crane
He bids go wade for fish and straight disgorge;
Also a sea-beast, lumpish, which he snared,
Blinded the eyes of, and brought somewhat tame,
And split its toe-webs, and now pens the drudge
In a hole o' the rock and calls him Caliban;
A bitter heart that bides its time and bites.
'Plays thus at being Prosper in a way,
Taketh his mirth with make-believes: so He.

His dam held that the Quiet made all things
Which Setebos vexed only: 'holds not so.
Who made them weak, meant weakness He might vex.
Had He meant other, while His hand was in,
Why not make horny eyes no thorn could prick,
Or plate my scalp with bone against the snow,
Or overscale my flesh 'neath joint and joint,
Like an orc's armour? Ay, – so spoil His sport!
He is the One now: only He doth all.
'Saith, He may like, perchance, what profits Him.
Ay, himself loves what does him good; but why?
'Gets good no otherwise. This blinded beast
Loves whoso places flesh-meat on his nose,
But, had he eyes, would want to help, but hate
Or love, just as it liked him: He hath eyes.
Also it pleaseth Setebos to work,

Use all His hands, and exercise much craft,
By no means for the love of what is worked.
'Tasteth, himself, no finer good i' the world
When all goes right, in this safe summer-time,
And he wants little, hungers, aches not much,
Than trying what to do with wit and strength.
'Falls to make something: 'piled yon pile of turfs,
And squared and stuck there squares of soft white chalk,
And, with a fish-tooth, scratched a moon on each,
And set up endwise certain spikes of tree,
And crowned the whole with a sloth's skull a-top,
Found dead i' the woods, too hard for one to kill.
No use at all i' the work, for work's sole sake;
'Shall some day knock it down again: so He.

'Saith He is terrible: watch His feats in proof!
One hurricane will spoil six good months' hope.
He hath a spite against me, that I know,
Just as He favours Prosper, who knows why?
So it is, all the same, as well I find.
'Wove wattles half the winter, fenced them firm
With stone and stake to stop she-tortoises
Crawling to lay their eggs here: well, one wave,
Feeling the foot of Him upon its neck,
Gaped as a snake does, lolled out its large tongue,
And licked the whole labour flat: so much for spite.
'Saw a ball flame down late (yonder it lies)
Where, half an hour before, I slept i' the shade:
Often they scatter sparkles: there is force!
'Dug up a newt He may have envied once
And turned to stone, shut up inside a stone.
Please Him and hinder this? – What Prosper does?
Aha, if He would tell me how! Not He!

There is the sport: discover how or die!
All need not die, for of the things o' the isle
Some flee afar, some dive, some run up trees;
Those at His mercy, – why, they please Him most
When . . . when . . . well, never try the same way twice!
Repeat what act has pleased, He may grow wroth.
You must not know His ways, and play Him off,
Sure of the issue. 'Doth the like himself:
'Spareth a squirrel that it nothing fears
But steals the nut from underneath my thumb,
And when I threat, bites stoutly in defence:
'Spareth an urchin that contrariwise,
Curls up into a ball, pretending death
For fright at my approach: the two ways please.
But what would move my choler more than this,
That either creature counted on its life
To-morrow and next day and all days to come,
Saying, forsooth, in the inmost of its heart,
'Because he did so yesterday with me,
And otherwise with such another brute,
So must he do henceforth and always.' – Ay?
Would teach the reasoning couple what 'must' means!
'Doth as he likes, or wherefore Lord? So He.

'Conceiveth all things will continue thus,
And we shall have to live in fear of Him
So long as He lives, keeps His strength: no change,
If He have done His best, make no new world
To please Him more, so leave off watching this, –
If He surprise not even the Quiet's self
Some strange day, – or, suppose, grow into it
As grubs grow butterflies: else, here are we,
And there is He, and nowhere help at all.

'Believeth with the life, the pain shall stop.
His dam held different, that after death
He both plagued enemies and feasted friends:
Idly! He doth His worst in this our life,
Giving just respite lest we die through pain,
Saving last pain for worst, – with which, an end.
Meanwhile, the best way to escape His ire
Is, not to seem too happy. 'Sees, himself,
Yonder two flies, with purple films and pink,
Bask on the pompion-bell above: kills both.
'Sees two black painful beetles roll their ball
On head and tail as if to save their lives:
Moves them the stick away they strive to clear.

Even so, 'would have Him misconceive, suppose
This Caliban strives hard and ails no less,
And always, above all else, envies Him;
Wherefore he mainly dances on dark nights,
Moans in the sun, gets under holes to laugh,
And never speaks his mind save housed as now:
Outside, 'groans, curses. If He caught me here,
O'erheard this speech, and asked 'What chucklest at?
'Would, to appease Him, cut a finger off,
Or of my three kid yearlings burn the best,
Or let the toothsome apples rot on tree,
Or push my tame beast for the orc to taste:
While myself lit a fire, and made a song
And sung it, '*What I hate, be consecrate
To celebrate Thee and Thy state, no mate
For Thee; what see for envy in poor me?*'
Hoping the while, since evils sometimes mend,
Warts rub away and sores are cured with slime,
That some strange day, will either the Quiet catch

And conquer Setebos, or likelier He
Decrepit may doze, doze, as good as die.

* * *

[What, what? A curtain o'er the world at once!
Crickets stop hissing; not a bird – or, yes,
There scuds His raven that has told Him all!
It was fool's play, this prattling! Ha! The wind
Shoulders the pillared dust, death's house o' the move,
And fast invading fires begin! White blaze –
A tree's head snaps – and there, there, there, there, there,
His thunder follows! Fool to gibe at Him!
Lo! 'Lieth flat and loveth Setebos!
'Maketh his teeth meet through his upper lip,
Will let those quails fly, will not eat this month
One little mess of whelks, so he may 'scape!]

CONFESSIONS

I

WHAT is he buzzing in my ears?
  'Now that I come to die,
Do I view the world as a vale of tears?'
  Ah, reverend sir, not I!

II

What I viewed there once, what I view again
  Where the physic bottles stand
On the table's edge, – is a suburb lane,
  With a wall to my bedside hand.

III

That lane sloped, much as the bottles do,
  From a house you could descry
O'er the garden-wall: is the curtain blue
  Or green to a healthy eye?

IV

To mine, it serves for the old June weather
  Blue above lane and wall;
And that farthest bottle labelled 'Ether'
  Is the house o'ertopping all.

V

At a terrace, somewhere near the stopper,
  There watched for me, one June,
A girl: I know, sir, it's improper,
  My poor mind's out of tune.

VI

Only, there was a way . . . you crept
   Close by the side, to dodge
Eyes in the house, two eyes except:
   They styled their house 'The Lodge'.

VII

What right had a lounger up their lane?
   But, by creeping very close,
With the good wall's help, – their eyes might strain
   And stretch themselves to Oes,

VIII

Yet never catch her and me together,
   As she left the attic, there,
By the rim of the bottle labelled 'Ether',
   And stole from stair to stair,

IX

And stood by the rose-wreathed gate. Alas,
   We loved, sir – used to meet:
How sad and bad and mad it was –
   But then, how it was sweet!

PROSPICE

FEAR death? – to feel the fog in my throat,
        The mist in my face,
When the snows begin, and the blasts denote
        I am nearing the place,
The power of the night, the press of the storm,
        The post of the foe;
Where he stands, the Arch Fear in a visible form,
        Yet the strong man must go:
For the journey is done and the summit attained,
        And the barriers fall,
Though a battle's to fight ere the guerdon be gained,
        The reward of it all.
I was ever a fighter, so – one fight more,
        The best and the last!
I would hate that death bandaged my eyes and forbore,
        And bade me creep past.
No! let me taste the whole of it, fare like my peers
        The heroes of old,
Bear the brunt, in a minute pay glad life's arrears
        Of pain, darkness and cold.
For sudden the worst turns the best to the brave,
        The black minute's at end,
And the elements' rage, the fiend-voices that rave,
        Shall dwindle, shall blend,
Shall change, shall become first a peace out of pain,
        Then a light, then thy breast,
O thou soul of my soul! I shall clasp thee again,
        And with God be the rest!

POMPILIA

['The Ring and the Book' is a poem 21,000 lines long which narrates, in two books, the murder by Count Guido Franceschini of his young wife Pompilia, and his subsequent trial and death. In successive Books the drama is unfolded from various points of view; and Book VII is Pompilia's narration, on her deathbed, of the story of her life.]

I AM just seventeen years and five months old,
And, if I lived one day more, three full weeks;
'Tis writ so in the church's register,
Lorenzo in Lucina, all my names
At length, so many names for one poor child,
– Francesca Camilla Vittoria Angela
Pompilia Comparini, – laughable!
Also 'tis writ that I was married there
Four years ago: and they will add, I hope,
When they insert my death, a word or two, –
Omitting all about the mode of death, –
This, in its place, this which one cares to know,
That I had been a mother of a son
Exactly two weeks. It will be through grace
O' the Curate, not through any claim I have;
Because the boy was born at, so baptized
Close to, the Villa, in the proper church:
A pretty church, I say no word against,
Yet stranger-like, – while this Lorenzo seems
My own particular place, I always say.
I used to wonder, when I stood scarce high
As the bed here, what the marble lion meant,
With half his body rushing from the wall,
Eating the figure of a prostrate man –

(To the right, it is, of entry by the door)
An ominous sign to one baptized like me,
Married, and to be buried there, I hope.
And they should add, to have my life complete,
He is a boy and Gaetan by name –
Gaetano, for a reason, – if the friar
Don Celestine will ask this grace for me
Of Curate Ottoboni: he it was
Baptized me: he remembers my whole life
As I do his grey hair.

                All these few things
I know are true, – will you remember them?
Because time flies. The surgeon cared for me,
To count my wounds, – twenty-two dagger-wounds,
Five deadly, but I do not suffer much –
Or too much pain, – and am to die to-night.

Oh how good God is that my babe was born,
– Better than born, baptized and hid away
Before this happened, safe from being hurt!
That had been sin God could not well forgive:
He was too young to smile and save himself.
When they took, two days after he was born,
My babe away from me to be baptized
And hidden awhile, for fear his foe should find, –
The country-woman, used to nursing babes,
Said 'Why take on so? where is the great loss?
These next three weeks he will but sleep and feed,
Only begin to smile at the month's end;
He would not know you, if you kept him here,
Sooner than that; so, spend three merry weeks
Snug in the Villa, getting strong and stout,

And then I bring him back to be your own,
And both of you may steal to – we know where!'
The month – there wants of it two weeks this day!
Still, I half fancied when I heard the knock
At the Villa in the dusk, it might prove she –
Come to say 'Since he smiles before the time,
Why should I cheat you out of one good hour?
Back I have brought him; speak to him and judge!'
Now I shall never see him; what is worse,
When he grows up and gets to be my age,
He will seem hardly more than a great boy;
And if he asks 'What was my mother like?'
People may answer 'Like girls of seventeen' –
And how can he but think of this and that,
Lucias, Marias, Sofias, who titter or blush
When he regards them as such boys may do?
Therefore I wish someone will please to say
I looked already old though I was young;
Do I not . . . say, if you are by to speak . . .
Look nearer twenty? No more like, at least,
Girls who look arch or redden when boys laugh,
Than the poor Virgin that I used to know
At our street-corner in a lonely niche, –
The babe, that sat upon her knees, broke off, –
Thin white glazed clay, you pitied her the more:
She, not the gay ones, always got my rose.

How happy those are who know how to write!
Such could write what their son should read in time,
Had they a whole day to live out like me.
Also my name is not a common name,
'Pompilia,' and may help to keep apart
A little the thing I am from what girls are.

But then how far away, how hard to find
Will anything about me have become,
Even if the boy bethink himself and ask!
No father that he ever knew at all,
Nor never had – no, never had, I say!
That is the truth, – nor any mother left,
Out of the little two weeks that she lived,
Fit for such memory as might assist:
As good too as no family, no name,
Not even poor old Pietro's name, nor hers,
Poor kind unwise Violante, since it seems
They must not be my parents any more.
That is why something put it in my head
To call the boy 'Gaetano' – no old name
For sorrow's sake; I looked up to the sky
And took a new saint to begin anew.
One who has only been made saint – how long?
Twenty-five years: so, carefuller, perhaps,
To guard a namesake than those old saints grow,
Tired out by this time, – see my own five saints!

On second thoughts, I hope he will regard
The history of me as what someone dreamed,
And get to disbelieve it at the last:
Since to myself it dwindles fast to that,
Sheer dreaming and impossibility, –
Just in four days too! All the seventeen years,
Not once did a suspicion visit me
IIow very different a lot is mine
From any other woman's in the world.
The reason must be, 'twas by step and step
It got to grow so terrible and strange.
These strange woes stole on tiptoe, as it were,

Into my neighbourhood and privacy,
Sat down where I sat, laid them where I lay;
And I was found familiarised with fear,
When friends broke in, held up a torch and cried
'Why, you Pompilia in the cavern thus,
How comes that arm of yours about a wolf?
And the soft length, – lies in and out your feet
And laps you round the knee, – a snake it is!'
And so on.

        Well, and they are right enough,
By the torch they hold up now: for first, observe,
I never had a father, – no, nor yet
A mother: my own boy can say at least
'I had a mother whom I kept two weeks!'
Not I, who little used to doubt . . . *I* doubt
Good Pietro, kind Violante, gave me birth?
They loved me always as I love my babe
(– Nearly so, that is – quite so could not be –)
Did for me all I meant to do for him,
Till one surprising day, three years ago,
They both declared, at Rome, before some judge
In some Court where the people flocked to hear,
That really I had never been their child,
Was a mere castaway, the careless crime
Of an unknown man, the crime and care too much
Of a woman known too well, – little to these,
Therefore, of whom I was the flesh and blood:
What then to Pietro and Violante, both
No more my relatives than you or you?
Nothing to them! You know what they declared.

So with my husband, – just such a surprise,
Such a mistake, in that relationship!

Everyone says that husbands love their wives,
Guard them and guide them, give them happiness;
'Tis duty, law, pleasure, religion: well,
You see how much of this comes true in mine!
People indeed would fain have somehow proved
He was no husband: but he did not hear,
Or would not wait, and so has killed us all.
Then there is . . . only let me name one more!
There is the friend, – men will not ask about,
But tell untruths of, and give nicknames to,
And think my lover, most surprise of all!
Do only hear, it is the priest they mean,
Giuseppe Caponsacchi: a priest – love,
And love me! Well, yet people think he did.
I am married, he has taken priestly vows,
They know that, and yet go on, say, the same,
'Yes, how he loves you!' 'That was love' – they
    say,
When anything is answered that they ask:
Or else 'No wonder you love him' – they say.
Then they shake heads, pity much, scarcely blame –
As if we neither of us lacked excuse,
And anyhow are punished to the full,
And downright love atones for everything!
Nay, I heard read out in the public Court
Before the judge, in presence of my friends,
Letters 'twas said the priest had sent to me,
And other letters sent him by myself,
We being lovers!
                    Listen what this is like!
When I was a mere child, my mother . . . that's
Violante, you must let me call her so
Nor waste time, trying to unlearn the word . . .

She brought a neighbour's child of my own age
To play with me of rainy afternoons;
And, since there hung a tapestry on the wall,
We two agreed to find each other out
Among the figures. 'Tisbe, that is you,
With half-moon on your hair-knot, spear in hand,
Flying, but no wings, only the great scarf
Blown to a bluish rainbow at your back:
Call off your hound and leave the stag alone!'
' – And there are you, Pompilia, such green leaves
Flourishing out of your five finger-ends,
And all the rest of you so brown and rough:
Why is it you are turned a sort of tree?'
You know the figures never were ourselves
Though we nicknamed them so. Thus, all my
    life, –
As well what was, as what, like this, was not, –
Looks old, fantastic and impossible:
I touch a fairy thing that fades and fades.
– Even to my babe! I thought, when he was born,
Something began for once that would not end,
Nor change into a laugh at me, but stay
For evermore, eternally quite mine.
Well, so he is, – but yet they bore him off,
The third day, lest my husband should lay traps
And catch him, and by means of him catch me.
Since they have saved him so, it was well done:
Yet thence comes such confusion of what was
With what will be, – that late seems long ago,
And, what years should bring round, already come,
Till even he withdraws into a dream
As the rest do: I fancy him grown great,
Strong, stern, a tall young man who tutors me,

Frowns with the others 'Poor imprudent child!
Why did you venture out of the safe street?
Why go so far from help to that lone house?
Why open at the whisper and the knock?'

Six days ago when it was New Year's day,
We bent above the fire and talked of him,
What he should do when he was grown and great.
Violante, Pietro, each had given the arm
I leant on, to walk by, from couch to chair
And fireside, – laughed, as I lay safe at last,
'Pompilia's march from bed to board is made,
Pompilia back again and with a babe,
Shall one day lend his arm and help her walk!'
Then we all wished each other more New Years.
Pietro began to scheme – 'Our cause is gained;
The law is stronger than a wicked man:
Let him henceforth go his way, leave us ours!
We will avoid the city, tempt no more
The greedy ones by feasting and parade, –
Live at the other villa, we know where,
Still farther off, and we can watch the babe
Grow fast in the good air; and wood is cheap
And wine sincere outside the city gate.
I still have two or three old friends will grope
Their way along the mere half-mile of road,
With staff and lantern on a moonless night
When one needs talk: they'll find me, never fear,
And I'll find them a flask of the old sort yet!'
Violante said 'You chatter like a crow:
Pompilia tires o' the tattle, and shall to bed:
Do not too much the first day, – somewhat more
To-morrow, and, the next, begin the cape

And hood and coat! I have spun wool enough.'
Oh what a happy friendly eve was that!

And, next day, about noon, out Pietro went –
He was so happy and would talk so much,
Until Violante pushed and laughed him forth
Sight-seeing in the cold, – 'So much to see
I' the churches! Swathe your throat three times!' she
    cried,
'And, above all, beware the slippery ways,
And bring us all the news by supper-time!'
He came back late, laid by cloak, staff and hat,
Powdered so thick with snow it made us laugh,
Rolled a great log upon the ash o' the hearth,
And bade Violante treat us to a flask,
Because he had obeyed her faithfully,
Gone sight-see through the seven, and found no church
To his mind like San Giovanni – 'There's the fold,
And all the sheep together, big as cats!
And such a shepherd, half the size of life,
Starts up and hears the angel' – when, at the door,
A tap: we started up: you know the rest.

Pietro at least had done no harm, I know;
Nor even Violante, so much harm as makes
Such revenge lawful. Certainly she erred –
Did wrong, how shall I dare say otherwise? –
In telling that first falsehood, buying me
From my poor faulty mother at a price,
To pass off upon Pietro as his child.
If one should take my babe, give him a name,
Say he was not Gaetano and my own,

But that some other woman made his mouth
And hands and feet, – how very false were that!
No good could come of that; and all harm did.
Yet if a stranger were to represent
'Needs must you either give your babe to me
And let me call him mine for evermore,
Or let your husband get him' – ah, my God,
That were a trial I refuse to face!
Well, just so here: it proved wrong but seemed right
To poor Violante – for there lay, she said,
My poor real dying mother in her rags,
Who put me from her with the life and all,
Poverty, pain, shame and disease at once,
To die the easier by what price I fetched –
Also (I hope) because I should be spared
Sorrow and sin, – why may not that have helped?
My father, – he was no one, any one, –
The worse, the likelier, – call him – he who came,
Was wicked for his pleasure, went his way,
And left no trace to track by; there remained
Nothing but me, the unnecessary life,
To catch up or let fall, – and yet a thing
She could make happy, be made happy with,
This poor Violante, – who would frown thereat?

Well, God, you see! God plants us where we grow.
It is not that because a bud is born
At a wild briar's end, full i' the wild beast's way,
We ought to pluck and put it out of reach
On the oak-tree top, – say 'There the bud belongs!'
She thought, moreover, real lies were lies told
For harm's sake; whereas this had good at heart,

Good for my mother, good for me, and good
For Pietro who was meant to love a babe,
And needed one to make his life of use,
Receive his house and land when he should die.
Wrong, wrong and always wrong! how plainly
    wrong!
For see, this fault kept pricking, as faults do,
All the same at her heart: this falsehood hatched,
She could not let it go nor keep it fast.
She told me so, – the first time I was found
Locked in her arms once more after the pain,
When the nuns let me leave them and go home,
And both of us cried all the cares away, –
This it was set her on to make amends,
This brought about the marriage – simply this!
Do let me speak for her you blame so much!
When Paul, my husband's brother, found me out,
Heard there was wealth for who should marry
    me,
So, came and made a speech to ask my hand
For Guido, – she, instead of piercing straight
Through the pretence of the ignoble truth,
Fancied she saw God's very finger point,
Designate just the time for planting me
(The wild-briar slip she plucked to love and wear)
In soil where I could strike real root, and grow,
And get to be the thing I called myself:
For, wife and husband are one flesh, God says,
And I, whose parents seemed such and were none,
Should in a husband have a husband now,
Find nothing, this time, but was what it seemed,
– All truth and no confusion any more.
I know she meant all good to me, all pain

To herself, – since how could it be aught but pain
To give me up, so, from her very breast,
The wilding flower-tree-branch that, all those years,
She had got used to feel for and find fixed?
She meant well: has it been so ill i' the main?
That is but fair to ask: one cannot judge
Of what has been the ill or well of life,
The day that one is dying, – sorrows change
Into not altogether sorrow-like;
I do see strangeness but scarce misery,
Now it is over, and no danger more.
My child is safe; there seems not so much pain.
It comes, most like, that I am just absolved,
Purged of the past, the foul in me, washed fair, –
One cannot both have and not have, you know, –
Being right now, I am happy and colour things.
Yes, everybody that leaves life sees all
Softened and bettered: so with other sights:
To me at least was never evening yet
But seemed far beautifuller than its day,
For past is past.

　　　　　　　There was a fancy came,
When somewhere, in the journey with my friend,
We stepped into a hovel to get food;
And there began a yelp here, a bark there, –
Misunderstanding creatures that were wroth
And vexed themselves and us till we retired.
The hovel is life: no matter what dogs bit
Or cats scratched in the hovel I break from,
All outside is lone field, moon and such peace –
Flowing in, filling up as with a sea
Whereon comes Someone, walks fast on the white,

Jesus Christ's self, Don Celestine declares,
To meet me and calm all things back again.

Beside, up to my marriage, thirteen years
Were, each day, happy as the day was long:
This may have made the change too terrible.
I know that when Violante told me first
The cavalier – she meant to bring next morn,
Whom I must also let take, kiss my hand –
Would be at San Lorenzo the same eve
And marry me, – which over, we should go
Home both of us without him as before,
And, till she bade speak, I must hold my tongue,
Such being the correct way with girl-brides,
From whom one word would make a father blush, –
I know, I say, that when she told me this,
– Well, I no more saw sense in what she said
Than a lamb does in people clipping wool;
Only lay down and let myself be clipped.
And when next day the cavalier who came –
(Tisbe had told me that the slim young man
With wings at head, and wings at feet, and sword
Threatening a monster, in our tapestry,
Would eat a girl else, – was a cavalier)
When he proved Guido Franceschini, – old
And nothing like so tall as I myself,
Hook-nosed and yellow in a bush of beard,
Much like a thing I saw on a boy's wrist,
He called an owl and used for catching birds, –
And when he took my hand and made a smile –
Why, the uncomfortableness of it all
Seemed hardly more important in the case
Than, – when one gives you, say, a coin to spend, –

Its newness or its oldness; if the piece
Weigh properly and buy you what you wish,
No matter whether you get grime or glare!
Men take the coin, return you grapes and figs.
Here, marriage was the coin, a dirty piece
Would purchase me the praise of those I loved:
About what else should I concern myself?

So, hardly knowing what a husband meant,
I supposed this or any man would serve,
No whit the worse for being so uncouth:
For I was ill once and a doctor came
With a great ugly hat, no plume thereto,
Black jerkin and black buckles and black sword,
And white sharp beard over the ruff in front,
And oh so lean, so sour-faced and austere! —
Who felt my pulse, made me put out my tongue,
Then oped a phial, dripped a drop or two
Of a black bitter something, — I was cured!
What mattered the fierce beard or the grim face?
It was the physic beautified the man,
Master Malpichi, — never met his match
In Rome, they said, — so ugly all the same!

However, I was hurried through a storm,
Next dark eve of December's deadest day —
How it rained! — through our street and the Lion's-
    mouth
And the bit of Corso, — cloaked round, covered close,
I was like something strange or contraband, —
Into blank San Lorenzo, up the aisle,
My mother keeping hold of me so tight,
I fancied we were come to see a corpse

Before the altar which she pulled me toward.
There we found waiting an unpleasant priest
Who proved the brother, not our parish friend,
But one with mischief-making mouth and eye,
Paul, whom I know since to my cost. And then
I heard the heavy church-door lock out help
Behind us: for the customary warmth,
Two tapers shivered on the altar. 'Quick –
Lose no time!' cried the priest. And straightway down
From . . . what's behind the altar where he hid –
Hawk-nose and yellowness and bush and all,
Stepped Guido, caught my hand, and there was I
O' the chancel, and the priest had opened book,
Read here and there, made me say that and this,
And after, told me I was now a wife,
Honoured indeed, since Christ thus weds the Church,
And therefore turned he water into wine,
To show I should obey my spouse like Christ.
Then the two slipped aside and talked apart,
And I, silent and scared, got down again
And joined my mother who was weeping now.
Nobody seemed to mind us any more,
And both of us on tiptoe found our way
To the door which was unlocked by this, and wide.
When we were in the street, the rain had stopped,
All things looked better. At our own house-door,
Violante whispered 'No one syllable
To Pietro! Girl-brides never breathe a word!'
' – Well treated to a wetting, draggle-tails!'
Laughed Pietro as he opened – 'Very near
You made me brave the gutter's roaring sea
To carry off from roost old dove and young,
Trussed up in church, the cote, by me, the kite!

What do these priests mean, praying folk to death
On stormy afternoons, with Christmas close
To wash our sins off nor require the rain?'
Violante gave my hand a timely squeeze,
Madonna saved me from immodest speech,
I kissed him and was quiet, being a bride.

When I saw nothing more, the next three weeks,
Of Guido – 'Nor the Church sees Christ' thought I:
'Nothing is changed however, wine is wine
And water only water in our house.
Nor did I see that ugly doctor since
That cure of the illness: just as I was cured,
I am married, – neither scarecrow will return.'

Three weeks, I chuckled – 'How would Giulia stare,
And Tecla smile and Tisbe laugh outright,
Were it not impudent for brides to talk!' –
Until one morning, as I sat and sang
At the broidery-frame alone i' the chamber, – loud
Voices, two, three together, sobbings too,
And my name, 'Guido', 'Paolo', flung like stones
From each to the other! In I ran to see.
There stood the very Guido and the priest
With sly face, – formal but nowise afraid, –
While Pietro seemed all red and angry, scarce
Able to stutter out his wrath in words;
And this it was that made my mother sob,
As he reproached her – 'You have murdered us,
Me and yourself and this our child beside!'
Then Guido interposed 'Murdered or not,
Be it enough your child is now my wife!

I claim and come to take her.' Paul put in,
'Consider – kinsman, dare I term you so? –
What is the good of your sagacity
Except to counsel in a strait like this?
I guarantee the parties man and wife
Whether you like or loathe it, bless or ban.
May spilt milk be put back within the bowl –
The done thing, undone? You, it is, we look
For counsel to, you fitliest will advise!
Since milk, though spilt and spoilt, does marble good,
Better we down on knees and scrub the floor,
Than sigh, 'the waste would make a syllabub!'
Help us so turn disaster to account,
So predispose the groom, he needs shall grace
The bride with favour from the very first,
Not begin marriage an embittered man!'
He smiled, – the game so wholly in his hands!
While fast and faster sobbed Violante – 'Ay,
All of us murdered, past averting now!
O my sin, O my secret!' and such like.

Then I began to half surmise the truth;
Something had happened, low, mean, underhand,
False, and my mother was to blame, and I
To pity, whom all spoke of, none addressed:
I was the chattel that had caused a crime.
I stood mute, – those who tangled must untie
The embroilment. Pietro cried 'Withdraw, my child!
She is not helpful to the sacrifice
At this stage, – do you want the victim by
While you discuss the value of her blood?
For her sake, I consent to hear you talk:
Go, child, and pray God help the innocent!'

I did go and was praying God, when came
Violante, with eyes swollen and red enough,
But movement on her mouth for make-believe
Matters were somehow getting right again.
She bade me sit down by her side and hear.
'You are too young and cannot understand,
Nor did your father understand at first.
I wished to benefit all three of us,
And when he failed to take my meaning, – why,
I tried to have my way at unaware –
Obtained him the advantage he refused.
As if I put before him wholesome food
Instead of broken victual, – he finds change
I' the viands, never cares to reason why,
But falls to blaming me, would fling the plate
From window, scandalize the neighborhood,
Even while he smacks his lips, – men's way, my child!
But either you have prayed him unperverse
Or I have talked him back into his wits:
And Paolo was a help in time of need, –
Guido, not much – my child, the way of men!
A priest is more a woman than a man,
And Paul did wonders to persuade. In short,
Yes, he was wrong, your father sees and says;
My scheme was worth attempting: and bears fruit,
Gives you a husband and a noble name,
A palace and no end of pleasant things.
What do you care about a handsome youth?
They are so volatile, and tease their wives!
This is the kind of man to keep the house.
We lose no daughter, – gain a son, that's all:
For 'tis arranged we never separate,
Nor miss, in our grey time of life, the tints

Of you that colour eve to match with morn.
In good or ill, we share and share alike,
And cast our lots into a common lap,
And all three die together as we lived!
Only, at Arezzo, – that's a Tuscan town,
Not so large as this noisy Rome, no doubt,
But older far and finer much, say folk, –
In a great palace where you will be queen,
Know the Archbishop and the Governor,
And we see homage done you ere we die.
Therefore, be good and pardon!' – 'Pardon what?
You know things, I am very ignorant:
All is right if you only will not cry!'

And so an end! Because a blank begins
From when, at the word, she kissed me hard and hot,
And took me back to where my father leaned
Opposite Guido – who stood eyeing him,
As eyes the butcher the cast panting ox
That feels his fate is come, nor struggles more, –
While Paul looked archly on, pricked brow at whiles
With the pen-point as to punish triumph there, –
And said 'Count Guido, take your lawful wife
Until death part you!'

                   All since is one blank,
Over and ended; a terrific dream.
It is the good of dreams – so soon they go!
Wake in a horror of heart-beats, you may –
Cry 'The dread thing will never from my thoughts!'
Still, a few daylight doses of plain life,
Cock-crow and sparrow-chirp, or bleat and bell
Of goats that trot by, tinkling, to be milked;

And when you rub your eyes awake and wide,
Where is the harm o' the horror? Gone! So here.
I know I wake, – but from what? Blank, I say!
This is the note of evil: for good lasts.
Even when Don Celestine bade 'Search and find!
For your soul's sake, remember what is past,
The better to forgive it,' – all in vain!
What was fast getting indistinct before,
Vanished outright. By special grace perhaps,
Between that first calm and this last, four years
Vanish, – one quarter of my life, you know.
I am held up, amid the nothingness,
By one or two truths only – thence I hang,
And there I live, – the rest is death or dream,
All but those points of my support. I think
Of what I saw at Rome once in the Square
O' the Spaniards, opposite the Spanish House:
There was a foreigner had trained a goat,
A shuddering white woman of a beast,
To climb up, stand straight on a pile of sticks
Put close, which gave the creature room enough:
When she was settled there he, one by one,
Took away all the sticks, left just the four
Whereon the little hoofs did really rest,
There she kept firm, all underneath was air.
So, what I hold by, are my prayer to God,
My hope, that came in answer to the prayer,
Some hand would interpose and save me – hand
Which proved to be my friend's hand: and, – blest
    bliss, –
That fancy which began so faint at first,
That thrill of dawn's suffusion through my dark,
Which I perceive was promise of my child,

The light his unborn face sent long before, –
God's way of breaking the good news to flesh.
That is all left now of those four bad years.
Don Celestine urged 'But remember more!
Other men's faults may help me find your own.
I need the cruelty exposed, explained,
Or how can I advise you to forgive?'
He thought I could not properly forgive
Unless I ceased forgetting, – which is true:
For, bringing back reluctantly to mind
My husband's treatment of me, – by a light
That's later than my life-time, I review
And comprehend much and imagine more,
And have but little to forgive at last.
For now, – be fair and say, – is it not true
He was ill-used and cheated of his hope
To get enriched by marriage? Marriage gave
Me and no money, broke the compact so:
He had a right to ask me on those terms,
As Pietro and Violante to declare
They would not give me: so the bargain stood:
They broke it, and he felt himself aggrieved,
Became unkind with me to punish them.
They said 'twas he began deception first,
Nor, in one point whereto he pledged himself,
Kept promise: what of that, suppose it were?
Echoes die off, scarcely reverberate
For ever, – why should ill keep echoing ill,
And never let our ears have done with noise?
Then my poor parents took the violent way
To thwart him, – he must needs retaliate, – wrong,
Wrong, and all wrong, – better say, all blind!
As I myself was, that is sure, who else

Had understood the mystery: for his wife
Was bound in some sort of help somehow there.
It seems as if I might have interposed,
Blunted the edge of their resentment so,
Since he vexed me because they first vexed him;
'I will entreat them to desist, submit,
Give him the money and be poor in peace, —
Certainly not go tell the world: perhaps
He will grow quiet with his gains.'

                                        Yes, say
Something to this effect and you do well!
But then you have to see first: I was blind.
That is the fruit of all such wormy ways,
The indirect, the unapproved of God:
You cannot find their author's end and aim,
Not even to substitute your good for bad,
Your straight for the irregular; you stand
Stupefied, profitless, as cow or sheep
That miss a man's mind, anger him just twice
By trial at repairing the first fault.
Thus, when he blamed me, 'You are a coquette,
A lure-owl posturing to attract birds,
You look love-lures at theatre and church,
In walk, at window!' – that, I knew, was false:
But why he charged me falsely, whither sought
To drive me by such charge, – how could I know?
So, unaware, I only made things worse.
I tried to soothe him by abjuring walk,
Window, church, theatre, for good and all,
As if he had been in earnest: that, you know,
Was nothing like the object of his charge.
Yes, when I got my maid to supplicate

The priest, whose name she read when she would
   read
Those feigned false letters I was forced to hear
Though I could read no word of, – he should cease
Writing, – nay, if he minded prayer of mine,
Cease from so much as even pass the street
Whereon our house looked, – in my ignorance
I was just thwarting Guido's true intent;
Which was, to bring about a wicked change
Of sport to earnest, tempt a thoughtless man
To write indeed, and pass the house, and more,
Till both of us were taken in a crime.
He ought not to have wished me thus act lies,
Simulate folly: but, – wrong or right, the wish, –
I failed to apprehend its drift. How plain
It follows, – if I fell into such fault,
He also may have overreached the mark,
Made mistake, by perversity of brain,
I' the whole sad strange plot, the grotesque intrigue
To make me and my friend unself ourselves,
Be other man and woman than we were!
Think it out, you who have the time! for me, –
I cannot say less; more I will not say.
Leave it to God to cover and undo!
Only, my dulness should not prove too much!
– Not prove that in a certain other point
Wherein my husband blamed me, – and you blame,
If I interpret smiles and shakes of head, –
I was dull too. Oh, if I dared but speak!
Must I speak? I am blamed that I forwent
A way to make my husband's favour come.
That is true: I was firm, withstood, refused . . .
– Women as you are, how can I find the words?

I felt there was just one thing Guido claimed
I had no right to give nor he to take;
We being in estrangement, soul from soul:
Till, when I sought help, the Archbishop smiled,
Inquiring into privacies of life,
– Said I was blameable – (he stands for God)
Nowise entitled to exemption there.
Then I obeyed, – as surely had obeyed
Were the injunction 'Since your husband bids,
Swallow the burning coal he proffers you!'
But I did wrong, and he gave wrong advice
Though he were thrice Archbishop, – that, I know! –
Now I have got to die and see things clear.
Remember I was barely twelve years old –
A child at marriage: I was let alone
For weeks I told you, lived my child-life still
Even at Arezzo, when I woke and found
First . . . but I need not think of that again –
Over and ended! Try and take the sense
Of what I signify, if it must be so.
After the first, my husband, for hate's sake,
Said one eve, when the simpler cruelty
Seemed somewhat dull at edge and fit to bear,
'We have been man and wife six months almost:
How long is this your comedy to last?
Go this night to my chamber, not your own!'
At which word, I did rush – most true the charge –
And gain the Archbishop's house – he stands for God –
And fall upon my knees and clasp his feet,
Praying him hinder what my estranged soul
Refused to bear, though patient of the rest:
'Place me within a convent,' I implored –
'Let me henceforward lead the virgin life

303

You praise in Her you bid me imitate!'
What did he answer? 'Folly of ignorance!
Know, daughter, circumstances make or mar
Virginity, – 'tis virtue or 'tis vice.
That which was glory in the Mother of God
Had been, for instance, damnable in Eve
Created to be mother of mankind.
Had Eve, in answer to her Maker's speech
"Be fruitful, multiply, replenish earth" –
Pouted "But I choose rather to remain
Single" – why, she had spared herself forthwith
Further probation by the apple and snake,
Been pushed straight out of Paradise! For see –
If motherhood be qualified impure,
I catch you making God command Eve sin!
– A blasphemy so like these Molinists',
I must suspect you dip into their books.'
Then he pursued ''Twas in your covenant!'

No! There my husband never used deceit.
He never did by speech nor act imply
'Because of our souls' yearning that we meet
And mix in soul through flesh, which yours and mine
Wear and impress, and make their visible selves,
– All which means, for the love of you and me,
Let us become one flesh, being one soul!'
He only stipulated for the wealth;
Honest so far. But when he spoke as plain –
Dreadfully honest also – 'Since our souls
Stand each from each, a whole world's width between,
Give me the fleshy vesture I can reach
And rend and leave just fit for hell to burn!' –
Why, in God's name, for Guido's soul's own sake

Imperilled by polluting mine, – I say,
I did resist; would I had overcome!

My heart died out at the Archbishop's smile;
– It seemed so stale and worn a way o' the world,
As though 'twere nature frowning – 'Here is Spring,
The sun shines as he shone at Adam's fall,
The earth requires that warmth reach everywhere:
What, must your patch of snow be saved forsooth
Because you rather fancy snow than flowers?'
Something in this style he began with me.
Last he said, savagely for a good man,
'This explains why you call your husband harsh,
Harsh to you, harsh to whom you love. God's Bread!
The poor Count has to manage a mere child
Whose parents leave untaught the simplest things
Their duty was and privilege to teach, –
Goodwives' instruction, gossips' lore: they laugh
And leave the Count the task, – or leave it me!'
Then I resolved to tell a frightful thing.
'I am not ignorant, – know what I say,
Declaring this is sought for hate, not love.
Sir, you may hear things like almighty God.
I tell you that my housemate, yes – the priest
My husband's brother, Canon Girolamo –
Has taught me what depraved and misnamed love
Means, and what outward signs denote the sin,
For he solicits me and says he loves,
The idle young priest with nought else to do.
My husband sees this, knows this, and lets be.
Is it your counsel I bear this beside?'
'– More scandal, and against a priest this time!
What, 'tis the Canon now?' – less snappishly –

'Rise up, my child, for such a child you are,
The rod were too advanced a punishment!
Let's try the honeyed cake. A parable!
"Without a parable spake He not to them."
There was a ripe round long black toothsome fruit,
Even a flower-fig, the prime boast of May:
And, to the tree, said . . . either the spirit o' the fig,
Or, if we bring in men, the gardener,
Archbishop of the orchard – had I time
To try o' the two which fits in best: indeed
It might be the Creator's self, but then
The tree should bear an apple, I suppose, –
Well, anyhow, one with authority said
"Ripe fig, burst skin, regale the fig-pecker –
The bird whereof thou art a perquisite!"
"Nay," with a flounce, replied the restif fig,
"I much prefer to keep my pulp myself:
He may go breakfastless and dinnerless,
Supperless of one crimson seed, for me!"
So, back she flopped into her bunch of leaves.
He flew off, left her, – did the natural lord, –
And lo, three hundred thousand bees and wasps
Found her out, feasted on her to the shuck:
Such gain the fig's that gave its bird no bite!
The moral, – fools elude their proper lot,
Tempt other fools, get ruined all alike.
Therefore go home, embrace your husband quick!
Which if his Canon brother chance to see,
He will the sooner back to book again.'

So, home I did go; so, the worst befell:
So, I had proof the Archbishop was just man,
And hardly that, and certainly no more.

For, miserable consequence to me,
My husband's hatred waxed nor waned at all,
His brother's boldness grew effrontery soon,
And my last stay and comfort in myself
Was forced from me: henceforth I looked to God
Only, nor cared my desecrated soul
Should have fair walls, gay windows for the world.
God's glimmer, that came through the ruin-top,
Was witness why all lights were quenched inside:
Henceforth I asked God counsel, not mankind.
So, when I made the effort, freed myself,
They said – 'No care to save appearance here!
How cynic, – when, how wanton, were enough!'
– Adding, it all came of my mother's life –
My own real mother, whom I never knew,
Who did wrong (if she needs must have done wrong)
Through being all her life, not my four years,
At mercy of the hateful: every beast
O' the field was wont to break that fountain-fence,
Trample the silver into mud so murk
Heaven could not find itself reflected there.
Now they cry 'Out on her, who, plashy pool,
Bequeathed turbidity and bitterness
To the daughter-stream where Guido dipt and drank!'

Well, since she had to bear this brand – let me!
The rather do I understand her now,
From my experience of what hate calls love, –
Much love might be in what their love called hate.
If she sold . . . what they call, sold . . . me her child –
I shall believe she hoped in her poor heart
That I at least might try be good and pure,
Begin to live untempted, not go doomed

And done with ere once found in fault, as she.
Oh and, my mother, it all came to this?
Why should I trust those that speak ill of you,
When I mistrust who speaks even well of them?
Why, since all bound to do me good, did harm,
May not you, seeming as you harmed me most,
Have meant to do most good – and feed your child
From bramble-bush, whom not one orchard-tree
But drew bough back from, nor let one fruit fall?
This it was for you sacrificed your babe?
Gained just this, giving your heart's hope away
As I might give mine, loving it as you,
If . . . but that never could be asked of me!

There, enough! I have my support again,
Again the knowledge that my babe was, is,
Will be mine only. Him, by death, I give
Outright to God, without a further care, –
But not to any parent in the world, –
So to be safe: why is it we repine?
What guardianship were sáfer could we choose?
All human plans and projects come to nought:
My life, and what I know of other lines,
Prove that: no plan nor project! God shall care!

And now you are not tired? How patient then
All of you, – Oh yes, patient this long while
Listening, and understanding, I am sure!
Four days ago, when I was sound and well
And like to live, no one would understand.
People were kind, but smiled 'And what of him,
Your friend, whose tonsure the rich dark-brown hides?
There, there! – your lover, do we dream he was?

308

A priest too – never were such naughtiness!
Still, he thinks many a long think, never fear,
After the shy pale lady, – lay so light
For a moment in his arms, the lucky one!'
And so on: wherefore should I blame you much?
So we are made, such difference in minds,
Such difference too in eyes that see the minds!
That man, you misinterpret and misprise –
The glory of his nature, I had thought,
Shot itself out in white light, blazed the truth
Through every atom of his act with me:
Yet where I point you, through the crystal shrine,
Purity in quintessence, one dew-drop,
You all descry a spider in the midst.
One says 'The head of it is plain to see,'
And one, 'They are the feet by which I judge,'
All say, 'Those films were spun by nothing else.'

Then, I must lay my babe away with God,
Nor think of him again, for gratitude.
Yes, my last breath shall wholly spend itself
In one attempt more to disperse the stain,
The mist from other breath fond mouths have made,
About a lustrous and pellucid soul:
So that, when I am gone but sorrow stays,
And people need assurance in their doubt
If God yet have a servant, man a friend,
The weak a saviour and the vile a foe, –
Let him be present, by the name invoked,
Giuseppe-Maria Caponsacchi!

      There,
Strength comes already with the utterance!
I will remember once more for his sake

The sorrow: for he lives and is belied.
Could he be here, how he would speak for me!

I had been miserable three drear years
In that dread palace and lay passive now.
When I first learned there could be such a man.
Thus it fell: I was at a public play,
In the last days of Carnival last March,
Brought there I knew not why, but now know well.
My husband put me where I sat, in front;
Then crouched down, breathed cold through me from
    behind,
Stationed i' the shadow, – none in front could see, –
I, it was, faced the stranger-throng beneath,
The crowd with upturned faces, eyes one stare,
Voices one buzz. I looked but to the stage,
Whereon two lovers sang and interchanged
'True life is only love, love only bliss;
I love thee – thee I love!' then they embraced.
I looked thence to the ceiling and the walls, –
Over the crowd, those voices and those eyes, –
My thoughts went through the roof and out, to Rome
On wings of music, waft of measured words, –
Set me down there, a happy child again
Sure that to-morrow would be festa-day,
Hearing my parents praise past festas more,
And seeing they were old if I was young,
Yet wondering why they still would end discourse
With 'We must soon go, you abide your time,
And, – might we haply see the proper friend
Throw his arm over you and make you safe!'

Sudden I saw him; into my lap there fell
A foolish twist of comfits, broke my dream

And brought me from the air and laid me low,
As ruined as the soaring bee that's reached
(So Pietro told me at the Villa once)
By the dust-handful. There the comfits lay:
I looked to see who flung them, and I faced
This Caponsacchi, looking up in turn.
Ere I could reason out why, I felt sure,
Whoever flung them, his was not the hand, —
Up rose the round face and good-natured grin
Of one who, in effect, had played the prank,
From covert close beside the earnest face, —
Fat waggish Conti, friend of all the world.
He was my husband's cousin, privileged
To throw the thing: the other, silent, grave,
Solemn almost, saw me, as I saw him.

There is a psalm Don Celestine recites,
'Had I a dove's wings, how I fain would flee!'
The psalm runs not 'I hope, I pray for wings,' —
Not 'If wings fall from heaven, I fix them fast,' —
Simply 'How good it were to fly and rest,
Have hope now, and one day expect content!
How well to do what I shall never do!'
So I said 'Had there been a man like that,
To lift me with his strength out of all strife
Into the calm, how I could fly and rest!
I have a keeper in the garden here
Whose sole employment is to strike me low
If ever I, for solace, seek the sun.
Life means with me successful feigning death,
Lying stone-like, eluding notice so,
Forgoing here the turf and there the sky.
Suppose that man had been instead of this!'

Presently Conti laughed into my ear,
– Had tripped up to the raised place where I sat –
'Cousin, I flung them brutishly and hard!
Because you must be hurt, to look austere
As Caponsacchi yonder, my tall friend
A-gazing now. Ah, Guido, you so close?
Keep on your knees, do! Beg her to forgive!
My cornet battered like a cannon-ball.
Good-bye, I'm gone!' – nor waited the reply.

That night at supper, out my husband broke,
'Why was that throwing, that buffoonery?
Do you think I am your dupe? What man would dare
Throw comfits in a stranger lady's lap?
'Twas knowledge of you bred such insolence
In Caponsacchi; he dared shoot the bolt,
Using that Conti for his stalking-horse.
How could you see him this once and no more,
When he is always haunting hereabout
At the street-corner or the palace-side,
Publishing my shame and your impudence?
You are a wanton, – I a dupe, you think?
O Christ, what hinders that I kill her quick?'
Whereat he drew his sword and feigned a thrust.

All this, now, – being not so strange to me,
Used to such misconception day by day
And broken-in to bear, – I bore, this time,
More quietly than woman should perhaps;
Repeated the mere truth and held my tongue.

Then he said, 'Since you play the ignorant,
I shall instruct you. This amour, – commenced

Or finished or midway in act, all's one, –
'Tis the town-talk; so my revenge shall be.
Does he presume because he is a priest?
I warn him that the sword I wear shall pink
His lily-scented cassock through and through,
Next time I catch him underneath your eaves!'
But he had threatened with the sword so oft
And, after all, not kept his promise. All
I said was 'Let God save the innocent!
Moreover death is far from a bad fate.
I shall go pray for you and me, not him;
And then I look to sleep, come death or, worse,
Life.' So, I slept.

There may have elapsed a week,
When Margherita, – called my waiting maid,
Whom it is said my husband found too fair –
Who stood and heard the charge and the reply,
Who never once would let the matter rest
From that night forward, but rang changes still
On this the thrust and that the shame, and how
Good cause for jealousy cures jealous fools,
And what a paragon was this same priest
She talked about until I stopped my ears, –
She said, 'A week is gone; you comb your hair,
Then go mope in a corner, cheek on palm,
Till night comes round again, – so, waste a week
As if your husband menaced you in sport.
Have not I some acquaintance with his tricks?
Oh no, he did not stab the serving-man
Who made and sang the rhymes about me once!
For why? They sent him to the wars next day.
Nor poisoned he the foreigner, my friend

Who wagered on the whiteness of my breast, –
The swarth skins of our city in dispute:
For, though he paid me proper compliment,
The Count well knew he was besotted with
Somebody else, a skin as black as ink,
(As all the town knew save my foreigner)
He found and wedded presently, – "Why need
Better revenge?" – the Count asked. But what's here?
A priest that does not fight, and cannot wed,
Yet must be dealt with! If the Count took fire
For the poor pastime of a minute, – me –
What were the conflagration for yourself,
Countess and lady-wife and all the rest?
The priest will perish; you will grieve too late:
So shall the city-ladies' handsomest
Frankest and liberalest gentleman
Die for you, to appease a scurvy dog
Hanging's too good for. Is there no escape?
Were it not simple Christian charity
To warn the priest be on his guard, – save him
Assured death, save yourself from causing it?
I meet him in the street. Give me a glove,
A ring to show for token! Mum's the word!'

I answered 'If you were, as styled, my maid,
I would command you: as you are, you say,
My husband's intimate, – assist his wife
Who can do nothing but entreat "Be still!"
Even if you speak truth and a crime is planned,
Leave help to God as I am forced to do!
There is no other help, or we should craze,
Seeing such evil with no human cure.
Reflect that God, who makes the storm desist,

Can make an angry violent heart subside.
Why should we venture teach Him governance?
Never address me on this subject more!'

Next night she said 'But I went, all the same,
– Ay, saw your Caponsacchi in his house,
And come back stuffed with news I must outpour.
I told him "Sir, my mistress is a stone:
Why should you harm her for no good you get?
For you do harm her – prowl about our place
With the Count never distant half the street,
Lurking at every corner, would you look!
'Tis certain she has witched you with a spell.
Are there not other beauties at your beck?
We all know, Donna This and Monna That
Die for a glance of yours, yet here you gaze!
Go make them grateful, leave the stone its cold!"
And he – oh, he turned first white and then red,
And then – "To her behest I bow myself,
Whom I love with my body and my soul:
Only a word i' the bowing! See, I write
One little word, no harm to see or hear!
Then, fear no further!" This is what he wrote.
I know you cannot read, – therefore, let me!
"*My idol!*" ' . . .

                  But I took it from her hand
And tore it into shreds. 'Why join the rest
Who harm me? Have I ever done you wrong?
People have told me 'tis you wrong myself:
Let it suffice I either feel no wrong
Or else forgive it, – yet you turn my foe!
The others hunt me and you throw a noose!'
She muttered 'Have your wilful way!' I slept.

Whereupon . . . no, I leave my husband out!
It is not to do him more hurt, I speak.
Let it suffice, when misery was most,
One day, I swooned and got a respite so.
She stooped as I was slowly coming to,
This Margherita, ever on my trace,
And whispered – 'Caponsacchi!'

                               If I drowned,
But woke afloat i' the wave with upturned eyes,
And found their first sight was a star! I turned –
For the first time, I let her have her will,
Heard passively, – 'The imposthume at such head,
One touch, one lancet-puncture would relieve, –
And still no glance the good physician's way
Who rids you of the torment in a trice!
Still he writes letters you refuse to hear.
He may prevent your husband, kill himself,
So desperate and all fordone is he!
Just hear the pretty verse he made to-day!
A sonnet from Mirtillo. "*Peerless fair* . . ."
All poetry is difficult to read,
– The sense of it is, anyhow, he seeks
Leave to contrive you an escape from hell,
And for that purpose asks an interview.
I can write, I can grant it in your name,
Or, what is better, lead you to his house.
Your husband dashes you against the stones;
This man would place each fragment in a shrine:
You hate him, love your husband!'

                                 I returned
'It is not true I love my husband, – no,
Nor hate this man. I listen while you speak,

– Assured that what you say is false, the same:
Much as when once, to me a little child,
A rough gaunt man in rags, with eyes on fire,
A crowd of boys and idlers at his heels,
Rushed as I crossed the Square, and held my head
In his two hands, "Here's she will let me speak!
You little girl, whose eyes do good to mine,
I am the Pope, am Sextus, now the Sixth;
And that Twelfth Innocent, proclaimed to-day,
Is Lucifer disguised in human flesh!
The angels, met in conclave, crowned me!" – thus
He gibbered and I listened; but I knew
All was delusion, ere folk interposed
"Unfasten him, the maniac!" Thus I know
All your report of Caponsacchi false,
Folly or dreaming; I have seen so much
By that adventure at the spectacle,
The face I fronted that one first, last time:
He would belie it by such words and thoughts.
Therefore while you profess to show him me,
I ever see his own face. Get you gone!'

' – That will I, nor once open mouth again, –
No, by Saint Joseph and the Holy Ghost!
On your head be the damage, so adieu!'

And so more days, more deeds I must forget,
Till . . . what a strange thing now is to declare!
Since I say anything, say all is true!
And how my life seems lengthened as to serve!
It may be idle or inopportune,
But, true? – why, what was all I said but truth,
Even when I found that such as are untrue
Could only take the truth in through a lie?

Now – I am speaking truth to the Truth's self:
God will lend credit to my words this time.

It had got half through April. I arose
One vivid daybreak, – who had gone to bed
In the old way my wont those last three years,
Careless until, the cup drained, I should die.
The last sound in my ear, the over-night,
Had been a something let drop on the sly
In prattle by Margherita, 'Soon enough
Gaieties end, now Easter's past: a week,
And the Archbishop gets him back to Rome, –
Everyone leaves the town for Rome, this Spring, –
Even Caponsacchi, out of heart and hope,
Resigns himself and follows with the flock.'
I heard this drop and drop like rain outside
Fast-falling through the darkness while she spoke:
So had I heard with like indifference,
'And Michael's pair of wings will arrive first
At Rome, to introduce the company,
And bear him from our picture where he fights
Satan, – expect to have that dragon loose
And never a defender!' – my sole thought
Being still, as night came, 'Done, another day!
How good to sleep and so get nearer death!'
When, what, first thing at daybreak, pierced the sleep
With a summons to me? Up I sprang alive,
Light in me, light without me, everywhere
Change! A broad yellow sunbeam was let fall
From heaven to earth, – a sudden drawbridge lay,
Along which marched a myriad merry motes,
Mocking the flies that crossed them and re-crossed
In rival dance, companions new-born too.

On the house-eaves, a dripping shag of weed
Shook diamonds on each dull grey lattice-square,
As first one, then another bird leapt by,
And light was off, and lo was back again,
Always with one voice, – where are two such joys? –
The blessed building-sparrow! I stepped forth,
Stood on the terrace, – o'er the roofs such sky!
My heart sang, 'I too am to go away,
I too have something I must care about,
Carry away with me to Rome, to Rome!
The bird brings hither sticks and hairs and wool,
And nowhere else i' the world; what fly breaks rank,
Falls out of the procession that befits,
From window here to window there, with all
The world to choose, – so well he knows his course?
I have my purpose and my motive too,
My march to Rome, like any bird or fly!
Had I been dead! How right to be alive!
Last night I almost prayed for leave to die,
Wished Guido all his pleasure with the sword
Or the poison, – poison, sword, was but a trick,
Harmless, may God forgive him the poor jest!
My life is charmed, will last till I reach Rome!
Yesterday, but for the sin, – ah, nameless be
The deed I could have dared against myself!
Now – see if I will touch an unripe fruit,
And risk the health I want to have and use!
Not to live, now, would be the wickedness, –
For life means to make haste and go to Rome
And leave Arezzo, leave all woes at once!'

Now understand here, by no means mistake!
Long ago had I tried to leave that house

319

When it seemed such procedure would stop sin;
And still failed more the more I tried – at first
The Archbishop, as I told you, – next, our lord
The Governor, – indeed I found my way,
I went to the great palace where he rules,
Though I knew well 'twas he who, – when I gave
A jewel or two, themselves had given me,
Back to my parents, – since they wanted bread,
They who had never let me want a nosegay, – he
Spoke of the jail for felons, if they kept
What was first theirs, then mine, so doubly theirs,
Though all the while my husband's most of all!
I knew well who had spoke the word wrought this:
Yet, being in extremity, I fled
To the Governor, as I say, – scarce opened lip
When – the cold cruel snicker close behind –
Guido was on my trace, already there,
Exchanging nod and wink for shrug and smile,
And I – pushed back to him and, for my pains
Paid with . . . but why remember what is past?
I sought out a poor friar the people call
The Roman, and confessed my sin which came
Of their sin, – that fact could not be repressed, –
The frightfulness of my despair in God:
And, feeling, through the grate, his horror shake,
Implored him, 'Write for me who cannot write,
Apprise my parents, make them rescue me!
You bid me be courageous and trust God:
Do you in turn dare somewhat, trust and write
"Dear friends, who used to be my parents once,
And now declare you have no part in me,
This is some riddle I want wit to solve,
Since you must love me with no difference.

Even suppose you altered, – there's your hate,
To ask for: hate of you two dearest ones
I shall find liker love than love found here,
If husbands love their wives. Take me away
And hate me as you do the gnats and fleas,
Even the scorpions! How I shall rejoice!"
Write that and save me!' And he promised – wrote
Or did not write; things never changed at all:
He was not like the Augustinian here!
Last, in a desperation I appealed
To friends, whoever wished me better days,
To Guillichini, that's of kin, – 'What, I –
Travel to Rome with you? A flying gout
Bids me deny my heart and mind my leg!'
Then I tried Conti, used to brave – laugh back
The louring thunder when his cousin scowled
At me protected by his presence: 'You –
Who well know what you cannot save me from, –
Carry me off! What frightens you, a priest?'
He shook his head, looked grave – 'Above my strength!
Guido has claws that scratch, shows feline teeth;
A formidabler foe than I dare fret:
Give me a dog to deal with, twice the size!
Of course I am a priest and Canon too,
But . . . by the bye . . . though both, not quite so bold
As he, my fellow-Canon, brother-priest,
The personage in such ill odour here
Because of the reports – pure birth o' the brain!
Our Caponsacchi, he's your true Saint George
To slay the monster, set the Princess free,
And have the whole High-Altar to himself:
I always think so when I see that piece

I' the Pieve, that's his church and mine, you know
Though you drop eyes at mention of his name!'

That name had got to take a half-grotesque
Half-ominous, wholly enigmatic sense,
Like any by-word, broken bit of song
Born with a meaning, changed by mouth and mouth
That mix it in a sneer or smile, as chance
Bids, till it now means nought but ugliness
And perhaps shame.

           – All this intends to say,
That, over-night, the notion of escape
Had seemed distemper, dreaming; and the name, –
Not the man, but the name of him, thus made
Into a mockery and disgrace, – why, she
Who uttered it persistently, had laughed,
'I name his name, and there you start and wince
As criminal from the red tongs' touch!' – yet now,
Now, as I stood letting morn bathe me bright,
Choosing which butterfly should bear my news, –
The white, the brown one, or that tinier blue, –
The Margherita, I detested so,
In she came – 'The fine day, the good Spring time!
What, up and out at window? That is best.
No thought of Caponsacchi? – who stood there
All night on one leg, like the sentry crane,
Under the pelting of your water-spout –
Looked last look at your lattice ere he leave
Our city, bury his dead hope at Rome.
Ay, go to looking-glass and make you fine,
While he may die ere touch one least loose hair
You drag at with the comb in such a rage!'

I turned – 'Tell Caponsacchi he may come!'

'Tell him to come? Ah, but, for charity,
A truce to fooling! Come? What, – come this eve?
Peter and Paul! But I see through the trick!
Yes, come, and take a flower-pot on his head,
Flung from your terrace! No joke, sincere truth?'

How plainly I perceived hell flash and fade
O' the face of her, – the doubt that first paled joy
Then, final reassurance I indeed
Was caught now, never to be free again!
What did I care? – who felt myself of force
To play with silk, and spurn the horsehair-springe.

'But – do you know that I have bade him come,
And in your own name? I presumed so much,
Knowing the thing you needed in your heart.
But somehow – what had I to show in proof?
He would not come: half-promised, that was all,
And wrote the letters you refused to read.
What is the message that shall move him now?'

'After the Ave Maria, at first dark,
I will be standing on the terrace, say!'

'I would I had a good long lock of hair
Should prove I was not lying! Never mind!'

Off she went – 'May he not refuse, that's all –
Fearing a trick!'

                    I answered, 'He will come.'
And, all day, I sent prayer like incense up

To God the strong, God the beneficent,
God ever mindful in all strife and strait,
Who, for our own good, makes the need extreme,
Till at the last He puts forth might and saves.
An old rhyme came into my head and rang
Of how a virgin, for the faith of God,
Hid herself, from the Paynims that pursued,
In a cave's heart; until a thunderstone,
Wrapped in a flame, revealed the couch and prey
And they laughed – 'Thanks to lightning, ours at last!'
And she cried 'Wrath of God, assert His love!
Servant of God, thou fire, befriended His child!'
And lo, the fire she grasped at, fixed its flash,
Lay in her hand a calm cold dreadful sword
She brandished till pursuers strewed the ground,
So did the souls within them die away,
As o'er the prostrate bodies, sworded, safe,
She walked forth to the solitudes and Christ:
So should I grasp the lightning and be saved!

And still, as the day wore, the trouble grew
Whereby I guessed there would be born a star,
Until at an intense throe of the dusk,
I started up, was pushed, I dare to say,
Out on the terrace, leaned and looked at last
Where the deliverer waited me: the same
Silent and solemn face, I first descried
At the spectacle, confronted mine once more.

So was that minute twice vouchsafed me, so
The manhood, wasted then, was still at watch
To save me yet a second time: no change
Here, though all else changed in the changing world!

324

I spoke on the instant, as my duty bade,
In some such sense as this, whatever the phrase.

'Friend, foolish words were borne from you to me;
Your soul behind them is the pure strong wind,
Not dust and feathers which its breath may bear:
These to the witless seem the wind itself,
Since proving thus the first of it they feel.
If by mischance you blew offence my way,
The straws are dropt, the wind desists no whit,
And how such strays were caught up in the street
And took a motion from you, why inquire?
I speak to the strong soul, no weak disguise.
If it be truth, – why should I doubt it truth? –
You serve God specially, as priests are bound,
And care about me, stranger as I am,
So far as wish my good, – that miracle
I take to intimate He wills you serve
By saving me, – what else can He direct?
Here is the service. Since a long while now,
I am in course of being put to death:
While death concerned nothing but me, I bowed
The head and bade, in heart, my husband strike.
Now I imperil something more, it seems,
Something that's truelier me than this myself,
Something I trust in God and you to save.
You go to Rome, they tell me: take me there,
Put me back with my people!'

                    He replied –
The first word I heard ever from his lips,
All himself in it, – an eternity
Of speech, to match the immeasurable depth
O' the soul that then broke silence – 'I am yours.'

So did the star rise, soon to lead my step,
Lead on, nor pause before it should stand still
Above the House o' the Babe, – my babe to be,
That knew me first and thus made me know him,
That had his right of life and claim on mine,
And would not let me die till he was born,
But pricked me at the heart to save us both,
Saying 'Have you the will? Leave God the way!'
And the way was Caponsacchi – 'mine', thank God!
He was mine, he is mine, he will be mine.

No pause i' the leading and the light! I know,
Next night there was a cloud came, and not he:
But I prayed through the darkness till it broke
And let him shine. The second night, he came.

'The plan is rash; the project desperate:
In such a flight needs must I risk your life,
Give food for falsehood, folly or mistake,
Ground for your husband's rancour and revenge' –
So he began again, with the same face.
I felt that, the same loyalty – one star
Turning now red that was so white before –
One service apprehended newly: just
A word of mine and there the white was back!

'No, friend, for you will take me! 'Tis yourself
Risk all, not I, – who let you, for I trust
In the compensating great God: enough!
I know you: when is it that you will come?'

'To-morrow at the day's dawn.' Then I heard
What I should do: how to prepare for flight
And where to fly.

That night my husband bade
'– You, whom I loathe, beware you break my sleep
This whole night! Couch beside me like the corpse
I would you were!' The rest you know, I think –
How I found Caponsacchi and escaped.

And this man, men called sinner? Jesus Christ!
Of whom men said, with mouth Thyself mad'st once,
'He hath a devil' – say he was Thy saint,
My Caponsacchi! Shield and show – unshroud
In Thine own time the glory of the soul
If aught obscure, – if ink-spot, from vile pens
Scribbling a charge against him – (I was glad
Then, for the first time, that I could not write) –
Flirted his way, have flecked the blaze!

                                    For me,
'Tis otherwise: let men take, sift my thoughts
– Thoughts I throw like the flax for sun to bleach!
I did pray, do pray, in the prayer shall die,
'Oh, to have Caponsacchi for my guide!'
Ever the face upturned to mine, the hand
Holding my hand across the world, – a sense
That reads, as only such can read, the mark
God sets on woman, signifying so
She should – shall peradventure – be divine;
Yet 'ware, the while, how weakness mars the print
And makes confusion, leaves the thing men see,
– Not this man sees, – who from his soul, rewrites
The obliterated charter, – love and strength
Mending what's marred. 'So kneels a votarist,
Weeds some poor waste traditionary plot
Where shrine once was, where temple yet may be,
Puring the place but worshipping the while,

By faith and not by sight, sight clearest so, –
Such way the saints work,' – says Don Celestine.
But I, not privileged to see a saint
Of old when such walked earth with crown and palm,
If I call 'saint' what saints call something else –
The saints must bear with me, impute the fault
To a soul i' the bud, so starved by ignorance,
Stinted of warmth, it will not blow this year
Nor recognize the orb which Spring-flowers know.
But if meanwhile some insect with a heart
Worth floods of lazy music, spendthrift joy –
Some fire-fly renounced Spring for my dwarfed cup,
Crept close to me, brought lustre for the dark,
Comfort against the cold, – what though excess
Of comfort should miscall the creature – sun?
What did the sun to hinder while harsh hands
Petal by petal, crude and colourless,
Tore me? This one heart gave me all the Spring!

Is all told? There's the journey: and where's time
To tell you how that heart burst out in shine?
Yet certain points do press on me too hard.
Each place must have a name, though I forget:
How strange it was – there where the plain begins
And the small river mitigates its flow –
When eve was fading fast, and my soul sank,
And he divined what surge of bitterness,
In overtaking me, would float me back
Whence I was carried by the striding day –
So, – 'This grey place was famous once,' said he –
And he began that legend of the place
As if in answer to the unspoken fear,
And told me all about a brave man dead,

Which lifted me and let my soul go on!
How did he know too, – at that town's approach
By the rock-side, – that in coming near the signs
Of life, the house-roofs and the church and tower,
I saw the old boundary and wall o' the world
Rise plain as ever round me, hard and cold,
As if the broken circlet joined again,
Tightened itself about me with no break, –
As if the town would turn Arezzo's self, –
The husband there, – the friends my enemies,
All ranged against me, not an avenue
To try, but would be blocked and drive me back
On him, – this other, . . . oh the heart in that!
Did not he find, bring, put into my arms
A new-born babe? – and I saw faces beam
Of the young mother proud to teach me joy,
And gossips round expecting my surprise
At the sudden hole through earth that lets in heaven.
I could believe himself by his strong will
Had woven around me what I thought the world
We went along in, every circumstance,
Towns, flowers and faces, all things helped so well!
For, through the journey, was it natural
Such comfort should arise from first to last?
As I look back, all is one milky way;
Still bettered more, the more remembered, so
Do new stars bud while I but search for old,
And fill all gaps i' the glory, and grow him –
Him I now see make the shine everywhere.
Even at the last when the bewildered flesh,
The cloud of weariness about my soul
Clogging too heavily, sucked down all sense, –
Still its last voice was, 'He will watch and care;

Let the strength go, I am content: he stays!'
I doubt not he did stay and care for all –
From that sick minute when the head swam round,
And the eyes looked their last and died on him,
As in his arms he caught me, and, you say,
Carried me in, that tragical red eve,
And laid me where I next returned to life
In the other red of morning, two red plates
That crushed together, crushed the time between,
And are since then a solid fire to me, –
When in, my dreadful husband and the world
Broke, – and I saw him, master, by hell's right,
And saw my angel helplessly held back
By guards that helped the malice – the lamb prone,
The serpent towering and triumphant – then
Came all the strength back in a sudden swell,
I did for once see right, do right, give tongue
The adequate protest: for a worm must turn
If it would have its wrong observed by God.
I did spring up, attempt to thrust aside
That ice-block 'twixt the sun and me, lay low
The neutralizer of all good and truth.
If I sinned so, – never obey voice more
O' the Just and Terrible, who bids us – 'Bear!'
Not – 'Stand by, bear to see my angels bear!'
I am clear it was on impulse to serve God
Not save myself, – no – nor my child unborn!
Had I else waited patiently till now? –
Who saw my old kind parents, silly-sooth
And too much trustful, for their worst of faults,
Cheated, brow-beaten, stripped and starved, cast out
Into the kennel: I remonstrated,
Then sank to silence, for, – their woes at end,

Themselves gone, – only I was left to plague.
If only I was threatened and belied,
What matter? I could bear it and did bear;
It was a comfort, still one lot for all:
They were not persecuted for my sake
And I, estranged, the single happy one.
But when at last, all by myself I stood
Obeying the clear voice which bade me rise,
Not for my own sake but my babe unborn,
And take the angel's hand was sent to help –
And found the old adversary athwart the path –
Not my hand simply struck from the angel's but
The very angel's self made foul i' the face
By the fiend who struck there, – that I would not bear,
That only I resisted! So, my first
And last resistance was invincible.
Prayers move God; threats, and nothing else, move
     men!
I must have prayed a man as he were God
When I implored the Governor to right
My parents' wrongs: the answer was a smile.
The Archbishop, – did I clasp his feet enough,
Hide my face hotly on them, while I told
More than I dared make my own mother know?
The profit was – compassion and a jest.
This time, the foolish prayers were done with, right
Used might, and solemnized the sport at once.
All was against the combat: vantage, mine?
The runaway avowed, the accomplice-wife,
In company with the plan-contriving priest?
Yet, shame thus rank and patent, I struck, bare,
At foe from head to foot in magic mail,
And off it withered, cobweb-armoury

Against the lightning! 'Twas truth singed the lies
And saved me, not the vain sword nor weak speech!

You see, I will not have the service fail!
I say, the angel saved me: I am safe!
Others may want and wish, I wish nor want
One point o' the circle plainer, where I stand
Traced round about with white to front the world.
What of the calumny I came across,
What o' the way to the end? – the end crowns all.
The judges judged aright i' the main, gave me
The uttermost of my heart's desire, a truce
From torture and Arezzo, balm for hurt,
With the quiet nuns, – God recompense the good!
Who said and sang away the ugly past.
And, when my final fortune was revealed,
What safety while, amid my parents' arms,
My babe was given me! Yes, he saved my babe:
It would not have peeped forth, the bird-like thing,
Through that Arezzo noise and trouble: back
Had it returned nor ever let me see!
But the sweet peace cured all, and let me live
And give my bird the life among the leaves
God meant him! Weeks and months of quietude,
I could lie in such peace and learn so much –
Begin the task, I see how needful now,
Of understanding somewhat of my past, –
Know life a little, I should leave so soon.
Therefore, because this man restored my soul,
All has been right; I have gained my gain, enjoyed
As well as suffered, – nay, got foretaste too
Of better life beginning where this ends –
All through the breathing-while allowed me thus,

Which let good premonitions reach my soul
Unthwarted, and benignant influence flow
And interpenetrate and change my heart,
Uncrossed by what was wicked, – nay, unkind.
For, as the weakness of my time drew nigh,
Nobody did me one disservice more,
Spoke coldly or looked strangely, broke the love
I lay in the arms of, till my boy was born,
Born all in love, with nought to spoil the bliss
A whole long fortnight: in a life like mine
A fortnight filled with bliss is long and much.
All women are not mothers of a boy,
Though they live twice the length of my whole life,
And, as they fancy, happily all the same.
There I lay, then, all my great fortnight long,
As if it would continue, broaden out
Happily more and more, and lead to heaven:
Christmas before me, – was not that a chance?
I never realized God's birth before –
How he grew likest God in being born.
This time I felt like Mary, had my babe
Lying a little on my breast like hers.
So all went on till, just four days ago –
The night and the tap.

                              Oh it shall be success
To the whole of our poor family! My friends
. . . Nay, father and mother, – give me back my
     word!
They have been rudely stripped of life, disgraced
Like children who must needs go clothed too fine,
Carry the garb of Carnival in Lent.

If they too much affected frippery,
They have been punished and submit themselves,
Say no word: all is over, they see God
Who will not be extreme to mark their fault
Or He had granted respite: they are safe.

For that most woeful man my husband once,
Who, needing respite, still draws vital breath,
I – pardon him? So far as lies in me,
I give him for his good the life he takes,
Praying the world will therefore acquiesce.
Let him make God amends, – none, none to me
Who thank him rather that, whereas strange fate
Mockingly styled him husband and me wife,
Himself this way at least pronounced divorce,
Blotted the marriage-bond: this blood of mine
Flies forth exultingly at any door,
Washes the parchment white, and thanks the blow.
We shall not meet in this world nor the next,
But where will God be absent? In His face
Is light, but in His shadow healing too:
Let Guido touch the shadow and be healed!
And as my presence was importunate, –
My earthly good, temptation and a snare, –
Nothing about me but drew somehow down
His hate upon me, – somewhat so excused
Therefore, since hate was thus the truth of him, –
May my evanishment for evermore
Help further to relieve the heart that cast
Such object of its natural loathing forth!
So he was made; he nowise made himself:
I could not love him, but his mother did.
His soul has never lain beside my soul:

But for the unresisting body, – thanks!
He burned that garment spotted by the flesh.
Whatever he touched is rightly ruined: plague
It caught, and disinfection it had craved
Still but for Guido; I am saved through him
So as by fire; to him – thanks and farewell!

Even for my babe, my boy, there's safety thence –
From the sudden death of me, I mean: we poor
Weak souls, how we endeavour to be strong!
I was already using up my life, –
This portion, now, should do him such a good,
This other go to keep off such an ill!
The great life; see, a breath and it is gone!
So is detached, so left all by itself
The little life, the fact which means so much.
Shall not God stoop the kindlier to His work,
His marvel of creation, foot would crush,
Now that the hand He trusted to receive
And hold it, lets the treasure fall perforce?
The better; He shall have in orphanage
His own way all the clearlier: if my babe
Outlived the hour – and he has lived two weeks –
It is through God who knows I am not by.
Who is it makes the soft gold hair turn black,
And sets the tongue, might lie so long at rest,
Trying to talk? Let us leave God alone!
Why should I doubt He will explain in time
What I feel now, but fail to find the words?
My babe nor was, nor is, nor yet shall be
Count Guido Franceschini's child at all –
Only his mother's, born of love not hate!
So shall I have my rights in after-time.

It seems absurd, impossible to-day;
So seems so much else, not explained but known!

Ah! Friends, I thank and bless you every one!
No more now: I withdraw from earth and man
To my own soul, compose myself for God.

Well, and there is more! Yes, my end of breath
Shall bear away my soul in being true!
He is still here, not outside with the world,
Here, here, I have him in his rightful place!
'Tis now, when I am most upon the move,
I feel for what I verily find – again
The face, again the eyes, again, through all,
The heart and its immeasurable love
Of my one friend, my only, all my own,
Who put his breast between the spears and me.
Ever with Caponsacchi! Otherwise
Here alone would be failure, loss to me –
How much more loss to him, with life debarred
From giving life, love locked from love's display,
The day-star stopped its task that makes night morn!
O lover of my life, O soldier-saint,
No work begun shall ever pause for death!
Love will be helpful to me more and more
I' the coming course, the new path I must tread –
My weak hand in thy strong hand, strong for that!
Tell him that if I seem without him now,
That's the world's insight! Oh, he understands!
He is at Civita – do I once doubt
The world again is holding us apart?
He had been here, displayed in my behalf
The broad brow that reverberates the truth,

And flashed the word God gave him, back to man!
I know where the free soul is flown! My fate
Will have been hard for even him to bear:
Let it confirm him in the trust of God,
Showing how holily he dared the deed!
And, for the rest, – say, from the deed, no touch
Of harm came, but all good, all happiness,
Not one faint fleck of failure! Why explain?
What I see, oh, he sees and how much more!
Tell him, – I know not wherefore the true word
Should fade and fall unuttered at the last –
It was the name of him I sprang to meet
When came the knock, the summons and the end.
'My great heart, my strong hand are back again!'
I would have sprung to these, beckoning across
Murder and hell gigantic and distinct
O' the threshold, posted to exclude me heaven:
He is ordained to call and I to come!
Do not the dead wear flowers when dressed for God?
Say, – I am all in flowers from head to foot!
Say, – not one flower of all he said and did,
Might seem to flit unnoticed, fade unknown,
But dropped a seed, has grown a balsam-tree
Whereof the blossoming perfumes the place
At this supreme of moments! He is a priest;
He cannot marry therefore, which is right:
I think he would not marry if he could.
Marriage on earth seems such a counterfeit,
Mere imitation of the inimitable:
In heaven we have the real and true and sure.
'Tis there they neither marry nor are given
In marriage but are as the angels: right,
Oh how right that is, how like Jesus Christ

To say that! Marriage-making for the earth,
With gold so much, – birth, power, repute so much,
Or beauty, youth so much, in lack of these!
Be as the angels rather, who, apart,
Know themselves into one, are found at length
Married, but marry never, no, nor give
In marriage; they are man and wife at once
When the true time is: here we have to wait
Not so long neither! Could we by a wish
Have what we will and get the future now,
Would we wish aught done undone in the past?
So, let him wait God's instant men call years;
Meantime hold hard by truth and his great soul.
Do out the duty! Through such souls alone
God stooping shows sufficient of His light
For us i' the dark to rise by. And I rise.

NEVER THE TIME AND THE PLACE

NEVER the time and the place
  And the loved one all together!
This path – how soft to pace!
  This May – what magic weather!
  Where is the loved one's face?
In a dream that loved one's face meets mine,
  But the house is narrow, the place is bleak
Where, outside, rain and wind combine
  With a furtive ear, if I strive to speak,
  With a hostile eye at my flushing cheek,
With a malice that marks each word, each sign!
O enemy sly and serpentine,
  Uncoil thee from the waking man!
     Do I hold the Past
     Thus firm and fast
  Yet doubt if the Future hold I can?
This path so soft to pace shall lead
Thro, the magic of May to herself indeed!
Or narrow if needs the house must be,
Outside are the storms and strangers: we –
Oh, close, safe, warm sleep I and she,
– I and she!

SUMMUM BONUM

ALL the breath and the bloom of the year in the bag of one
   bee:
   All the wonder and wealth of the mine in the heart of
   one gem:
In the core of one pearl all the shade and the shine of the
   sea:
   Breath and bloom, shade and shine, – wonder, wealth,
   and – how far above them –
      Truth, that's brighter than gem,
      Trust, that's purer than pearl, –
Brightest truth, purest trust in the universe – all were for
   me
      In the kiss of one girl.

EPILOGUE

TO 'ASOLANDO'

At the midnight in the silence of the sleeptime,
  When you set your fancies free,
Will they pass to where – by death, fools think, imprisoned –
Low he lies who once so loved you, whom you loved so,
      – Pity me?

Oh to love so, be so loved, yet so mistaken!
  What had I on earth to do
With the slothful, with the mawkish, the unmanly?
Like the aimless, helpless, hopeless, did I drivel
      – Being – who?

One who never turned his back but marched breast forward,
  Never doubted clouds would break,
Never dreamed, though right were worsted, wrong would triumph,
Held we fall to rise, are baffled to fight better,
      Sleep to wake.

No, at noonday in the bustle of man's worktime
  Greet the unseen with a cheer!
Bid him forward, breast and back as either should be,
'Strive and thrive!' cry 'Speed, – fight on, fare ever
      There as here!'

INDEX OF FIRST LINES

MORE ABOUT PENGUINS
AND PELICANS

Penguinews, which appears every month, contains details of all the new books issued by Penguins as they are published. From time to time it is supplemented by *Penguins in Print*, which is our complete list of almost 5,000 titles.

A specimen copy of *Penguinews* will be sent to you free on request. Please write to Dept EP, Penguin Books Ltd, Harmondsworth, Middlesex, for your copy.

In the U.S.A.: For a complete list of books available from Penguins in the United States write to Dept CS, Penguin Books, 625 Madison Avenue, New York, New York 10022.

In Canada: For a complete list of books available from Penguins in Canada write to Penguin Books Canada Ltd, 2801 John Street, Markham, Ontario L3R 1B4.

PENGUIN ENGLISH POETS

General Editor: Christopher Ricks
Professor of English, University of Cambridge

—

Robert Browning: The Ring and the Book
Edited by Richard D. Altick

William Blake: The Complete Poems
Edited by Alicia Ostriker

John Donne: The Complete English Poems
Edited by A. J. Smith

Sir Gawain and the Green Knight
Edited by J. A. Burrow

Samuel Johnson: The Complete English Poems
Edited by J. D. Fleeman

Ben Jonson: The Complete English Poems
Edited by George Parfitt

John Keats: The Complete Poems
Edited by John Barnard

Christopher Marlowe: The Complete Poems and Translations
Edited by Stephen Orgel

Edmund Spenser: The Faerie Queene
Edited by Thomas P. Roche Jnr and C. Patrick O'Donnell Jnr

Henry Vaughan: The Complete Poems
Edited by Alan Rudrum

Walt Whitman: The Complete Poems
Edited by Francis Murphy

William Wordsworth: The Prelude (A Parallel Text)
Edited by J. C. Maxwell

Penguin Modern Poets

Poetry Anthologies in Penguins

The Pelican Guide to English Literature

EDITED BY BORIS FORD

What this work sets out to offer is a guide to the history and traditions of English literature, a contour-map of the literary scene. It attempts, that is, to draw up an ordered account of literature that is concerned, first and foremost, with value for the present, and this as a direct encouragement to people to read for themselves.

Each volume sets out to present the reader with four kinds of related material:

(i) An account of the social context of literature in each period.

(ii) A literary survey of the period.

(iii) Detailed studies of some of the chief writers and works in the period.

(iv) An appendix of essential facts for reference purposes.

The *Guide* consists of seven volumes, as follows:

1. *The Age of Chaucer*
2. *The Age of Shakespeare*
3. *From Donne to Marvell*
4. *From Dryden to Johnson*
5. *From Blake to Byron*
6. *From Dickens to Hardy*
7. *The Modern Age*